TALES FROM THE ...FERNO

VOLUME

II

By

JAY DARKMOORE

Also by Jay Darkmoore –

The Space Between Heaven and Hell

The Space Between Heaven and Hell – The Shadow Man

Tales From the Inferno Volume One

Tales From the Inferno Volume Two

The Everlife Chronicles – Hunted

If you're interested in getting exclusive content, giveaways, early releases and news, not to mention blog posts written by yours truly, click here –

Website –

https://jaydarkmooreauthor.com

If you want to see my social media and be part of the community and even hear a terrible joke or two, then click here –

Instagram –

https://www.instagram.com/jay_darkmoore_author/

Please leave a review for this title. It helps authors

like me keep making content to be devoured up by

hungry readers. You can do this by clicking here

From the author –

Dear reader,

I would like to thank you for taking the time to pick up this book. I have loved writing short stories. I feel they let you expand on those lurking ideas in the back of your mind.

In this book there are six stories, each ranging from Novella length to flash fiction, from tragic romance to horror and psychological thriller. I hope you like them.

Welcome to my nightmare.

-    **Jay Darkmoore**

Tales From the Inferno

Volume

II

Lorna

1

Then

The first time you told me you loved me you broke my nose. It was dripping onto the kitchen floor in a steady stream of crimson like a leaking water balloon. My face was on fire, and I remember when you pressed the cold compress on my skin and telling me how sorry you were. How sorry that you had hurt me. That I drove you to do it. The way your mascara ran from your eyelids and smeared your cheeks. You had been drinking gin again, even though you told me that you had given it up because of how it made you act.

It was New Year's eve. Things hadn't been great recently but you told me it was because you were stressed out at work at the office, and I had asked about who the guy always blowing up your phone was. You shrugged the comment off and gave me some excuse, but you knew that it was still on my mind.

When your work friends came to join us to drink, eat and laugh as we said goodbye to the year and hello to the next one, you looked so happy. So beautiful. But then Mark walked in, and I knew your eyes were more focused on him rather than me. And you could sense mine too, lingering on Cara. You know our past. What I told you anyway. You were always for appearances. The way you smiled, the way you stood. It was all for a show, and it was my show to witness. You made sure of that, laughing, drink in hand, touching Mark's arm more times than my liking. But you knew what you were doing, *always* knew what you were doing. You saw me watching you whilst you did it, and those beautiful eyes turned cold, and I saw you look at him for the first time, saw you *really* look at him, the same way you had looked at me the first time we had met each other, and you knew that I would think things which I should have never thought. Because it was all for show. It was for me, and not for him. He, maybe not so innocently, leant in and kissed your cheek. Your eyes on me at all times as I sat in the corner rocking a whisky.

That night, I think it was around two in the morning, you had been drinking heavily and when the cohort left and the music died, you, not me, decided to bring it up.

"I don't care," I said, knowing better than to argue with you when you had been drinking. You had never been aggressive, not physically anyway, before. But that temper was always there, just waiting to come out and bite me like sharks under still water. One little dip past the surface and the teeth were ready to sink into you.

Naturally you said it was me. Conflating, projecting as always. But I knew that sinister smile behind those crocodile tears too well by now.

"Talk to me!" You shouted. You're across the kitchen, nursing the last drops of prosecco. You pick up the half empty bottle. It was round, black. The expensive stuff to celebrate our first New Years together. You reminded me of the first time we met, on the car park of Rubens café that day. You weren't in your work attire tonight obviously, but you looked incredible, and as I look at you from across the room tonight, your hair still made up, glitter and sequins clinging to your black dress from the poppers and balloons in the main from when the new year was officially here, you looked as dangerous, as deadly, and as alluring as ever, like a poisoned rose with thorns dripping with venom.

"I don't want to talk about it," I said with more contemptment than I should have. "I think you need to go to bed." There I was, doing it again. I know you hated that. You thought I was trying to run from the conversation, not trying to work things through. Whereas I knew better than to taunt the bull with a red rag when it was already angry. "We can talk in the morning. You're drunk, and I don't like it when you drink."

"You calling me an alcoholic?" Again, you did this often. Jumping to conclusions. Reading between the lines to find meanings that weren't there. I felt myself growing tort, rigid. I stopped cleaning the dinner plates with half eaten icing clinging to the porcelain. I washed off the suds and let the water run a moment to clear the sink, before putting the cutlery on the draining board. I didn't want to look at you any longer. I didn't like seeing you like this, because it's what I normally saw before the bad side of you came out. I often wondered how something so beautiful, so wonderful to everyone else, could be so cruel. Like Faustus selling his soul to the Devil, the illusion of beauty, until it's too late.

I think you stood up, or stumbled, I can't quite remember. But I remember you coming up to me and putting your hands on my waist and nestling your head into my back. Something else you liked to do so often. When you know my guard was up, when you know I don't want to talk about things, you want to try a different tactic. You throw affection, use it as a weapon to break through the wall around my heart. I shrugged you off with a grunt. I know you too well, and as good as you are at acting, I know your pattens. You're beautiful, but very predictable. I think I went to the other side of the kitchen to get a clean glass for some water, I can't remember properly. I had had a couple of beers. Not as many as you though, given by how much you were swaying and how you were slurring your words.

"I fucking hate you, you know." *There we go* I remember

thinking to myself. That, I remember very clearly. *This is where the sharks start jumping out the water to catch the birds hovering above, too afraid to go near the deep black below them.*

"You're drunk, you need to go to bed. I will talk to you in the morning." I was trying to keep things calm, relaxed. I stood by you as those eyes bored into me. You didn't need to say anything further, I could feel the heat from your blood boiling as I filled the glass with cold water. "Please Lorna," I said quietly. If I was too loud, you might tell the police I was shouting at you. That I provoked you. That I *caused* the fight. It wouldn't be the first time. I had learned to adapt the way I move, talk and even think around you. I was better at acting than you. Skills I had learned to fine tune since being with you. I was an actor in my own rite, and I was going to win the Oscar tonight. I took another drink and went to move past you.

"I'm fucking Mark." You bit so sharply, and I felt the venom lingering on the skin. I tried so hard not to let it in. But I stood there, body turned to rock, staring at the couch through the kitchen door where I was going to be spending my night. "And I fucking loved it." That little twist of the knife at the end, just to make the pain that little deeper, to open me up, to let the venom really find its way into my blood stream. I bit down hard, and took a breath. I knew better than to react right away. When I turned to face you, you had a smile on your face. *Gotcha* those eyes said. I didn't say much, or if I did, I can't recall. The next thing I remember was pouring the glass of water away and putting it back in the sink. I took the bottle of Prosecco, took one last long drink, felt the bubbles burn my throat, and then took another long gulp to make the fire in my gullet that little more painful. I had been used to pain since being with you. At first it was alien to me, but over time, you have made me want it. *To crave it.* Still the bull was scooping the dirt with its hooves, and you really wanted me to start waving that red rag so you could charge.

You came to me, to take the bottle from my hand, but I was already emptying it into the sink. "You need to go to bed Lorna. I don't want to do this tonight." I moved to the living room. As I passed you, I got a hint of your perfume. I had always hated that brand, and you knew it. "Happy New Year baby," I said. *Red rag waved, come at me with those horns.*

You pushed me to the back. Thankfully, I wasn't as drunk as you, and I stopped myself from falling over, catching myself on the door frame. I turned to you. I think I was laughing. Reservation now gone. "You're disgusting," I said. "Childish. Trying to get a rise out of me? You haven't been fucking anyone. You're easy, but you aren't that special."

"Oh really?" You said, then that smile splayed across your

face. You know the one? The one that says *I know your hurting and this gives me joy.* You turned and spread your hands on the kitchen counter and bent over. "He did me like this first," and you lifted your leg onto the counter, the bottom of your skirt riding up. You were wearing a thong. You told me you didn't like wearing those. "And then like this." You hopped on the counter, skirt around your waist, legs wide open. You held my gaze, then scoffed, laughed, and dropped back to the floor, your heels clicking on the tiled kitchen. *My* tiled kitchen. You took out a cigarette from the packet next to the toaster and sparked up the poison, taking a deep inhale and holding it. "He's not as big as you," you said, blowing the smoke from those rouge lips. "But he's much better." You shrugged, arms folded, the smoke burning into the air. "I didn't know I was a squirter."

I remember turning, shaking my head, walking to the living room again. The heat in my chest rising, my hands beginning to tremble. But I couldn't let you see it. I couldn't let you know you had cut me. I had to get away from you before I did something I regretted, or before I fed your desire for pain. But it was too late. I was in the kitchen again, and I was screaming. Something, anything. I called you a slut, I called you a whore, a liar, manipulator. I told you your outfit looked stupid. I told you that no one could love you because you're incapable of such things. I said so much, and I knew you loved it. I knew you enjoyed seeing me get like this. I could tell with that look in your eyes, my pain feeding that overflowing cup in your black heart. I had failed again to hold myself together. You knew what to press and how hard. Too much too fast and I'd just walk away. You were good, I knew your patterns, and you got me every time I tried to get away.

You threw the cigarette into the sink and it died with a hiss. I moved to you, rage gripping me. I grabbed your hair and pulled your head back. You smiled and slapped me across the face. Heat pushed itself down to my stomach and then a little farther. I spat in your face, right in that laughing mouth. You tore open my shirt and pulled the buttons apart, those long red nails dragging down my chest, blood pushing from the gouges. I turned you away from me and you pressed your ass against my throbbing dick. I got myself out and you yanked your thong down to your ankles.

"I fucking hate you," I whispered in your ear as I entered you. I was hard, harder than I had been in so long. I pushed your head into the work surface and took handfuls of your hair. I swung hard, trying to hurt you. Trying to make you feel my pain. You gritted your teeth and screamed my name. Screamed *his* name. I thought of my ex-girlfriend. Any other girl I had dated before you. And then another. Every hot girl I had ever loved, fucked or hated. Everyone I could think of being inside other than who I was inside of. You pulled away and pushed me onto the kitchen table and moved on top. I grabbed your throat as you climbed on. You thrashed half empty wine glasses onto the ground and plates onto the floor. I wrapped my fingers around your neck and you let me fill you up. Biting your lips. You bit my chest hard, my pecs cheek stinging like hot iron. I called you a whore. You called me worthless as you laughed and fucked me harder, the table shaking. You took handfuls of me and I you, hot breath in my mouth and in yours until I felt you tighten and dig those nails into my chest once more.

You were always quiet when you came. A slight whimper and holding tight. But tonight you howled in ecstasy, your nipples hard, body rigid like an electric bolt had struck you. You were wet and quivering, a flush of the skin and nails drawing blood from my chest. I gripped you tighter and filled you up. We lay on the table for a few moments, heavy breathing, body racing with euphoria and endorphins dancing along our minds. Stallions racing through our blood streams. Tracing the blood across my chest, you giggled. Red lips smudged on perfect teeth.

"I must have gotten a little rough," you said smiling as you climbed off me and put your underwear back on, stepping over the broken glass. "I'll get something for that." You got the towel doused in cold water and I saw that look in your eyes again as you nursed my wounds. The look I saw the day I met you. The look that kept me coming back to you. "I love you." You whispered under your breath.

The sound made me feel sick. I didn't reply, and for my penance, the tears began to linger on those black eye lids. You hit me for the first time then, punched me in the nose in an explosion of bone and blood. You moved from me, leaving me bleeding. You slept alone that night, and I didn't sleep at all.

2

Now

"Good morning baby." You were wearing those joggers which squoze your ass like a peach. You didn't have any makeup on, your skin pale, hair like a wire brush. Something you didn't like to broadcast, all of your photos online filtered, done up and with perfect straight hair. I saw something in you which no one else did, the *real* you and not the façade which you portray to the rest of the world. I lifted my head and found that my nose had pooled onto the couch. Thankfully we had a dark brown leather suite, so the dried blood would come off easily enough with some wet wipes and elbow grease. "I'm sorry about last night," you took a seat next to me, touching my face. Your fingertips were like razor blades on my skin. You looked like warmed up shit.

"How long has it been going on?" I bit, the memory of your infidelity pushing through the haze like a wrecking ball through glass. Your face contorted like you were suffering a worse hangover than the throbbing in my nose.

"Has what been going on?" You said, your face slapped with confusion.

"You and Mark?" I said, nearly puking at the taste of his name. You shook your head.

"Nothing has been going on Chris," you said softly. "I was angry. Upset. Don't you trust me?" You said, those eyes turning angry.

"I do trust you," I said, "But last night you –"

"Last night I was drunk and you started a fight because of your jealousy, remember?" You held my gaze, my stomach clenching and knotting. You could see me searching my mind, my memory fractured, trying to piece together what had happened. "Nothing has been going on," you spat.

"Okay," I said. I didn't apologize. I never apologized. I know I hadn't gotten it wrong, but it was often easier to keep your mouth firmly shut sometimes. I stood then. Slowly at first, still dazed. I checked my watch and it had just gone mid-day. I hadn't slept in this late for a long time and I had work in a couple of hours. Foolishly, I had decided to opt for the double time on New Year's Day at work. In hindsight I was thankful; it was an excuse to get away from you. "I need to get ready." I spat. You stood, a worried look in your eyes. Why wasn't I fighting with you? Why was I not complimenting you? Telling you how beautiful you looked? Because I don't think that. Not right now. I could feel my lip tight with the dried blood. I touched it. It was swollen, and I hoped I didn't have a black eye too.

In the kitchen I saw the broken plates and destroyed wine glasses that littered the floor. Thankfully, I was still in my shoes from the night before. I walked over the glass lightly, feeling the odd stray shard crunch under my feet like walking on morning snow. I took out the brush and got to work on the mess. You stood at the kitchen door holding yourself. Those puppy dog eyes looking at me from afar.

"Do you need to go to work today?" You said standing at the doorway. Your voice was slight, soft, like you were a child asking for an extra cupcake after dinner. "I think you should stay home. We need to talk about last night. I don't want you to go. You can't leave me in the house after what happened." There was vulnerability in your voice, meek and mild. Something you usually did after a fight. I knew the score. We would talk. We would get nowhere. We would fight, we would fuck, and it would be another 'do not disturb' in the locked box of unsettled arguments over flowing with black tar.

As usual, I held back, as you dangled the bait. I wanted to say so much. I could feel the bitterness on my tongue, the drunken fury still there in the pit of my stomach like a train of bile wanting to come out. I continued to sweep up the regret from the night before. I took a panful of glass and porcelain and depressed the handle of the bin. There, staring me in the face, rags and bundles of bloodied tissues. The searing pain in my nose pushing to the front of my mind once more. I don't know how long I was standing there staring at the blood sodden rags, but it was long enough for the glass to fall from the pan onto the floor once more. I pulled myself from my daze. I turned but you were gone. I could hear the sound of water running upstairs and music playing. It would appear agony is only one sided.

I finished cleaning up the shards once more and took the bin outside. The afternoon air was cool and the sky above was a dull grey. No doubt there would be snow later. The weather forecast had predicted as much. I had always hated snow. Even when we went out to the local forest and built snowmen in late November. The memory lingered in my mind like a sunny afternoon in the harshest of winters. The break in the storm of my mind.

I closed the bin and stared back at the house. It wasn't anything fancy, but it was my home. The shower leaked a little and it was always fucking cold, but it was my home none the less. My place where I could retreat from the world. Retreat there with you, and the cold of your heart often made the bitter chill of winter a little less bearable. I stopped as I caught a glimpse of myself in the kitchen window as I went to go back inside. I looked like emaciated shit: my face was puffy, my eyes sunken and my nose, God, I wasn't the best-looking guy in the world anyway, and you had me looking like a Picasso painting. I felt the pain begin to well once more. Not from my face, but deeper in my stomach. It began to dance and bubble, and in a second, I let my insides paint the concrete flagging. I tried to aim, but the splatter caught my shoes and painted the bottom of my jeans in last night's booze.

I reeled up, wiping my mouth on my hand and flicked the dangling mucus onto the ground. Wiping myself on my already destroyed jeans, I gagged once more at the smell of bile and acid pushing into my nose. Booze tastes much worse the second time round.

In the kitchen I took a long drink of water, swirled my mouth out and spat into the sink basin. The bile and saliva was marred with blood like a painter's water running off the canvas. The shower was still running. You were upstairs, either that or you had vanished into thin air, the water dissolving you like the witch from the Wizard of Oz. I took some painkillers out of the drawer and moved past your boxes of anti-depressants, something which you told me you were trying to get yourself off. We had differing views about Pharmacopeia, and you gave into the narrative of it's something you had no control over. That you were simply born broken. I disagreed, but you didn't like that, so now I just let you get on with doping yourself up. It's better to feel sad than feel nothing at all. In my warped mind anyway. Maybe that was why I stayed with you? Even after the fights? The crazy arguments? The insults? I had gotten used to feeling numb, and the misery was better than fading into the grey of the sky above.

I walked upstairs slowly. The steam was pushing from under the bathroom door and filling the landing like I was stuck in a burning building. I put my ear to the door and heard the faint sound of music playing and the sound of water cascading. In the bedroom I looked at myself properly in the mirror. My eye was beginning to swell and darken. *Great* I thought. There was no way I could go into work looking like this. Wouldn't be the first time I had had to dodge work because of you. There's only so many times you can use the excuse of *my car has broken down* or *sorry, I'm not feeling well. Bad fish. Again yes.* I was already on a warning for me not coming in enough. Not to mention it was New Year's Eve last night. To call in sick would scream being hungover. I could always tell the truth? I laughed at myself. Now *that* was pure insanity.

I took out one of your makeup wipes from your dresser. The smell of fragrance made my eyes sting. I eyed the little cotton bastard with trepidation, like going to wash your hands with alcohol gel knowing you have been biting your fingers too much. I put the fabric to my nose and sweet holy hell danced across my skin. I bit down and clenched my teeth, letting out some curse word sequences I didn't know existed. The fire danced on my skin and crawled into the open wounds. I picked the dried blood from my nostrils and had to wipe my eyes a few times so I could still see myself in the dresser mirror. After a few minutes of agony, I was done. I looked and felt a little better. I heard the shower turn off. Quickly, I stuffed the rag into my pocket. Finally I could get showered and changed. Maybe then you would let me use your phone to call work. We only had one phone. Mine had broken so I had to use yours.

The bathroom door pulled open and the steam bellowed out onto the landing and you emerged naked in the bedroom like a rock star onstage at a glam concert. The razor blade in your hand. The blood dripped down your arms like red snakes. You soaked into the carpet. Eyes red. The crimson smearing along your pale skin. The steam dancing off your skin like you had emerged from the fire.

"We need to talk about last night." You said, as you held up your arms and showed me your lacerated forearms, peeling open to the grey bone inside.

3

Then

"It's hot as dick today," John said as he tucked into his second McDonalds of the day. He saw me eyeing the greasy burger with contempt. I didn't say anything, but the look on my face said it all for me. "Hey," he said, with lettuce sticking out of his mouth and his digits digging into the bun. "I told you, I'm bulking. I need the calories. Don't look at me like that." I smiled and continued to eat my lentils and chicken. "Looks better than that rabbit food you're eating!" I took another mouthful and swallowed, trying to hide the grimace on my face but John saw it and laughed. "Bet you wish you had one of these babies now!" I smiled, forcing down the tasteless mush down my throat.

"I suppose. But I don't think eating your body weight in fast food is how you're supposed to bulk up." John punched me to the arm from the driver's seat. The thud left a lingering sting, but it wasn't something I wasn't used to by now. I had been working with John for the past three months on the early shift at the delivery warehouse. Casual punches were how him and his brother had always greeted each other. Old habits die hard I suppose.

"What would you know eating that rabbit food Chris? How many calories are in that thing? About three fifty? Max?" He scoffed. "More than that in my milkshake." To demonstrate his point, he picked up the large plastic cup from the drinks holder and took a heavy gulp and finished with a satisfied sigh. "See!" He flexed his right bicep. "Can feel them growing already."

"You're fucking weird," I laughed as I scraped the last few lentils from the bottom of the plastic tub. I wound down the window and let some air in. The day was hot and it was only late morning. We still had a long way to go before we could complete our work for the day, but John insisted on making a pit stop at the place of nuggets and happy meals. I was hoping to wait until we got back to the warehouse because I had had to eat my food cold, but given I had been late for work this morning due to my alarm deciding it didn't want to work (I hadn't just overslept honestly boss), I hadn't had chance to make anything before I came in. I needed to get more shopping in and I would take a trip tonight when I got home before getting ready to head to the party. "Whose going tonight?" I asked as I gazed out the window to the afternoon sun. The soft wind kissed my sweating forehead and I lit a cigarette from my pocket. John instinctively reached out his hand for one. I eyed his fat fingers with a disgruntled grin. Still, the hand stayed. "You need to start buying your own." I said as I relinquished the smoke.

"I'm trying to quit, I told you this."

"Bullshit." I leant over and passed him the lighter and he tried to put it in his pocket before I snatched it out his hand. "So whose coming later? Cara's birthday?"

"Just a few friends. Half of them I've never met despite us being together for a few years." *You'd be surprised what people can hide from you* I thought. I wonder if he knew? About *The Girl Next Door?* I breathed the smoke into my lungs, letting the sounds of the birds above me nesting carry me away into more provocative times.

"A few of her work colleagues, some business people," he continued, lost in his own monologue.

"Sounds like it would be a good night," I say. I turn to him and smile, reaching into my pocket I pull out the pack of smokes again. "You want another?" John eyed me like a kid in a candy shop of lollipops coated in arsenic. He took it without question and took the lighter too. He put it in his pocket. I didn't protest. "So a few women are going to be there?" I said with a smirk. John nodded. He was a heavy-set man in his early thirties. He had a couple of very badly done tattoos, and he weighed about the same as a small elephant. His hair was pitch black and he always seemed to wear the same pair of jeans and white Tee Shirt, other than one year at a work function where he opted for shorts. His wife on the other hand, Cara, was way out of his league, and he knew it. She was tall, slim, brunette. Fucking gorgeous. He tells me that they met on a night out and were both drunk and hit it off from there. I often tease him if she ever sobered up she would realise what a dumb arse he was and bolt.

"Say," he said, licking the left-over barbeque sauce from his fingers. "Do you have any plans tonight?" As it happened, I *did* have plans tonight: Pilates at the Crunch Gym, an appointment at the sauna and then was looking to go for a swim for a few hours at the pool. Maybe a face mask in the evening as I chilled on my Egyptian satin bed sheets, nursing a cool glass of Merlot wine with a facemask form the Body Shop. Kale mixed with ginger extract for that smooth, clean skin texture that keeps your face hydrated.

"As it happens John," I say, "I don't have anything on this evening. What're you suggesting?" John takes a big gulp of his disgusting sloppy milkshake that must have gone warm in the sun by now. Didn't he know that as the milk evaporated the sugar content went up? His insulin levels must be shot at it is. I doubt he would live past the age of forty-five.

"Well," he began, mouth still full of sugar and cream. "Why

don't you come by? I'm sure Cara won't mind if I bring a friend from work." I liked this idea. It would be good to see her again.

"That sounds great," I say, trying to not sound too eager about the idea of having a night of fun. I could always do my crunches when I got home and some press ups too before jumping in a cold shower to keep the muscles nice and tight. Makes the fitted shirts fit better. Makes my arms and chest stand out that little more.

We sat there a minute smoking and watching the world go by on the carpark of the fast-food restaurant. A mother with two kids trying to quell the argument over who got the toy from the happy meal. A tall man in a black suit taking selfies in the front of a Mercedes and then walk to the banged up Corsa next to it and get inside. A flock of pigeons cleaning the scraps of food that had been lazily discarded on the ground.

And then, I saw *you*.

You didn't see me, but I saw you walking to your car. You had a large bag of food with you and you were fumbling with your keys trying to hit the right button. I watched you for a couple of seconds; your red hair dancing in the wind, straight and pristine. Your pencil dress cut low both for modesty, but also because you knew guys would be checking out your ass. You wore a small blue blazer that went well with your white shirt. I figured you must work in an office or be some kind of lawyer. However the car you were driving, a twelve-year-old Nissan Micra which had more dirt on it than a Labrador in the woods on the first day of autumn, made me think you had a modest side.

I watched you, I would even say admired you, for a few moments more. John was talking about some bullshit story that was on the radio, but his droning tone was just a blur with you in my eye. I saw you and *only* you. Nothing else: not the birds, not the screaming kids and certainly not the guy taking selfies. You were my eye then, and I enjoyed watching you. I felt something inside me, and I had never believed in love at first sight. It was a romantic concept I had no time for, I didn't believe in fairy tales. And yet here you were, at this exact moment. In my eye, in my life when I had no one else to call my own, and by the lack of an engagement ring, you were the same.

You dropped your keys on the ground and fumbled to pick them up. The bag fell open and your milkshake tumbled onto the ground and splattered on the floor and onto your now not so clean blue blazer. You muttered something that didn't need a genius to understand.

"I mean, the damn government need to get a grip with this shit!" John barked, pointing at the radio, shouting at the presenter like he could hear him. I touched the handle, toyed with it. Do I go to help you? What would you say? What would *I* say? I was out the van and walking towards you before I realised, like I was walking on a cloud as you fumbled with the food, milkshake and fallen keys.

"Let me help you with that," I said as calmly as possible, a little smirk on my face, trying to seem just as embarrassed as you were. I was glad I decided to wear a tight Tee shirt today. I tried to keep you looking at my good side as my left bicep was a little bigger than my right. It was probably just in my mind, but we can never be too careful.

"Oh god thank you," you said. Your voice was local but eloquent. You weren't from common upbringings, you were different. Well educated, maybe an only child. I think you liked Coldplay or some other kind of indie band. Maybe you played an instrument yourself? I couldn't see any calluses on your fingertips so not the guitar. The violin perhaps? I think you play the violin, but I couldn't ask right now. I knelt down and fished the keys out of the melting puddle of cream and sugar.

"Here," I said. I wiped the keys off and you took them gracefully. You met my eyes. The deepest green emeralds. "I've never met a red head with green eyes before." I actually had, a few times, but you didn't need to know that.

"It's one in a hundred thousand." You said, those thin lips stretching to your ears.

"Oh really?" I say flabbergasted. "That rare huh?" We share a look for a moment, maybe a second, maybe an hour. Time stood still for me then, looking into those eyes, feeling like I wanted the world to swallow me whole and float into the sky at the same time. I point to the small platter of cream on your blazer. "You seem to have spilt a little bit," I said laughing. Be playful, be funny. Don't take yourself too seriously. You followed my finger and checked yourself out and your jaw dropped.

"Oh no!" You screeched. You shook your head and placed your ripped food bag on the top of your car. In a frenzy, you began licking your finger and rubbing the fabric, making the smudge bigger. You laughed, trying to make light of the situation. *Were you nervous? Was I making you nervous?* Shrugging and flicking your hair back, eyebrows jumping, you took the jacket off. You locked eyes with me again then, only for a second, but I knew you wanted me to know you were taking clothes off. Maybe something you wanted to do in the future for me? Maybe this was the appetiser before the full meal.

"Hey it's okay!" I said laughing. I reached down into the gloop and took a scoop full of milkshake and wiped it on my face. You laughed and twirled your hair through your fingers, the blue jacket accompanying your now cold food. I doubt you wanted to eat it now it was tainted. Given by how slender you were, I doubted it was for you. Some of the milkshake had found its way to my lips. I licked it and tried to hide my disgust. Banana. I hate banana.

"I hate banana!" I laughed. Your eyes widened.

"So do I! I asked for vanilla!" We both laughed again then. You pointed to the van which John was leaning forward in the driver's seat, watching intently at me rubbing milkshake on my face whilst the hot red head undresses for me in the McDonald's car park. I went to ask you your name, for your number, to marry me right there and then, but you let out a long breath and spun the keys in your fingers. "Thanks for the help." You took hold of the ripped McDonalds bag and walked and placed it in the bin.

"You not hungry?" I said.

"I don't eat that crap," you laughed, walking back to your car. So I was right. *It wasn't for you.* Your heels click on the asphalt as you move to the driver's side. "It was for my friend at work. He wanted me to grab him something whilst I was out. I'll tell him I ran out of time or something," you lie. You're a liar? You opened your door and at the risk of blowing it completely, I decided to grow a pair. I opened the door for you as you unlocked it and you smiled again. You look me over and get into the driver's seat with no much as a *thank you.* I wonder if you were used to having guys fall over you? Or if you were typically the damsel in distress?

"Was great meeting you," you say as you put the jacket in the back of the car. You closed your door and fired up the engine. The window was still open.

"You're welcome." I took in a sharp breath. "I'm Chris."

"Nice to meet you." You gave me another glance and began to reverse, before turning and leaving me in your rear-view mirror standing in the car park with banana milkshake on my face with pigeons walking around my feet. I turned and walked back to the van. I felt so deflated, like every footstep was weighted by chains. John was smiling widely as I got into the van.

"Not a fucking word." I bit, embarrassed.

"Dude she was hot!" He made an obscene gesture with his fingers and his tongue.

"She blew me off man. Didn't give me her name."

"Maybe you came on too strong?"

"Fuck her," I say. "Her loss." John doesn't back me up with the comment. I thought that's what guy friends do? Or have I got that wrong?

"Nah," John said. "I saw a guy on the internet talk about

dating. He said if you're too nice, women will see you as their gay male friend. You gotta be an arsehole with them. Call em fat. Tell em they look ugly."

"And you have a wife how?" I laughed, reaching for another cigarette.

"Hey," he said, hand reaching out once more. I eyed the greasy palm. "I'm quitting tomorrow I swear!" I laughed and flicked the cigarette at his bulging belly.

"I'll pick you some up tonight for letting me come later. Sweeten the deal a little."

"Sounds great," John said firing up the engine. We left the car park then, turned the corner and I hoped to see you parked up and waiting for me. But the road was bare. No Nissan Micra, no trail of milkshake. I looked out the window as we joined the busy traffic. It was like you had never existed, and the thought of you in my mind lingered there for the rest of the afternoon.

"Treat them mean," I whispered to myself. "I can do that."

4

Now

My face was fixed with horror. Hands shaking, mind racing and lip quivering. "Lorna what the fuck have you done!" I screamed as I got to my feet. Your skin had turned dull, your lips turning blue.

"Don't go to work," you rasped. "We need to talk about last night." You collapsed to the carpet, your open arms mixing with the blue fabric, threads and dust clinging to the flowing wound. I thrust open the drawer and took out a shirt. One of my less expensive ones, and snagged it with my teeth, shredding the fabric. I took your left arm first, and tied the bandage tight around your bicep. Then onto the right arm. I was covered in you. You were so warm, drenching me in red heat. Your skin so cold. Breath shallow. I looked for your phone, to call for help. I could hear the sound of music playing, echoing.

I lept to my feet and bolted to the bathroom like a gazelle fleeing a cheetah. Grabbing the phone, I tapped the screen wildly but you had changed your password again. I held it in front of your face for the facial recognition and the code vanished and a home screen filled with apps for social media filled my eyes like different types of ice cream. Your eyes began to sink into your head and your hair matted with the blood and water over your face. So much hair, so much blood. My fingers coated like grabbing a swollen strawberry doughnut.

I pulled the duvet off the bed. Thankfully I had changed the sheets from white to dark blue a few days before. I drowned you in its king-size arms and with all my might; harbouring onto what little strength I had, I scooped your slender wet body into my arms and hurdled downstairs.

"Stay with me baby," I soothed. "Stay with me, we'll get help soon." I bundled you in the passenger seat of the car and stabbed the keys in the ignition. I fired up the engine and stomped on the accelerator, driving the needle deep into the red. The machine screamed and popped and I snapped the car into second. At the junction, I didn't look. It was busy but I went for it anyway. I held my breath as I banked hard around the corner, snapping the gear into fourth to the sound of blaring horns and shouts of motorists. I didn't care, I gave them a quick glance in the rear-view mirror to make sure blue lights and sirens weren't chasing me. I couldn't stop. The hospital was less than two miles away, but I doubt you had long left.

My heart hammered in my chest and I stole a look at you in between swerving slower moving cars. Houses blurred as I clocked double the speed limit. You were turning paler, your skin the colour of candle wax.

"Lorna!" I shouted, pushing you to the head. "Stay with me!" You gave a low moan. *Good* I thought. If you are in pain, it means you're still alive. I could hear the dripping of your wounds pooling onto the ground like Spring rain.

A red light in front. Standing traffic and cars flying across my path. I revved the engine and slammed it back into second for that extra burst of power. The car hurtled through the barrage of oncoming metal. We made it across, swerving and clipping a kerb. I heard something pop and the engine begin to stammer and sparks fly in my wing mirror. I couldn't slow down. You were fading quickly and the hospital was in sight. The smell of rubber burning, metal screeching. In the wing mirror sparks erupted as the wheel rim coursed and carved into the gravel. The steering wheel shook violently but I kept my foot to the floor.

I got to the car park. The barrier was up and out of order for maintenance and I thanked God, Buddha or Jeff from the local supermarket for a break in my shitty day. I turned into the car park, narrowly missing a patient with a drip that should definitely not have been out smoking in the cool January air. At the front door to the emergency department entrance, I slammed on the breaks and dove out of the driver's door like a drowning man clutches the shore. Racing, eyes on me, the stench of burning rubber and the engine smoking, I pulled open the passenger door and took you into my arms. I raced faster than I knew I could, my arms burning, my legs aching, adrenalin flooding my veins as blood drained out of yours. "I need some help!"

5

Then

I got in from a quick sauna and Pilates class holding some shopping from the farmer's store. I only ate the best cuts of meat straight from the field: grass fed beef, free range chicken and pigs that have been able to roll in their own shit for their whole lives. Not only that, but Mary, the owner, had finally come through with her promise of getting me cut of lean venison. As well as that, I purchased a large quantity of whole foods and grains and legumes, not to mention the rainbow assorted fruits and vegetables I had picked. Some still had soil on them, the organic carrots that had been picked that morning especially.

I called a cab and they told me I would be waiting around fifty minutes for someone to pick me up. Normally I would have called the call taker a fucking whore and slammed the phone down, but I restrained myself. It gave me chance to clean and prune my food, separate and freeze the meats, and to roll the venison in pepper, salt and herbs of oregano and parsley, before wrapping it tight with cling film and put it in the fridge to marinate and chill for my meal tomorrow following a chest workout at the Crunch gym. In another bag, I had a bottle of fifteen years aged scotch which I poured in a tumbler and let the whisky swirl a little. Then, I pulled out some mineral water and put just a drop in the amber liquid, before taking a sip and letting it dance around my gums, before swallowing.

I got a quick cold shower which let me oxygenate my blood from the deep breathing exercises I had been practising a few times a day, then washed my hair in a lavender and ginger extract shampoo, before lathering it with a coconut based conditioner. Finally, I moisturised and put some talc on my hair to dry out any of the residue suds and moisture, blow dried and slicked it back where it stayed. I took out a sharp looking royal blue long sleeved shirt and left the two top buttons undone so my pecks could be seen popping from the top, and finally threw on a pair of tight-fitting denim jeans which made my ass look like a rounded peach. A pair of black Louis Vuitton dress shoes with brown laces. I trimmed the stray hairs that were poking from the sides of my beard with an electronic razor I had bought myself. It had a five-year guarantee don't you know. I looked myself in the mirror and told myself that if I were gay or a woman, I would fuck my brains out, before returning to the kitchen a couple of minutes before the time the taxi was meant to be here, taking another scotch into my hand.

Then, like an uninvited guest, you walked right into my mind again. I hadn't thought about you much after I saw you. Not because I didn't want to, but because the thought of never seeing you again made my heart sombre. Maybe you had a boyfriend? Maybe you were gay and weren't interested? But that smile, the taking off your jacket, the way your eyes met mine under that afternoon sun, made me wonder otherwise. I imagine you got a lot of guys checking you out and wanting to speak to you, to get to know you, to fuck you. I was indeed one of those guys, but I wanted much more of you from that.

Firstly, I wanted to know your name. I wanted to put a name to the memory of you. Because it was much easier to create something, to make an attachment to something if it has a name. It's like when you first buy a pet from the pet store, as soon as you give it a name it becomes part of the family. It then has an identity. I wanted to know *your* identity. Who and *what* you were? I wanted to know everything about you, where you liked to eat, what you liked to drink, the taste of your cunt and how deep you could put my cock to the back of your throat.

Was I afraid of you? Was it that I didn't feel good enough for you? That was why you didn't want to tell me your name after I offered mine? After I gave myself to you, opened up to you and made myself vulnerable? I didn't get your name, not even your number. Even after the universe threw us together by chance, and I was left the one with the questions and wondering. I wonder if you were thinking of me? If when your boyfriend came home this evening and fucked you, if a thought of me crept into your mind as he entered you? And you lied too. You were a liar. A woman of little morals and of disregard about your own reputation. But that made you much more perfect to me. I wanted to know you. To love you. To make you mine all mine.

I finished the scotch and checked my watch. The cab was three minutes late. I wouldn't have another scotch, so I opted for a glass of water from the kitchen sink. I had just had a new filter installed. The water in this part of the country was hard, and I heard that it was the cause of bowel problems in the local community. There had been a story about it in the news.

I open up my phone and click on the usual socials: Facebook, Instagram. The picture of me looking hot in the bedroom had gotten over three hundred likes already, and that put a smile on my face. I scrolled and found John's latest post. Him and his wife Cara, looking as stunning as ever, both having a drink of wine in the kitchen and smiling for the world to see. The caption 'Birthday party!' with a few emoji balloons to accompany it. I can't wait to be in those photos, to be part of the party.

I scalded myself as I ran upstairs. I had forgotten to throw on some aftershave and my cufflinks. The thought of you in my mind, already making me loose it.

Whilst in the bedroom I took another selfie, deleted it, and then took a few more. I sat on the bed cycling through them. I added a filter, changed the lighting and cropped some of the background. Highlighted my teeth, smoothed out the wrinkles on my forehead. Which reminded me, Botox. I needed more Botox. When I was happy with the picture I uploaded it and checked my watch. The cab was now fourteen minutes late and I was starting to grow impatient. I dialled the company back –

"Express taxis," the woman said on the other side of the phone. I bet she was fat. She sounded fat.

"Hi, I ordered a taxi over an hour ago. Where is it?" I gave her my address and I heard the sound of those fingers tapping on the keyboard that was probably littered with crust from devoured sausage roles and cheap nail varnish.

"The driver has arrived but left after you didn't go out to him sir," she said. I squoze the phone tight in my hands.

"What the fuck did you say?" I seethed. "The fucking taxi has left? I have somewhere to be!" I demanded she turn the taxi around and send him back immediately or I will make an official complaint to the company director. She quickly tapped on the keyboard.

"Okay sir, it's on its way," she said, her voice quick, feeble. I hung up the phone and checked my news feed once more. The photo from earlier had now gotten over four hundred likes, the one I had just taken creeping up to one hundred. I saw John's birthday post once more and I nearly like and commented, but saw that he had tagged Cara in the photo too. I refrained myself. The post had only gotten fifteen likes and a couple of comments. I checked the pages of those that had bothered to write something, none of them attractive. Not even worth a desperate drunken screw.

The taxi arrived a short while later. Two more whisky's deep and I was feeling a little buzzed. I got in and eyed the driver.

"You're late," I said. "Don't think you're getting a tip." The driver didn't respond, simply asked for the address which again pissed me off. "You mean they didn't tell you when you took the job?"

"No sir," he said, with a little attitude to his voice which I didn't like. I told him the address and the cab set off. I heard the latest single from Ed Sheeran play on the radio.

"Hey, turn that up will ya?" I asked politely. The cabbie did as he was instructed. I began to dance a little in my seat, my body getting into the groove of the music. I was thinking of making the usual small talk: *Been busy? What time you working till?* But I figured that to be bad manners.

I bet I could gut him at a red light.

"Ever had a murderer in your car before?" I asked. It was a good ice breaker. In my opinion anyway. He lifted his head and eyed me in his rear-view mirror. I smiled at him innocently.

"A lot of serial killers drove taxis to lure victims," the cabbie said with a smirk. "Don't get too comfortable. And don't check the glove box." We both laughed, both assured in our mutual respect that at any moment, we could choke the life out of each other. It was a comforting feeling, knowing you were on the verge of annihilation at any one time. Kept things interesting.

I arrived at John's home a few minutes later. I paid the driver and we laughed a little more at the conversation. I even threw him an extra ten percent for the joke he made about Ted Bundy. He too complimented me, but on my shoes and not my hair.

"Are you this complimentary to everyone who gets in your car?" I asked jokingly.

"Only the ones that escape!" I closed the door and he drove off into the night. I imagine he would be on the news in a few years. Guys like that have a story to tell. They don't go unnoticed for very long.

I looked up at the house. The driveway was paved in bronze and grey slabs that formed a circle in the centre pulling from the high hedges on the perimeter. A nice new Mercedes sat on the driveway behind the high front gates. Behind the Mercedes was a new Range rover, metallic green and no doubt had all the gadgets. The house itself was brightly lit, and the feint sound of laughter and music crept into the evening air. The sky was clear and the stars twinkled above in the dusk of the evening. No moon tonight. A good Omen. Feint clouds fell over the top of the three-story town house which sat alone, with a perimeter of high walls that gave way to a luxuriously spaced garden. John didn't have a penny to his name, but Cara on the other hand had come from wealth. Her mother was a divorcee, and she had played the courts well to get what she wanted. Deservedly or not. Cara's father was a tyrant. Unloving till the end. From what I had heard in the conversations with John on our morning rounds, he had been a complete bastard with her and her mother, and she still had the scars to prove it. She paid for her time with blood, and he paid with his wallet when it was over, and ended it all with a hosepipe and a running engine. That explained a lot about Cara and her psyche. *We date our parents* Freud had said, and there was, in Cara's case, certainly some truth to that.

I pushed the gate and it gave way. Not a single creek of the hinges. It was heavy, and it fell back quickly but then slowed to a slight clatter of metal. Barely noticeable. Walking to the front door, I caught a glimpse of the security camera perched at the top, my face for the world to see in high definition. I smiled for the camera, turning my face to the left so they captured my good side, the one where the lack of Botox was less noticeable.

I knocked on the door and waited. I checked my watch and tapped my fingers on the neck of the wine bottle in my hand. Couldn't turn up empty handed could I? That's what people did at parties wasn't it? Bring gifts? Alcohol? Severed heads? A few moments later the door opened and the heat from inside was welcoming on the chilly night as it pushed through into the night sky. John was standing there with his usual white top and bottle of Budweiser in his hand.

"About time you got here!" He slurred, and gestured me in with the bottle. He closed the door behind me and eyed the wine. "Nice one mate. Cara loves red." He took the bottle from my hand and I followed him into the kitchen. The spread was impressive to say the least: Pasta, fruit cocktails, chocolate, finger food, sandwiches, olives stuffed with garlic, shrimp, sea bass cakes, even a Thai green curry with basmati rice with lemon grass. Appeasing to all appetites and diets it would seem.

Cara was standing there with her back to me. She looked

amazing, and that was only from the back. Her hair was long and fell past her bare shoulders that were wrapped in a tight pencil dress that stopped just above the knees. Her heals black also, and her slim frame holding her weight in all the right places. She had lost a little weight around her neck since I last saw her. I'd be able to fit my hands around it that little easier.

"Babe!" John shouted. I got the first hit of stale booze then. This was going to be a rough night. John was already shit faced, and it had only just gone 9PM. He could hold his own though. He seemed to 'peak' about fifteen bottles in and you wouldn't notice he was drunk. 'Irish Gold,' they called it. The ability to drink yourself sober. I believed it a myth though, if not biologically impossible. Not because I was a scientist, but because I have seen John utterly shit faced drunk dancing in a crowded room with a tie around his head thinking he was 'fat Rambo.' The worst part is, John didn't own a tie. "Look what the cat dragged in!" He announced, turning to me. One hand wrapping the bottle of wine around its neck so tight you would think he was an eighteen-year-old with a free porn hub account and he couldn't jerk hard enough anymore.

Cara turned to me with a smile spread across her face. Her eyes met mine and it quivered and slipped away like a gust of wind.

"Hi," I said, outstretching my hand. "Cara is it? A pleasure to meet you."

6

Then

"You okay babe?" John said. He touched Cara's arm as she stood, her face draining of colour. She jolted when his fingers met her shoulder. I still had my smile fixed on my face and my hand outstretched. Cara snapped out of her stupor.

"Sorry...I..."

"You feeling okay?" John said concerned. Cara looked at him, then at me, then at him again.

"Yeah," she said flatly. She ran her fingers through her hair. "I'm just tired. Lots of guests, lots of things to do!" The smile that followed was more fake than a porn stars tits, and I knew that smile well.

"I told you, you're working too hard! Relax!" John said, handing her a glass of wine and kissing her on the cheek. My hand still outstretched, she eyed it like a rattle snake with its fangs dripping. She snaked her arm out and took mine softly.

"A pleasure to meet you," I said, my smile and white teeth gleaming in her eyes. Cara didn't respond. She let go of my hand and turned from me and began cleaning, putting dishes and spent glasses on the white marble work tops that sat adjacent to a stainless-steel oven and hob. John put his arm around me and ushered me away from the kitchen area.

"Sorry mate, don't know what's up with her. She'll be alright though," John said. I shrugged.

"A lot of pressure isn't it, but the work you've put into the evening is amazing," I said, eyes kind. "I'll grab a drink." John was already halfway through a glass of the red I had bought. He slapped me on the back and then grabbed another.

I stood there in the middle of a mingling marauding of people, some hot, some not. Some healthy, some not. Some well-dressed, some not. I could feel Cara's eyes burning into my back. I turned over my shoulder and we met each other's eyes for a second, before she looked away to the floor. A moment later, I saw her speaking to a tall blonde in a white dress. Her hair in curls and her lips obviously newly done. Badly. She was hot though, and I could see her eyes flitting to mine and then back to Cara. I smiled back and she touched her ear, playing with those golden ear rings of hers. *Eighty percent of communication was body language* I thought. And she was communicating very clearly. Maybe I could speak to her later? But then, my eyes drifted, and the floor around me caved in.

You were sat there in the back of the room nursing a glass of gin. The rim of the glass frosted with sugar and a piece of cucumber swimming in the liquid. The music and chatter around me dulled. I focused in on you. I could see the fresh manicure, the highlights in your hair, even the clinking of the ice in your glass. You hadn't noticed me, your attention on the guy sat opposite you. He was built, a black jumper turning his back like a tort kite. He was tanned and had the styled five o'clock shadow. But you didn't seem that interested in him? He was leaning forward, his legs spread to let his manhood breathe and his heavy silver watch strapped to those tattooed arms that coated the glass of amber in his hand. He was the only one talking however and you played with the straw in your glass, smiling politely. No teeth though. A thin smile that barely met the eyes. His eyes were of course falling on your bare legs that were exposed under that green dress you wore. No pattern? You don't want to be noticed, but the way you had your hair said otherwise. He roared a laugh and you smiled again; the straw being played with between those fingers. He was peacocking. Trying to show you he's funny, charming and has a big dick. The best version of himself, a fraud from the start, but his chizzled jaw and sharp humour wasn't breaking your armour. He was falling, drowning in his own confidence, and you weren't offering him a life ring.

I took a seat at the kitchen bar and watched you from across the dimly lit room, people dancing, obscuring my view. I could look at you all night. I thought I had lost you, your part in my life over like a candle in the wind. And yet, here you were. Fate, it would seem, had brought us closer together. I wonder how you knew Cara? A friend maybe? And just like that, Cara stood opposite me, and I wondered if I had been thinking out loud?

"What are you doing here?" She bit. I was taken back, I thought she would have had more to drink before we had this conversation.

"I was invited."

"Leave now." She said fiercely. Her eyes didn't leave mine, and the world behind her blurred. I smiled broadly and took a bottle of Coors from the counter and cracked the cap with my teeth, taking a long swig. I held her gaze, and just as expected, when John came close, her gaze wavered. I let out a satisfying breath as the booze tickled the back of my throat.

"I think I'll stay. Maybe for a few beers. Maybe even spend the night." I touched Cara's hand and she recoiled like being bitten by a snake. I laughed to myself. "I thought as much." I finished the bottle right there in front of her and passed her the empty. "Get me another one."

7

Then

I have always enjoyed people watching. The way others interact when someone is trying to hit on them, and they are feigning interest. They might never outrightly say those magic words that would send even Satan himself running back to his hellish pit, but the body and the eyes can't lie. I have found that most people, when they are not interested in what you are saying or not wanting to engage with you will either look away, sometimes for a while, sometimes for a few moments but more frequently, like trying to find some way to escape from the uncomfortable interaction they are in. That's one of the reasons I love going to parties, gatherings and even cafés on my own. Whereas the rest of the world is distracted in their own lives, I sit and watch. I am like a hunter. A hunter in a world full of zombies.

I think that's why I couldn't take my eyes off you. Not once while you were sitting there with the big bravado tanned sasquatch did you pull out your phone, did you look away. But I could still see those subtleties. We all have them: the slight crinkle of the eye brows when he would move closer to you, the slight widening of your eyes as he would laugh loudly and boast broadly about the women he had conquered and how you would be in for such a 'good time' if you would only relax a little more. The way your fingertips pinched the top of the Gin glass, holding it to your mouth like it was some kind of barrier between you and the obviously puffed-up lips and fake tanned arsehole that tried to draw closer to you with his 3mm designer beard which had been manscaped to perfection.

The guy you're speaking to, or more accurately, who was talking *at you*, was clearly a façade of a man. He was built, and would no doubt think he could have whoever and whatever he wanted, simply because he wanted it. I bet his father was a dick head, and his mother a whore. I doubted he went to university or did anything meaningful with his life other than posting online and trying to look buff. Probably used bath bombs too.

He may have the world fooled, but I could see straight through him, through his efforts to hide the wrinkles, the lines, the steroids, the three shakes a day with protein powder, creatine for that pre pump, the post workout with low sugars, the cod liver oil for his aching joints, the multi vitamins, the three-step facial routine he did every morning, the hair tweezering to hide the grey, the Instagram profile with the filters and the whitening tooth paste he used twice morning and night, the designer clothes and the overdrawn bank balance, the Audi on finance, the rings and jewellery that weren't his, the dyed hair and the beard trimmed with a razor that didn't come with a five year guarantee. He wasn't good for you, and you knew it. You just needed a way to get away from him.

"So what do you say?" The plastic man said loudly, as he grew a pair, or drank too much scotch, and reached his arm out to touch you. *There.* If I was unsure before, that was all I needed to see. You had a mouthful of gin, and it stuck in your throat as his large hands wrapped around your bare shoulder. You smiled politely, putting your hand to your mouth. You're wearing a lighter shade of foundation since we last met.

"I think you've had a little much to drink Mark," you said, moving away from him and crossing your legs tighter, taking a sip of the gin through the straw. Plastic man had a name after all. He didn't like that. I could tell from how that bolstering smile wavered like a crinkled kite of white in a sudden change of wind. His hand lingered in the air, and you eyed it like it was a leech that hadn't gotten its fill just yet. "I need to use the bathroom."

You stood and turned my way. I don't know why, but I looked away. I had been peering over my shoulder at you, hands resting on the bar with the bottle of beer that Cara had reluctantly brought me. Putting my head down, I let my eyes follow those freshly tanned legs as you walked out of the room. Just as predicted, 'Mark,' sat back in his chair nestling the glass of scotch in his hand, whilst pulling out his smart phone and cracking open his social media feed. The folly of Man is we believe we are the masters of this Earth. But when we see the wrinkles on our skin, the grey in our hair, and the seasons change and the aches emerge, we find we are no more than the ground under our feet. That we are simply clever apes and not Gods amongst worms.

"How's the beer going down man?" John said, breaking my train of thought. He was opposite me, another beer in his hand. He had had more than a few, and in true John fashion, sounded as sober and as stoic as ever. I was just waiting for that one beer that broke the dam.

"Not bad man," I said, gesturing the bottle. "Cara got it for me." John smirked.

"I've got her well trained!" My face stayed stoic as he barked and laughed at the misogynistic comment. "Sink it down and I'll get her to fetch us a couple more." With that, and without a moment's hesitation, he took a long drink, lifting the green bottle to his mouth and tipping it back like a thirsty man in a desert. A satisfied sigh and a slight belch later, he called over his wife who was busy speaking to other guests. She turned and smiled at John, and of course, avoided eye contact with me. I held the smile anyway. "Get us a couple more please darling."

Cara nodded, knelt down, letting that tight dress cup her ass even tighter. She almost wanted me to see it. What kind of game was she playing here? She wants me, she doesn't want me, but she couldn't make her mind up. A moment later, two fresh beers were uncapped and handed to us. Her eyes lingered on mine. I nodded a *thank you*, and she turned back to John that was already half way through.

"Are you not drinking?" I said. Cara froze with the comment. "Why don't you grab a glass of red? I heard it's your favourite," I said with a wink. Her body stuck like a frozen cartoon on television. She turned quickly, running her fingers through her hair.

"I don't drink anymore. It doesn't agree with me." I leant in. I could feel the room closing in on her, and dare I say, I was enjoying watching her squirm.

"But," I said, and touched her finger tips away from John's inebriated gaze, away from the busy eyes of the rest of the room that either stared at cell phones, the bottom of beer bottles, or at each other. "You get so, *loose,* when you have a drink. Sober, you're so stiff, rigid, but when you've had a few drinks down you," I bit lightly on my lip. "You're like a different person."

"You need to leave now Chris." She said, fighting that internal scream that was begging to come out of her throat. "I know what you're doing, and you can't. I can't risk it." She leaned in. I could smell the slight hint on her breath. It definitely there, if you could tease past the mint and lavish appetisers.

"You said you don't drink?" She knew I knew. And I could tell from how her eyes widened. Only slightly, but certainly there.

"I don't know what you're talking about..." She said, trying to hide her guilt. I took a drink and my thumb caressed the top of her hand. I was cool. I didn't care who saw. I kept my gaze on her, and her skin looked like it was about to peel away from her bone and show the world what she was underneath. A fraud and a liar.

"Please," she said under her breath. "I'll do anything you want..." She stole a glance at John who was tucking into a large plate of rolls. "I don't want him to know." I moved my gaze from hers and observed John a moment. What a strong, happy man he was. I wonder how strong? How strong is a pane of glass when the rain hits it? What about something stronger, like a cannon ball?

"I won't tell him," I teased through a slight grin. I saw the tension move from her chest and the hit of vodka exhaled over me. "But..." That released breath ceased once more. Those dark eyes under those carefully sculpted eye brows met mine. The tears beginning to gather on the lip of her eye lid. "Don't let your mascara run Cara," I whispered. "You'll draw attention to yourself." I took out a napkin from my pocket and passed it her and she lightly dabbed her eyes and handed it back to me. I gestured my eye to my pocket, then back to her.

"What do you want?" Ahh the forbidden question, coming from the mouth of the spoiled fruit. The snake in the garden of Eden. *What does your heart desire?* I leaned in, inches from her mouth. Those sweet lips. I could put one on her right now in front of everyone. She was drinking, and we *all* knew what Cara Sheppard got like when she'd had a few too many drinks. *The Girl Next Door.* I had the hospital appointments saved on my computer, and the aftercare kit at the abortion clinic to prove it. I looked to the door where you had gone. When you had wanted me to follow you. But I couldn't go uninvited. I needed someone to put in a good word for me.

"I want you to introduce me to someone."

8

Now

The world flitted by like a movie on double speed. The nurses and doctor's dove into action and raced to help you as you faded away in my arms, the very essence of you draining onto the linoleum flooring and soaking my trousers in hot red. The look of terror on patients faces that were waiting for some innocuous ailment, and then wondered why the NHS waiting times were seven hours or more.

One nurse, a heavy-set man with more tattoos than you could shake a stick at, pushed a rickety trolley bed which banged on door frames and screwed down chairs as he raced to get you onto it. Another nurse, a small petite woman with a bowl like brunette haircut, wrapped rubber around your biceps to stop the bleeding and she jammed an IV drip into your pulsing blue veins.

I followed you as the rabble of aprons and scrubs matted in red and sweat and pushed you through the double doors from the waiting area. I ran down the hallway with you as I saw signs for

'Theatre.' 'The show must go on' it would seem, and you were playing the part brilliantly. I answered as many questions as I could: name, birthday next of kin, address, blood type, medical history etc etc, the doctor standing next to me with a clipboard writing down details as fast as they came out my mouth. It was no wonder a doctors handwriting was notoriously hard to read, they had to be used to writing fast and moving on to something else.

We approached two large white doors with plastic windows and sanitising stations on each flank. You were hurdled down the corridor like a rollercoaster flying through a tunnel before heading towards the big drop of thrills and screams. I only wondered if you would be met by angels or the fires of hell when you made it to the other side.

I tried to follow you, to watch you under the knife, under the operating table as they sewed you back together, but I was met by two nurses that acted like bouncers to a VIP club I wasn't welcome too. They shouted that I couldn't go in, because I wasn't able to, because it was the doctors and surgeons that needed to work now and that I should go and wait in the waiting area. I protested; I called your name. I screamed that I loved you, even though the words lingered on my tongue, laced in acid.

My third coffee tasted worse than the first two. The first went down smoothly. The cream was fresher, newer, albeit powdered and then brought back to life with a splash of hot water. The second, more bitter. And the third sat in my hand like a man stares at his eighteenth shot of Tequila on the night of his 21st birthday, wondering why he had gone so far.

"It'll be okay mate," John said as he put his hand on my shoulder. "She'll pull through." He hadn't been here long. I had a small amount of change in my pocket which I had used to call him on the hospital phone. Archaic, stiff metal buttons that numbed your fingertips as you pressed them. The cord thick like a titanium snake left out in the cold too long. I knew his number, because I wasn't able to have my own phone.

I think it's better if we share a phone you had said to me after a tirade of insults following a girl I work with texting me how my day had gone. *I just think it will make things better, more transparent. I think it will help us move past what you have done.* Obviously I agreed to that, because I knew the consequences of fighting my own corner. The next time I went to use the phone, I had asked why you had changed your password. *Why? Do you want to go snooping?* You had said. I opted to remain quiet once more. I had seen the way you had flirted with Mark, ever since the first day I met. You were just being modest then, seeing if there was any one else you could sink your fangs into first, and boy, did you find the juiciest, more rump steak with me that night.

I rarely, if ever won an argument with you, and even if I did score a slight win, you would retaliate in a deplorable, desperate fashion, like slicing your own arms open. The audacity! To think we couldn't have a civilised debate, a disagreement like *normal* couples. That you would resort to such extremes to try and *win*. But then again, this was all a game to you, every last detail for show. You knew what you were doing, and I take my hat off to you.

"What happened man?" The look in John's eyes was genuine. I could tell. His eyes were soft and he was leaning in. He wanted to hear the truth, about what had happened the night before. He looked like shit, but then again he had drunk his bodyweight the night before.

He had already noticed the marks on my face but he hadn't asked about them yet. He had seen the fucked-up state my car was in, which was going to be towed away soon by the police. I had narrowly avoided being arrested for dangerous driving, but the constable had a heart and let me off with a strong warning. So at least that was something good.

"I don't know," I felt tears beginning to well up which stung my swollen eye lid more than it was already hurting. That's what people did when they were sad, right? They cried? "We were completely fine last night. After you all left, we cleaned up, went to bed in good spirits and we fucked until the morning. Things have been going a little downhill recently. I know we have only been seeing each other a little while, but something in her has changed, you know? She's not the loving happy girl I have fallen in love with, the same one I met at your party. But instead, she's turned into something unstable. I found her anti-depressants; she had been hiding them from me."

"Really?" John said, leaning in as he listened to my tale.

"So much has happened," I continued. "I supported her, loved her, through it, thinking things would get better. And then, she kept talking about hurting herself. Never out right in the open, but always insinuated if you get me? Under her breath, like she wanted me to hear it and then question if she had ever said anything." I let a tear fall from my eye. John put his hand on my shoulder.

"You weren't to know what she was going through mate," he said tentatively.

"I know, but I blame myself. When we got up today, she seemed a little off, made a couple of innocuous comments that I should have taken more note of. That she couldn't go on, that she felt trapped, she wanted to leave me, leave everything." I put my head in my hands. That's what people did right? When the love of their life was hanging on the verge of death? Didn't they cry? Didn't they show pain like everyone else? Not just pain but utter unhinged despair? I couldn't lay it on too much though, and given that John put his hand on my back and told me it was *okay to be upset* and *I couldn't have known what she was thinking,* I felt like I was doing it just right. I wiped my eyes and sat back in my chair. "She needs to be sectioned or something," I said, holding his gaze, my eyes puffy and red. "Oh god, did I just say that?" I put my head back in my hands.

"Hey," John said, closing those big flabby arms around me. I got a hit of his body odour then, and that nearly broke my concentration. "Don't be like that. You didn't know! The doctors will have a talk with her and ask exactly what happened and they will do some kind of assessment on her head, make sure she isn't cracking up completely." This made me smile.

"So she'll be able to come home you think? Will everyone think she's gone crazy?" John huffed again.

"I don't know man," he said, "But I think people will be more cautious around her in the future if I'm honest. I think people will be more concerned about you in the long run. You gotta leave her man!" He said with conviction laced in guilt. "You can't be around someone like that! It's not safe!"

Perfect, I thought. I nodded, the lump in my throat growing bigger and swelling.

"Thanks man," I said. "I'll need to have a think. Maybe she does need some time in a hospital." My expression turned grave as I picked up my coffee." She did say something last night which was worrying." John's ears pricked and he leant in. Not too close thankfully.

"Like what?"

"She said she was thinking things. *Bad things*, about people." John's expression turned grave.

"Like what?"

"Like," I said, licking my lips. "Like she wants to *hurt* someone. She was drunk and spoke about a lot about Mark. That he was coming on to her a lot at work and it had been stressing her out, making her feel really uncomfortable. That she felt like she needed to *do something a*bout it."

"You mean like report him? Go to the police?" John said. I shook my head.

"No. Like she wanted to *do* something about it. I don't know what she meant, but after today, that could mean anything." I let the silence drag out then, let that seed sprout in John's mind. Then, almost detached from the vines spreading around his subconscious, he spoke.

"I'm worried about Cara." The words pulled me out of my thoughts, took me away from the pattern of dirt engrained into the flooring and the blinding reflection of the overhead lights.

"What do you mean?" I said, my heart rate starting to pick up. John shook his head.

"I think she's having an affair." I nodded and saw the pain well up in his fat face. Now the right thing to do in this situation would be to console your friend, place a reassuring hand on his shoulder, maybe even tell him that she isn't, that she isn't like that and that if she is then he should leave. But that isn't what I did. Like opening a tightly wrapped chest in thick chains, I turned the key.

"I don't know how to tell you this man." I said. My words must have been laced in razor blades because John's large face contorted and the vein at the top of his forehead began to push through his flabby skin, and that would have taken some serious blood flow. For a second, I worried if he was going to pass out.

"Just say it..." He said resounded. Then, I touched his shoulder.

"I know what's been going on. I didn't know how to tell you

and I am sorry. I didn't know what to say or how to say it. I wanted to tell you so many times but…"

"But what Chris? Spit it out!" John barked. I saw some eyes of the room falling on us. Whispers and curious looks that averted when they had been discovered. I licked my lips, them drying by the second. *I want a vodka* I thought. *I could kill for a vodka. Maybe a lime too. I like limes. A vodka and lime. That would do me right about now.*

"I know she has been sleeping with someone. Lorna told me," I said. "She's been sleeping with someone called Mark. He was at her birthday party. Big guy, nice teeth. I haven't seen them, but Lorna works with him, and she told me that she has been seeing him for a short while now." The tears began to flow then, and I placed my hand firmly on the big guys back as he cried uncontrollably at his lover, his wife, in the arms of another man. "I'm so sorry John," I soothed. "I honestly had no idea." He let it all out then. The sight of him in utter despair made me a little uncomfortable. I haven't ever been able to deal with emotions very well. I tried my best of course: was attentive when I was supposed to be, caring but firm in other places. Tough love, and loved tough, but loved all the same.

A nurse came over with some tissues and I thanked her silently before she went to complete the rest of her long shift. We sat there for a moment or two whilst John finished blubbering. I got him a fresh coffee. He took it silently, and then pushing through the lump in his throat, he roused his arid throat to speak.

"How long have you known?" He croaked. The question was loaded. The stages of grief, the cycle. He had gone through denial, and now with the sharpness of his tone, and with his knuckles turning white around the plastic cup, he was heading into anger.

"Last night" I lied. "I saw Cara talking to Mark, and I asked Lorna about it. She told me that she had seen them a few times touching hands, letting those stares linger longer than a simple 'platonic' relationship. But also that she had seen texts on his phone at work, and that they had been meeting for some time." I could see the words tormenting him, like each syllable of distrust and betrayal was a silver bullet into his monstrous heart haemorrhaging with love that was all misplaced. "They met on a website," I said, pulling out my phone. "Have you ever heard of the site *The Girl Next Door?*" John didn't say anything, instead he let that jaw hang loose like he was expecting a cookie or something. I took out my phone and google the site. It loaded up in reds and blacks, half naked women with their profiles on display, women holding sex toys and touching themselves, a question-and-answer tab to the left where you could speak your darkest and most deprived fantasies from the comfort of your home with complete strangers on the internet. I began to scroll, his eyes fixated on the screen. "You can speak to people, meet up with people and fuck them for the night and then leave. No real names, only user names. Like this one –" I click on a profile of some babe wearing a leather cat outfit holding a leather flail between her teeth. "Hook ups wanted. Safe sex only. Drinks acceptable. Couples welcome." I closed the profile and continued to scroll. Then, did I find the profile I had been looking for. "CBABEXX," I said, opening up Cara's profile. I flicked through some of the photos and John began to turn white, his hands shaking. "I like to be tied up and fucked from behind, the rougher, the better. Spit on me if you want, I'm a dirty girl waiting for you." I clicked on a couple of photos of her in her underwear, some without. John didn't try to stop me, his spirit too broken inside to tell me to stop looking at pictures of his whore wife. I didn't have the heart to tell him I had seen all of these pictures anyway, and had even taken some of them myself. He went to speak, but then a doctor appeared. The same one from before. Same clip board. Same set of scrubs. Same tiny coffee stain on his left cuff which he either hadn't noticed or hadn't been bothered to get changed. I noticed, but I noticed a lot of things.

"She's out of surgery now Mr. Peters." The Doctor sounded pleased. My eyes widened. She had survived... but how?

"That's amazing news!" I smiled widely. I put my arm around

John. "John! She's going to be okay!" I said joyfully. The Doctor nodded and smiled. "When can I see her?" I asked as politely and as hopeful as I could. Hands clasped together in like a weak prayer, leaning forward so I had his attention. Body language speaks louder than tone, and tone speaks louder than words.

"Soon," he said tiredly. "She is out of surgery, but she won't be ready for visitors just yet. We would like to keep her in overnight for observations. I hope you understand?" I let out a sigh. I nodded. I thanked the Doctor and he left us.

"I can't believe it," John said, his voice heavy.

"I know!" I said ecstatic. "Come on," I said, springing to my feet. "Let's get out of here for a little while." He looked up at me from the space between his feet and the floor. "We'll have to take your car, but I need to get some things out of the back of mine first before its towed away."

"Where are we going?" He queried with reddening eyes. I gestured to the exit.

"For a drive."

9

Then

John and Cara had really gone all out for the birthday party. Their home was prestigious enough, much better than my tiny apartment in the bad area of town, where if you didn't lock your doors at night you would wake up to find your place ransacked and the words 'Stupid Bastard' smeared on your wall in faeces. Not Cara and John though. With the money she had gotten from her mother, a hefty inheritance to her and her two brothers. They were wealthy of course, the price of the curtains hanging over the patio doors and the marble kitchen flooring that led into the half acre back garden filled with tiki torches and fairy lights around the jacuzzi with bottles of champagne on ice told me that. But money couldn't count for happiness, especially when it came from such a loveless place.

I saw you there sitting with your back to me. Your dress falling from your shoulders and your waist. As much as you tried to hide, you wanted to be noticed. Sitting here alone in the dark, cut away from the world, both real and digital, yet your soul screamed for attention. Were you simply playing a part? Or was there something much deeper going on under those calm waters?

You sat there quietly. No mobile phone, no Instagram or Facebook scrolling. Just you on the edge of the decking like someone watching the ships roll by on a dock. Your heels placed next to you like a child that had finally fallen to sleep and you could enjoy the relaxing evening bliss by yourself. The night was cool but the slight breeze that meandered through the grounds licked your skin with its warming tongue. Above us, Saturn was coming out. You knew which one I meant right? The one that sits on the horizon and twinkles a slight blue. And Venus, the brightest star in the night sky, shining down on me and you. Cara, as per my request, approached you with tears in her eyes.

"I Can't believe it!" She barked as she moved towards you. She stood behind you but you barely seemed to notice. I however stood back, touching the leaves of some exotic plant in a terracotta pot that stood just outside the back door. The wind licked the back of your neck and your red hair danced lightly, but you didn't turn your head. Cara stood there dumbfounded. She turned to me and I eyed her sternly. Her lip quivered more. "I don't know what's happened! It's everywhere!" You turned your head away from her, this woman dressed in black screaming incoherent rabble that had

had way too much to drink already. You took out a cigarette and lit it, exhaling a plume of blue smoke into the night air that disappeared into the dark sky.

"What do you want Cara?" You bit. Not the response either of us was looking for, and given the surprised look on Cara's face, and the distasteful one on mine, what we were expecting either. You two weren't as good friends as I was left to believe after all. *Interesting.* That made Cara seem more disgusting, and you, much more enticing.

Cara looked at me once more like an actress that had forgotten her lines. I took out the kitchen rag I had taken from the counter and walked to her, the sounds of the decking clicking under my heals, the laughter and sloppy kisses mixing with the sound of splashing water of the couple in the hot tub, its steam dancing around the overhead lights. Let's just hope they were tied in properly and didn't fall in. Then the night would get interesting. Nothing says a first date like obliterated genitals.

"Oh my god Cara!" I blurted. Attentive, concerned, almost embarrassed *for* her. "How could you spill such expensive stuff on that beautiful dress!" Both of us keeping an eye on you as you smoked away. I cleaned up the 'damp' on her dress, her body recoiling from my touch.

"Thanks Chris," she said through clenched teeth. "That's cleaned it up just right." Without missing a step, Cara turned and went inside, not looking back. She had done what I had asked, she was safe for another night. You however, still seemed uninterested. This was not how this was supposed to go down. You were to show concern for your friend and then me, the strong saviour type, who came to help her. You were to look at me, put the pieces together and then *Hey! You're the guy from earlier! Small world!* Then we would laugh and we would talk, and we would fall in love. I was the one you needed in your life. You just had to realise it.

That, apparently, was not how this was going to work. Now, I was stood behind you with a kitchen rag staring at you smoking. Not at all awkward...

"Are you going to stand there all night looking at me or are you going to grow a pair and say something?" You were abrupt. Not a hint of laughter in there either. Serious, stoic. Not the friendly girl I had seen before. This was either a façade, a defence, or the charade you put on earlier was. Only one way to find out. I sat next to you and without asking, took one of your cigarettes, lit it and we sat there a moment smoking. "Most people ask if they want to steal a smoke," you said, still looking out into the darkness that prevailed us.

"I'm not most people," I said, looking into the black. They

say to get someone's attention you should mirror their behaviour. Its psychology. So, I sat there, and I acted like an uninterested bitch. A few moments later, you exhaled deeply.

"I fucking hate parties." So you curse. That's good to know.

"Same. Can't stand the fucking things. 'Hey let's all get together, get drunk and pretend that we like each other for the night.' It seems so forced doesn't it?" You laughed a little. *Fuck the world. That's my way in. Not some reunification of two souls. Fuck the world, and maybe, you can fuck me too...*

"It's the noise most of the time. That's why I like to sit out here and think."

"I get that. Work is chaotic. I work with John, and I find he talks a hell of a lot. And then at the end of the long week working with him, I get to spend my time off with him and his wife." You took another drag of your smoke and held the poison inside.

"It's funny," you said, the smoke creeping out of your nostrils like a dragon about to destroy a castle.

"What is?" I asked. You turned to me.

"I don't remember asking about your day." You didn't miss a beat. You turned, no eye contact, and took one of the beers from my hand, cracked it open, a devoured a long gulp. "But, I completely get you," you continued. "Like Mark, the guy with the white teeth and who blatantly loves himself. He just talks and talks, and tries it on with me all the time. Sometimes, people don't get the damn hint you just aren't interested." Your eyes fell onto me then, before returning to the prevailing darkness ahead of us.

"Yeah I saw him in there talking to you," I said, cracking the second beer in my hand and taking a drink. "How many steroids and selfies do you think he takes in a 24-hour period?" You let out a slight laugh and touch your hair. This was good. I was getting somewhere.

"So you were watching me?" You said slyly, your eyes falling into mine. I held my breath as those daggers of green pierced my soul. You were the most stunning woman I had ever seen, the complexion of your skin under the moonlight making it soft and light. Your eyes that held the twinkle of the stars, and your lips, plump and smooth, holding that smile of pearls.

"Maybe I was?" I teased. "I recognised you from earlier today. Milkshake girl?" I laughed. You held that's smile but I saw the corners crumple a little, like throwing a love note on the fire.

"I thought I recognised you..." You let the statement linger a little. Testing me? I should say something bold, funny, smart arse, but I sat there with my drink in my hand like a truck was heading towards me and I couldn't find my legs.

"You didn't give me your name earlier?" Fuck, that was desperate. You turned away from me.

"What makes me so special to want to be known?" So you *do* like being hidden away. You enjoy being the recluse. You don't want to be noticed. "There's tonnes of beautiful women in there and you come out here to sit with me because I spilt a milkshake on my top. Why?" *Daggers laced in venom. Tread lightly.* I turned to you and held that gaze once more. The wind blew gently and the sound of the music and the party faded away. It was just you and me, and time stood still.

"Because when I look at you, I see someone who wants to be seen. Someone who tries to hide away, but because the world is artificial now. Filled with bullshit and fake laughter. Memes and likes, zombies trapped in the cages of their smart phones. I see you and feel you don't think you belong, like you're the only real flower in a Boquete of plastic ones." You hold my stare a moment. I wouldn't look away. Strong people don't look away. Fighters going into the ring, lions squaring up to each other, hell even narcissist CEO's, they don't break the gaze. To break is weakness, so I held firm. Something about you spoke to me. I enjoyed the tenseness in the air, the not knowing what to say, the game of chess. Was this what flirting was like? Is this what people did? Maybe love wasn't just an *idea* I had seen so much about in the movies or on the lips of those I didn't care to listen too. Maybe this was what I had been missing? What I had had before wasn't love, it was a façade, a fake, an oil painting left in acid rain to sour and dissolve, letting its colours run down the drains of barren streets long deserted.

"Do you tell that to all the women you meet?" You said, taking a another drag of your smoke.

"Only the fucked-up ones." Your stoic complexion cracked then and you roared a laugh. I must have hit the bullseye.

"Nice," you say, taking another drink. "I don't think you could handle me Chris." The name struck me.

"You remembered my name?" I say, a little more needy than I would have liked. You turn your head away.

"I remember all the details." You leaned in then. "So, how many red flags can you handle?"

"I'm not scared of a little wind burn." Again you laughed and stubbed the smoke out. That stare, that silence, was powerful. Something you had practise with, making men eat out the palm of your hand. Not me though. Mine would fit better under that dress, in between those toned thighs...

"I'm not that special." You said flatly and took hold of your heels. You went to stand and I took your hand. You turned to me, a look of fire. You didn't pull away though, and you sat back down next to me, closer this time, our legs touching.

I went to speak, to say something I had heard from the movies. *'Be the flame; not the moth'* no, that would be too cheesy. My eyes searched yours tyring to find my in. I opened my mouth to speak, when you leaned in and kissed me. Only a flitting one, enough to leave me wanting more, like the first drag off a cigarette following a year of craving.

"I believe in myself and going for what I want. Come whatever may, I always win."

"Is that a challenge?" I smiled, touching the top of your back. Your skin was so warm, so soft, and I let my eyes fall onto you even more. You held your stare on my lips and leaned in closer, touching your hand to the inside of my thigh.

"Depends how good you are at playing," you whispered as you drew closer. I could smell your perfume and it pulled me in with ethereal fingers. "I'm Lorna, by the way." You said as you got closer, as your whisper was carried by the breeze. Our lips touched, and I felt the smooth of your tongue slide into my mouth. Behind us, I saw Cara standing there with a drink in her hand behind the curtains. She put her hand to her mouth then moved inside. I smiled slightly and ran my fingers through your hair. *You're mine.*

10

Now

The ride to the other side of town was arduous at best. We hit every red light and I saw more homeless bums than I could keep count of, sitting in doorways covered in their own filth. John was still whining about Cara and her infidelity. He had even gone so far as to create a profile on *The Girl Next Door* website to troll though the profile of his lover. Funny how one small bit of information can completely destroy someone's whole life.

"How could she do this to me?" He blubbered, staring at his phone. I cracked a window open, letting the sound of the air pushing through the gap and the meandering drunks that fell over themselves on the pavement, stuffing their faces with take away food, even some whores in tiny dresses dropped their underwear to relieve themselves against the doorways where the homeless slept. Still, it was better sound than listening to John whimper.

She's out of your fucking league anyway you fat fuck. Don't you see that? Of course she was going to go with a real man, one that takes care of himself, one that doesn't have a waist size greater than his age.

"I'm sorry man," I say, trying my hardest to not stomp on the accelerator and drive as fast as I could into the crowd of drunken dick heads stumbling in the middle of the road. I blared my horn at them and one bitch with last years Vogue's featured winter dress gave me the finger, before falling over her heels. It was incredible what alcohol could do to someone. I thought of you in that moment. About how you told me you loved me after beating me with your fists.

Why did you cut your arms? I wasn't that bad to love was I? *No* I thought. *It's not me that's the problem. The issue is clearly in your own mind. In your own soul I remember the night at the party when we met, the things you said, the way you sat like an empty shell wanting me to come and find you, to fill you up, to breathe life back into you. You were clearly unstable. You needed to be locked away in a psyche hospital. I* clenched the steering wheel tighter. *All you had to do if you weren't happy was tell me that you wanted to leave the relationship. I would have understood, almost welcomed the idea. But I know you would never leave me. And after tonight, you'd never be able too.*

"Cara!" John wailed, his face in his hands. I turn to him, enraged.

"Shut the fuck up!" He snapped his eyes open, staring at me

stunned. His mouth tries to speak, the tears now dried up. I rebuke, take a breath. "I just can't think with you making so much noise." He leans forward, taking out a pack of smokes from his pocket. He fires one up and offers me one. I take it warmly.

"I'm sorry Chris," he says. "I'm having a bad time, but nothing compared to what you're going through." He goes back to the phone, silently sobbing to himself whilst his face glistens once again in the tiny light of the screen. I look over to him, slumped over next to the passenger side window, his frame blotting out the passing streetlights. "I just…." He tried, before taking another drag of the cigarette. He coughed loudly and cracked the window, huffing gulps of city air. "I can't believe she would do this to me Christian!" He slammed his hand off the dashboard. I didn't mind, it was his fucking car after all. I opted to drive for the fact of in his state, he was more likely to drive us off the edge of a cliff than to where we needed to go.

"Bitch." I stabbed. I didn't need to consider any other response. That's what friends did right? Bad mouth those that have hurt their friends? Take their sides, regardless of what the whole story was? We have our loyalties, and our loyalties lie further than facts and conjecture. Projection of opinions are nothing when it came to the tight bonds of blood and friendships. I looked at him there, sitting and wallowing in his own tears. Firstly I thought of the salt content in his tears wouldn't do his impending diabetes any good, and not to mention the moisture expended would worsen his headache. But I figured that crying was considered something helpful and therapeutic, something I had never done.

"How did you know about the website?" John said, dragging the words out.

"Which website?" I said, deflecting. John eyed me as I continued down the main street through the town.

"The fucking site Chris," he spat. "The one she is on; how did you know?"

"Oh," I say, thinking of a response. "Lorna told me she used to use it. She used to be in a bad place a long time ago. Makes sense with how she is now, when you think of it." I let the lie sprout and embed in John's mind. Of course he would believe me, they always did. He fell again into his mind, the torment of his thoughts and imagination turning him inside and out.

"Where are we going Christian?" I hated it when he used my full name. It sounded so pretentious. I had always despised my parents for giving me such a name that conjects aristocracy and double crested cotton sweaters. But hey, I can't choose what sound people use with their mouths to address me, I can only ask that they modify it to suit my own needs. That's what friends would do right?

"Call me Chris, John. You know I don't like being called my full name."

"Sorry." He said. He didn't redact his previous comment, and I gripped the steering wheel a little tighter, the lyrics of Elton John's *Rocket man* creeping through the stereo. When was the last time he had cleaned this damn car anyway? Fuck my face still hurt. That bitch had done a real number on me. Thankfully the painkillers from the hospital kept me on a level. I probably shouldn't be driving, but I figured with it being Friday night, the police would be busier breaking up Jack and Jill's third domestic incident of the week.

I look over to John again. This is the product of love. I am the product of love. You, Lorna, in my mind right now, are the product of love. A wasteful emotion. Something that is considered beautiful and destructive. The poets were right. Without love, there would be no pain, and without pain, there would be no art.

"We're going to your home," I say, turning down the A road leading to the outskirts of the city. His eyes snapped from the picture of his wife giving a blow job to my face coated in shadow.

"What? Why?"

"Don't you want answers? To confront that whore?" I laced the last comment in venom, because as much as I may be overstepping the mark, I knew he wouldn't correct me. There was something inside him that had died, something that had broken him into two. Something that I knew, given the chance, would want to watch the light vanish from his cheating wife's eyes.

We continue driving a little while longer. He didn't protest, instead stared vacantly out the window, flexing and clenching his knuckles. He was rehearsing what he was going to say, I could see his tongue moving behind those flabby lips. He was thinking what insults he would hurl, what old arguments he would throw back in her face, and most importantly, how much he was going to ruin her life after this. That's what I would be thinking. And again, I thought of you.

We pass over the motorway bridge to a quieter part of town, just outside the city centre. Large industrial buildings flank our right whilst a reservoir filled with black water and meandering ducks sit ominously to our left.

"Where are we?" We pull into a court yard to a large building. No lighting in the yard, and the headlights from the SUV pulse over gravel and a fleeing black cat whose eyes light up the night. In front of us is a tall building with a couple of lights on. Its grey, plated with metal. Out of the way and remote, just the way I like it. "This isn't the way to my house?" He says, touching the window.

"Detour," I say. "I just have to collect some bits. We won't be long." John goes to speak once more but I kill the engine and step outside into the cool night air. Above me, I see no stars. No cloud coverage, but no night diamonds are placed on the black canvas overhead. No moon either. Just a prevailing of black, like someone staring into the abyss, waiting for the monster from the deep to creep towards them, teeth sneering with dead eyes. I move to the boot and pop it open. The heavy sound of gravel crunches in my ears, and soon, John is standing next to me. His big white Tee shirt sodden with sweat. God he stinks like shit. His face is withered, his eyes sunken and red. A thought crosses my mind to let him free of the string he was being pulled on. *Soon,* I thought. *Soon, it will be over.* This way, I could rally all the rats and snakes into a pit, and watch them devour each other.

"What are we doing here Christian?" A flare of annoyance hits me. I stab my eyes to him, and he rebukes instantly. "Chris." I smile.

"That building?" I nod with my head to the small metal huts connected to each other with crude brick work. "That is where the fucker that's been sleeping with your wife works." I see the anger flare in John's eyes, burning red. A pain born from shattered dreams and raped realities. An unchained and unforgiving rage. Unbridled, true and honest fury. He goes to step, like a bull released from the pen charging at the red rag and the man with the funny boots. I take his arm. "Wait!"

"Let go of me!" He tries to pull away, but he doesn't get far. I didn't go heavy on arm day for no reason, nor did I wear tight sleeved shirts because I found them more comfortable.

"Don't be stupid," I bit. He stopped, his breath hot in the cool air. Again I wondered where the stars were, hiding their beautiful eyes from the spilling of blood the hairless apes below were about to partake in. I pull him back and point my finger. "CCTV cameras. You'll be caught." John looks at the single bleeping black eye mounted above the building, and defeated frustration leaves his mouth.

"So what then?" I pull out a bag from the boot of the car.

"I took these out of my car earlier. I have them for when I go hunting in the Lakes." I opened up the bag and took out a balaclava, a slingshot, gloves and tie wraps.

"Jesus Christian!" *Anger hitting boiling point.* "I didn't think you were allowed to carry things like this?" He looked over to the unit, his rage suddenly diminishing. "Wait... what are you going to do to him?" I laugh. He was so worried it was almost cute, like seeing a bear afraid of the sight of blood.

"Relax," I reassure. "We're not going to hurt him," I whisper.

"Just scare him. Nothing more I promise." A few moments later, we both have balaclavas on, and I use my slingshot on the CCTV camera which explodes into shards of metal and glass, falling limply like a 21-year-olds dick when his mum catches him looking at vomit porn on his dad's computer.

We move fast, low. John loves the rush, as without thinking, he bursts through the front door of the office screaming bloody murder. The room is bare, only a single chair alone in the centre of the room, with a desk a phone and a single lamp that illuminates the dull white walls.

"The fuck?" John sighs. He removes the balaclava and turns to me. "There's nobody here?" I take the baseball bat from behind the front door and swing a home run across his jaw. His fat flabby disgusting face snaps to the side and a row of teeth and blood redecorate the walls. He hits the ground hard, taking a couple of chairs and monitors with him on his way down. I close the door, pull out the tie wraps, and get to work.

11

Now

It had been a while since I last tied someone up and didn't put my cock in them. It was tougher when they struggled. John was a big guy, but I forgot just *how* big he was. His arms were flabby, his man boobs so big it would make most women blush, and the size of his stomach was the stuff of legend. His breath, fuck, that was the worst part, laying him on his side so he didn't choke on his tongue, making sure I didn't hit him hard enough to kill the fat bastard. That wouldn't do me any good. I was a saviour, not a killer. And I had a job to do. But just know, that I am doing all of this for you. To help you. To show you how much I love you.

I bind his legs first, after making sure the liquid seeping out of his hair was sweat and not brain fluid, I checked my watch. It was late, and it wouldn't be long before you would wake up from the surgery. You had cut pretty fucking deep Lorna. I'll give you that. You knew how to make a scene, how to make a show. A true performer for all the world to see. The helpless victim in a world filled with monsters. But you wear the mask well, and I would soon show you the ugliness underneath it all. I will show you what a true monster is.

Getting him on the chair took a lot of effort. I can dead lift over 160KG in the gym easily, but lifting a huge bodied man all by myself, even onto a chair two feet off the ground, was a real struggle. If my mother could hear the words that came out of my mouth, she would have scrubbed my tongue harder than a cheating wife scrubs her underwear after forgetting to use a condom. Finally, after nearly pulling my back out and my hair fusing to my drenched scalp, I secure John to the office chair. I head back to the car boot and take out the rest of my equipment and place it inside the room next to the sleeping mound. I check the small black box in the back, and I am thankful that I know where John keeps his spare key, and Cara keeps her work computer. You should always secure you passwords and belongings away kids. You never know who is looking.

I place the items on a table, laid out for my next visitor. John wouldn't wake up for a couple of hours yet, which would give me plenty of time to go and get you. I just had a couple of things to do first, a few more chairs to fill, before I bring you to the party.

When I'm done with John, making sure that I hadn't caused serious damage to his head, more than I wanted to anyway. He might talk with a lisp the rest of his life and not be able to clench his left hand, but at least that will help him lose weight. Can't eat if you can't pick things up or chew. I clean my face off with a zero-alcohol wet wipe and wipe my hands, making sure to get under the nails thoroughly. I heard that's where most bacteria can gather and if left unchecked, can cause gangrene. Lastly, I wash the handle of the baseball bat with a ninety nine percent alcohol solution, being sure to get right in the grooves of the handle and along the shaft and head.

Satisfied, I turn off the lights and head back to the car, put my balaclava in the glove compartment and set the sat nav for my next destination. I take out John's phone and type in *your* name, then type out a simple message –

I KNOW ABOUT THE WEBSITE. I wait a moment, see the message gets read, followed by a quick –

WHAT?

THE WEBSITE. THE GIRL NEXT DOOR. I KNOW.

You try to call John but I put the phone down. I know he wouldn't do this, the little lap dog, but I do it anyway. Makes you confused. And just as I thought, those little dots appeared once more, telling me you were writing.

ANSWER THE PHONE JOHN you say. No emojis. Nice to know you're taking this seriously. I smile, my straight teeth reflecting back in the darkened window of the SUV.

I'LL SPEAK IN PERSON. MEET ME HERE. I say, and text her the address. I know it's around fifty-eight minutes with a little leeway for traffic lights and drunks, so I give myself fifty to be sure. I turn the phone off for the time being, before starting the ignition again. I make a mental note to burn the sat nav when I am done.

I turned out the carpark and set on my way to my next destination. A song comes on the radio. I don't know who it is by, but I turn it up anyway. You enter my thoughts once more. Your tight black dress, your long dark hair, the way your face looked side on in the camera. I loved you so much. I fucking adored the ground you walked on. I would have cut my throat open and poured all of my life into your veins if it meant having you, giving you another moment with me. The way it ended between us. Before I knew the truth about you, knew the truth about you being a dirty girl, rotten to the core. The betrayal in my mind like a fucking hot spike that the Devil himself is hammering into my eyes. And then *You* appeared in my life, and I thought you were different. But no, you were always the same, every fucking one of you just the same as the one before. I loved you, I wanted you, I would have done anything to have you, for you to throw it back in my face for some testosterone filled Instagram filtered gold watch wearing designer beards flaunting tight black shirt shit teeth-stained cunt! I slam my hands on the wheel. Good, I thought. I need to be angry. I need to want pain.

12

Then

"I can see you two are getting along well?" John said, stumbling out of the patio doors. He had caught me and you leaning into each other. We hadn't kissed yet, but I could feel your breath lingering on my lips, and I know that you wanted me, almost as bad as I wanted you. I didn't believe in fate until today. I had been unlucky in love. Never anything longer than a few months at best: a casual affair, fling or cheeky handy under a restaurant table here and there. Never anything real. Never anything like what I felt for *you*. Pure fire. A fire that ravaged my insides from the moment I laid my eyes on that inferno of red hair and those deep green eyes.

"Thanks for the cock block," I laughed, "We were just about to get it on!" I watched your expression as I said this. You didn't seem to flinch. In fact, you squoze my hand a little tighter and then, in front of John and some other guests that had made their way onto the patio, sitting near us and nestled in each other's hands, swaying and singing gently to the music that floated from the kitchen, you put your lips to mine and my body erupted in euphoria.

Was it too early to tell you, even in my own mind, that I was crazy for you? Madly in love with you? From the moment I saw you all the way until now? Would that make you run from me? Or would it make you feel the same? A secret connection we had with each other right from the offset? Did you believe in soul mates? Twin flames? Two people destined to be brought together? String theory, chaos theory, or some other sequence of seemingly random events that have led me to be here, right here, right now, and you the same, to find you in my arms with your breath in my nostrils and caressing my tongue with yours. I put my hand to the back of your head and ran my fingers through those soft auburn locks. I cracked an eye open. All eyes were on us: drunk couples with their mouths falling open, John with a huge fucking smile, big bad tight top guy who stood in the porch with a face of jealousy and rage, and of course, Cara, whose face could sink ships and feed drowning sailors to the sharks. I closed my eyes and kissed you harder. I was nearly there already. I would have you all to myself. I could feel it. You were the one I would have forever. You were *mine*.

"You want a refill?" I ask, politely, not too presumptuous. You nodded and gave me that killer smile. The smile you know I already loved. That's why you did it wasn't it? Even now, you knew me, knew who I was, and you knew that you were the one I wanted and the one I needed. But you couldn't let me know so soon that you knew. That would give the game away. That's what this was after all, *a game.* It's all these things ever are. The dating game, the career game, the love game, the friendship game. Was anything serious anymore? Or is it just who wins, who loses, and how badly the rules are broken? *All is fair in love and war?* Whoever wrote that must have known this whole thing is nothing more than a game. Luckily for you, I like to win. And I *don't* like to play fairly.

"That would be nice," you said, the smile meeting the corners of your eyes, the crows feet that were only slightly there grew a little more. You knew exactly who I was, and you couldn't wait for me to show you later. I leant in. Took my chance. Fuck it, I didn't care. I wanted what you had to offer and I knew before even moving that you would welcome it, and welcome it you did. Our lips met and fucking hell, my cock began to swell right then and there. If it wasn't for the people watching I would have torn that dress off and now and fucked you until your cunt fractured. I pulled myself away, I needed to control myself, *must* control myself. I was getting too carried away *again.* I didn't want a repeat of what happened last time. But that was just practise. I didn't win that game, but I learnt a lot of lessons.

You smiled at me again and touched my arm. "Where did that come from?" You giggled. Not mockingly, but genuine, sincere, even. I shook my head and smiled, looking at the decking below me like a blushing school boy. I knew all eyes were on us. Everyone was thinking about us fucking, what our children would look like, how big our wedding day was going to be. I stole a glance around me; they must have been looking away at that moment, because when I looked back at you, I could feel the eyes on me again.

"I just got a little carried away I guess." I laugh quietly. You reciprocated, then leant in and kissed me back. I feel our lips gliding, and you slip your tongue into my mouth, the feint taste of malibu lingers on my lips. Your finger nails find the back of my scalp, and I pull you in and put my arm around you. We kiss loudly and passionately in front of the crowd for a few minutes. I don't care if people are imagining us naked, I want them to see me and you and how good we look together. I pull away, hear you panting and I get to my feet, pushing my erection down. My dick is throbbing and aching for you, but you knew that already didn't you? We exchange a smile. "I'll be right back."

I go around the side of the house and slip through the side gate when nobody is looking. I walk back through the front door and slip upstairs. The upper deck is dead, and I peer into a couple of bedrooms, looking for what I am after. Someone was coming, and I pull out my phone and the two guests, two men who were talking about politics or some shit, walk right passed me like I wasn't there.

They vanish into the upper floor of the house and I hear a door close. Maybe they were fucking, maybe they were using the bathroom. I didn't care, I was already inside Cara's office, installing the spyware in her computer from the USB I had in my pocket. I watched as the upload bar crept along silently, before it completed its work. I removed it, putting it in my pocket. Next, I moved back downstairs, conscious of onlookers, and moved to John's car. I took out the blank key from my pocket and using an app from my phone, routed the key through the WIFI and the bluetooth of the existing key, before syncing it to John's vehicle. That would come in handy later. Just a contingency, something I hoped I would never have to use. Unless I thought you were pulling away from me, from my love. To break my heart Lorna. That would be a foolish thing indeed.

In the kitchen, John didn't look happy. His nostrils are flared and he is stroking the back of his neck. All signs of frustration and stress. I have read about them in a magazine: *Psychology today?* I think that was it. Studying body language. The April edition was about stress and anger, and how the level of cortisol rises in the blood and adrenaline, and how this accounts for a lot of stress in the work place, as our body doesn't know the difference between a sabre tooth tiger and a threatening email. The brain simply sees a threat and the body responds: sweaty palms, shaking legs, adrenal gland activates and cortisol floods the blood stream. Also when people are hungry, the body produces adrenaline and cortisol. I found that particularly interesting. I wonder how far someone will push themselves in the name of grabbing a fucking cheese burger?

"Hot?" I say, leaning into John. He shakes his head. I don't know if he even knows who is speaking to him, his eyes are shut solid and his forehead is leaning on the bar. He stinks of booze, and I am surprised he hasn't done his drunk Rambo routine yet.

"Cara's pissed at me." I try to hide my smile.

"Why?" I ask, leaning in. His voice is muffled as his face is buried in his flabby armpit. *God, you need to go to the fucking gym man* I think to myself *You're going to die of a heart attack before you reach the age of forty at this rate. Have you ever heard of Pilates? A skipping rope? A fucking salad?* "Is everything okay? You want me to go and speak to her for you?" He mumbles something I doubt even he can understand. I take that as a queue to help him in his current love dilemma. I scan the room and find Cara talking to the prick in the black jumper. The guy looked like a well-trimmed ape who clearly spends way too much time man scaping and watching reality TV shows. She looked happy, unlike her husband. Her dress tight around that rocking bod, and holding a glass of Pinot Noir in her hand and twirling her finger around her hair. The slut.

I march over, moving past the group sitting in the living

room speaking about some bullshit politics and history of some third world country nobody gives a fuck about.

"Can I talk to you for a second?" I say, nodding to her, taking her by the elbow. She recoils at my touch, the look on her face like that of a bulldog that's chewing on a wasp.

"What do you want Chris?" She spits, giving the big chizzled oaf a look of bemusement. He puffs his chest out and looks me up and down. Naturally, I don't entertain his gaze.

"Can I borrow you for a moment?" She eyed me like I was offering her a knife to go and maim a small child. I try not to laugh at the thought of her with a knife. She's already tried that once before. "Well?" I say after a moment. Big and bold must be able to sense the feelings between us, the chemistry, the tension, because he puffs out his chest and I see his jaw about to clench. He might not know he's even doing it, but I certainly do, and I have my eye on the centre of his chest. My peripheral vision anyway. I don't want to give anything away. Assuming he can throw a decent punch, he will pull backwards first and then go for the swing. A fighter basically warns you of an impending assault before they actually throw a hit, you just have to know how to look for the danger signs: dropping of the jaw, narrowing of the stance, making one's self seem larger, as with the rabid dogs fighting over a meal, we are but animals in clothing and who make interesting sounds with our mouths. I know people like him, I have met them before. I like it when they try to run from me, but I enjoy it more when they try to fight.

I eye Cara a second longer. "I said I need you for a second." She was rigid like stone. The thought of being alone with me obviously making her pussy wet. The jock strap in the black jumper could obviously sense she was getting the horn for me, and naturally, his testosterone injected ball sack swelled and he piped up.

"She's not into you. I would leave if I were you." He eyed me up and down like I was a mannequin wearing last summer's clothing range, and added "Freak." I laugh slightly at the comment. He didn't like that. Not used to people being smaller than him but not afraid of him and his ten thousand Instagram follower count. Fucking oversized dick head.

"If I wanted the dog to bark I would have thrown you a treat," I say, not taking my eye of Cara and her quivering lip. His eyebrow raised and he touched his chin with the hand wearing that big 'I have a small dick' watch of his.

"What you fucking say?" He said, and stepped towards me.

"Put your mutt back on a leash Cara, before I choke him with it." My words stabbed into his ears and Cara's jaw dropped in shock. He uttered some bullshit through his turka teeth and filled with booze and blue balls seeing me take *his* woman, he throws that punch I was waiting for. I side step, taking him off balance and drive my foot into his shin, sending him off balance, aided by my arm under his shoulder. He cascades through the glass table, knocking over drinks and glasses onto the ground and onto the laps of other guests that turn to him in distain and horror. They look at him, a giant large oaf whose had one too many whiskeys and has been trying to fuck every woman at the party all night, and then at me, the new guy, twelve stone wearing a nice-looking shirt and who hasn't made so much as a peep all evening. They make the right choice.

Two guests, big dudes with arms the sizes of small watermelons take Mark and haul him to his feet. He shouts something incoherent as they drag him out of the front door and toss him into the street like the fucking garbage he is. The guests clean themselves up, ask if I am okay, to which I give them a cursory

–

"Yes thanks," before the party resumes, like he was never here in the first place. Rule number one kids, remember, you are not as important to other people as you think, and no one really gives that much of a fuck about you, and if they do, its until they either forget you or replace you. Often at the same time.

I turn to Cara who is still standing there utterly bewildered and holding the same glass of white champagne she has been nursing for the last fifteen minutes.

"What do you want Chris?" She whispers, tears in her eyes. "Why are you here? Why did John invite you? When did you start working with him? I thought you had moved out of town!" I study her and then look back to John who is now completely comatose on the kitchen bar.

"Someone should really put him in the recovery position," I joke, taking the glass off Cara and downing it myself. I nod in approval. "Expensive. Bubbly. I like it."

"Why are you here Chris?" She whispers again, her heart filling with dread. "You shouldn't be here. I'll call the police. You need to leave." My face turns dark, and I see that familiar look of fear in her eyes.

"You called the police once on me before, when you thought I was going to *tell* on you." I eyed her, and I watched her shrivel a little smaller. "What happened, happened. You were the one that cheated, not me. I was on that site to hook up, you were on there to get something extra."

"I was drinking a lot back then," she said, her face turning hard. "I still have nightmares from what you did."

"But you didn't press charges Cara?"

"Because I!" You started, then, catching your volume, resumed your whisper. "Because I didn't want you to tell John. You told me you would go, leave forever. Why are you back? Why don't you leave us alone Christian!" I took another drink of the champagne.

"I will leave when I leave Cara, and there is nothing you can do about it. Me and your husband are friends, and your other friend wants to fuck me. How does that feel?" She shakes her head and puts her hand to her face.

"You're sick. A monster."

"Stop being so dramatic. You knew when the time had come I would find you again." I take out my hand and touch her face. She stays still, allowing my touch. Her skin like it should be bubbling, like my hand is a hot iron burning her, scarring her once more. "See," I whisper, "Just like we used to do." I feel wetness around my feet and the potent smell hits my nose. I look down at my shoes and find a stream of clear liquid soaking into the carpet falling from Cara's hips. I smile. "At least you're hydrated. That would leave a bad stain otherwise."

"Please just leave Christian," She pleads, her mascara beginning to run. The room around us completely unaware of what is happening, of the connection we have. Me and you, here in this moment, reliving old times. I lean in for a kiss and you let me. Those lips just like I remember.

"This time will be different, I promise," I say. "You won't get away from me again."

13

Now

Driving to your work is quick enough, now the night has drawn on a little and the traffic has died down. My mind runs a thousand miles an hour, but to see me on the surface you wouldn't be able to tell. I am calm, stoic, relaxed. The lights are on, the touch of my skin would yield the feeling of flesh. To shine a torch in my eyes and the pupils will react, and cut my arm open and you will see real blood pouring from the wound. But me? Me on the other hand, I am simply a concept. An enigma. A word people make with their mouths to address me. My gaze is warm but my thoughts are cold. My smile bright but my voice of razors. I am both your devil and your angel. I will give you everything, and I will take it from you with a smile.

I pull up outside the office. The car park is empty except for a couple of cars that look like they haven't moved all day. Stirrup Enterprises is a huge building filled with glass windows and over eighteen floors that I could see from the entrance to the carpark.

The perimeter of the building is lined with tall fences with sharpened spikes on top, and the security hut had an automatic barrier system in place. I pull up to the security terminal and an elderly gentleman who had worked too many night shifts sat lazily with his feet up, big nose buried in a copy of some bullshit newspaper.

"Can I help you?" He croaks, barely looking up. I smile, nod my head and then show him your ID card. Thankfully, your place hadn't modernised just yet to need up to date photographs, so with my hood up and with a hint of darkness, the guard doesn't think too much about it and waves me through. I pull up close to the entrance, get out of the car and stretch, my back and hips clicking. I hadn't figured out how to adjust the seat of John's car yet. My posture would suffer. Thankfully I was great at Pilates, and I drank more water a day than recommended to keep me nice and supple.

With a spring in my step, I walk straight through those big glass double doors to the place you like to spend so much of your time rather than spend it at home with me. Why don't you love me? Why don't you want to spend your time with me? Is this the place where Mark fucks you? Is this the place where he makes you cum?

I move up the stairs quickly and get a good burn in my chizzled quads. I have been working on them a lot recently, making that nice little diamond shape in the middle of them. Have you noticed? Have you noticed me working out in the morning? Have you bothered to see the calorie counter app on my phone where I track my macros? Have you noticed how my black polo shirt you said you like fits tighter around my shoulders and waist? No, you haven't. And why would you? You're already getting drilled by the fancy beard with the ten thousand Instagram followers. So why the fuck would you notice what I have done to try and salvage our relationship? I punch one of the walls with the side of my fist as I make it up to the fifth floor. I look at my smart watch.

"50 calories burnt" I say to myself. I quickly press the *save workout* option on the watch, before slowing to a walk and look for the *records* section.

The corridors are quiet, dead and dark. They stretch on for what seems to be miles, flanked by empty office rooms and lifeless windows. I follow the signs and eventually make my way into the small office marked 'HR.' Using your pass, I swipe the key card on the small terminal and the solid red light flashes an inviting solid green. I push the door open. Thank you for telling me that you have access to most of the building's offices and rooms. You often let things slip when you had been drinking. A few nuggets of information which most people wouldn't bat an eye lid at: the town you grew up in, the name of your first pet, the school you went to as a child. Just some simple things that would be innocuous to most people. But to me, I have been planning this for a while, a night of fun, a night to end *all* nights, and to bring this whole thing to an end. You will love me Lorna, even if it kills me.

I check my watch. I didn't have much time. Cara had no doubt set out on her way by now. She would be cursing John for the traffic as she needed to head downtown to get to him. Through the busy pissed up pedestrian high streets filled with bars and restaurants. I still had so much to do, so I hurried my step.

I pull up an office chair and fire up one of the computers which comes to life. I press the *log in* option and slot the key card into the keyboard. Your credentials came up, that smile of yours filling up the screen. "LORNA WITHERS." I look over the keys, a billion possibilities for the password. I feel like a kid again playing spy movies, or secret agents. I just hoped the guard downstairs hadn't gotten some kind of epiphany and wasn't realising that the records unit had been swiped into by a very masculine sounding LORNA with an obscure face. I had to be quick, the wolves would be coming for me soon.

I try a couple of things first, like my name, the place we met or even what our first meal was together. All wrong, and I nearly smash up the keyboard in fury. *Bitch* I think. I lean back and take a breath, then, try a few combinations. The name of your first dog

'Suzie,' was the magic bullet. Not me. Not my name. But your fucking mutt that ran away from home.

The terminal logged in and folders of information stared me in the face. First things first, I type in the name of your fancy man –

MARK WOOD. I find his profile, and more importantly, I find his address.

I note the address down, and before I am finished, I upload the USB that I plugged into Cara's computer at the party. I move the software through a VPN, through some more sophisticated channels and log into her online banking. She was a wealthy girl indeed and I nearly salivate as I click the DEPOSIT button and watch the loading bar fill. Finally, I send an email of your resignation to your boss, dated the day before. It wasn't hard if you knew how to do it.

'I'M REALLY STRUGGLING AT THE MINUTE. I DON'T KNOW WHAT TO DO. MARK HAS BEEN HARRASSING ME. IM SORRY I DIDN'T BRING THIS UP SOONER. I WILL TAKE CARE OF IT. YOU WONT SEE ME AGAIN.'

-    LORNA WITHERS

I look at my watch. Nearly time. Just one more stop to make before I come and see you.

14

Then

"Goodnight!" I say, leaving the party. You're firmly gripping my arm as we stumble drunkenly into the night air. The taxi driver from earlier has come back to pick us up. 01:00 sharp, just like we agreed. He was right on time, and I liked that. I opened the back passenger door and you slipped inside, smiling at me.

"Nobody has ever held a door for me before," you said, a sound of wonder in your voice.

"Trust me Lorna," I say with a smile. "I guarantee, you haven't ever met anyone like me before." I close the door. As I move around the rear of the cab, its brake lights lighting up my jeans and I see you looking at me through the top bedroom window. You're shaking your head Cara, and I don't like that. What if your friend sees you? I imagine you never told her about us? You are gold to me, and I love every second of watching you squirm under the weight of your own guilt.

I slide in next to you. There is a slight hint of vomit and anti-bac lingering in the air of the cab, but then again, it is Friday night and the kids of today can't handle their drink. Too busy taking shit drugs and getting fingered on sticky dancefloors. I was always the best at drinking, stuntman tequila shots, martinis made from Rum and not Vodka. Spinning in circles, drinking bottles of wine and fuck it, even a cheap cider on top of an even cheaper bottle of Vodka would get me into a good buzz. I could drink for the country. I was a champion, and given with how straight I felt right now, looking into your drunken eyes, your hair still neat and the smell of the cocktails emanating from your breath as you leaned into me, I knew I could have you in whatever way I wanted. You weren't completely shit faced, I'm not a total fucking creep. But the look in those eyes that shone in the moonlight told me that you wanted me, and you were as sure of that as you have been sure of anything in your whole life.

"Take me back," you whispered, putting your hand on my thigh. "Take me back with you." You leant in, your lips an inch from mine. The smell of your perfume making my cock wake up. I knew you could feel it, growing, getting harder under those fingertips. You squoze them around it, and you heard my breath intake sharply. The cab driver asked where too, and I told him the address not breaking our gaze. United, finally, like we were lovers from past lives, twin souls destined to dance through this world together, through each life until the moon turned black and the sun grew cold. Me and you forever and ever, until the night sky turned blank and the earth died, our souls would still be there, searching for each other for eons to come.

You pressed into my chest with your hands as the engine fired to life and the wheels began to turn. I didn't know if the cab had CCTV, but that didn't seem to bother you. It would only show the back of your head anyway, those lips wrapped around me, your knees on the floor of the cab. Your tongue glided and caressed my throbbing head, and those lips, plump and smooth, tightened around me and glided over me, extracting me into you, pumping me, making me harder. You gripped me with your right hand, softly at first but then tightly as you sucked hard on the end, those green eyes locking with mine. You could feel me getting close, my legs twitching, my breath going heavy, fingers buried in your hair. You pushed me away from you, reaching your tongue down to my balls and ran through them like licking ice cream. I heard you moan, that free hand tucked under your dress, sank deeply between your legs, finding the wet softness that lingered underneath. You took those offending fingers out and pushed them into my mouth. You tasted sweet, delicious, like a flavour you always wanted but could never find, the taste of it on my tongue intoxicating. You kept going with your mouth, not caring as we drove back through the busy streets of town. Some onlookers caught a glance of us when we idled at traffic lights, but you just smiled at them and gave them a front row seat, knowing they wished it was their cock you were sucking on and not mine. I gripped the back of your head as I came, and you kept going, not missing a beat, the cum filling your mouth and you swallowed it up whole, licking me clean, nibbling the insides of my thighs as you smiled at my heavy breath. And like that, you sat back next to me, touching up your hair, holding me.

"I love you," I said. I didn't mean to say it, but I did anyway. It felt right, felt like destiny. Your face didn't match mine. You told the driver to stop. I asked what was wrong, but you got your bag and you jumped out of the taxi at the next set of lights. I tried to go after you but you disappeared in the crowd of party goers. You were gone, and I didn't know why. You used me, you slut. You fucking whore. You used me, and you were going to pay for it.

15

Now

I exit the building and leave the car park, the security guard too busy to notice with his big nose buried into a copy of 'Razzle.' His fingers vanishing into a bag of butter popcorn, no doubt telling himself how much he will pleasure the gals in the magazine he is reading more than the studs and models that actually took care of themselves.

I put in Mark's address and move down the dark streets. My skin is damp with sweat, so I take out a pack of facial wipes, unscented, and wipe myself dry. Then, I rub some super dry roll on under my arm pits.

The drive was shorter than expected. I arrived outside his house and looked upon it with surprise. Considering how expensive and huge Mark's personality would seem to an outsider, his house was nothing special: a terrace house on a street littered with empty beer cans, discarded cigarette packages, and the odd mound of dog shit matted into the pavement. The houses on either side of the road had several windows boarded up, and most of the cars on the streets had their black plastic bags over their windows where they had been broken into. This, was not the Instagram lifestyle which I would expect you to have in real life. I pull up his socials and check out his page.

He is jacked, tanned and has his shirt off on most photos, supporting a designer beard in the glow of the evening sun on some beach somewhere, the wide blue ocean in the background, next to some tall brunette or blonde in a bikini and a flat stomach. This must be some kind of mistake, because I look at the guy standing on the beach of Malta, and then at the home where he lived, and these cannot be the same lives of the man in the photos.

I park around the back of his house, a small alley way littered with overflowing blue and black bins. A black cat moves towards me as I get out of the truck and look into the back of my trunk. I pull out my duffel bag and the little fur ball begins purring and pawing me, rubbing its face on my leg and tail caressing my thighs and knees as it weaves in and out of my legs. It makes me smile a little, my heart a little warmer. I stroke the top of the precious things head as it glides between my legs. It nestles into my ankle, and with a smile, I decide to only stamp on the creatures' front legs, rather than kill it outright. The damn thing was too cute.

I count down the houses and find which one is Mark's. It's

the one with the low back gate with the bolt securing it to the wall without a padlock. The house is all in darkness and the back door is made of PVC and a single pane of glass. I see no security cameras, and I see no intruder lights protecting the back of the home. I walk to the back door and check the lock. It's a simple mechanism, and with a screwdriver, a hammer and a piece of wood for torque, comes away quite easily. I have placed a small cloth on the ground to cushion the sound of the barrel falling from the door, less the rattling of metal on concrete flags give me away. I depress the handle and step inside the house.

Inside, the kitchen is pretty big: a flimsy black wooden table sits next to the radiator on the far wall, no doubt from Ikea or Walmart. The sink is filled with dishes and there are half empty boxes of pizza and stacks of protein powder on the counters, also a plastic tub filled with empty syringes.

Steroids I think to myself. So even when Mr. Big was getting you in his bedroom, he would no doubt need a lot of 'help' getting it up, and he would be flat out of breath by the time he was finished, if he finished at all. I see the photo then and I nearly scream the place down. You and him, holding each other, smiling away, smiling at the camera, laughing together, having a great fucking time. When was this taken? *Where* was this taken? Had this affair been going on for longer than I thought? I take the photo out of the frame and stuff the photo in my pocket. I snap the frame in two and toss it in the trash can.

I listen to the night, and I can hear the sound of someone upstairs. I stand at the bottom of the narrow staircase. I breathe slowly, steadying my hand. Carefully, I begin to ascend.

One step at a time, I listen for any change in your breathing. You snore so loudly; you basically ring a dinner bell for anyone wanting to come into your house at night. This isn't my fault, it's yours. You put yourself in this position with your diet and your over exercising, not to mention the shit you clearly pump into your system each day. You are in such a deep sleep; it shouldn't be too hard for me to complete the next part of my plan.

On the landing, I see Mark's bedroom door is slightly ajar. I step in, and I see a figure lying in a single bed in a room that is almost bare: lamp and a bedside table, a small dresser with a mirror on the top of it with a jumper, pants and some other clothes that are folded neatly. The mattress is thin on a metal frame which creaked with every breath. You sleep next to the large window with thick drapes over the glass. I take out the rag and the chloroform and douse it. The smell is potent, and I feel the sharp scent push into my nose. I push it away, feeling the gas burn the top of my sinus'. I lean over and pull the covers away.

It wasn't you. I was in the wrong fucking house. Before me lay an old man, maybe in his eighties, sleeping soundly, his tiny frame rattling with the volume of his snoring. I let out a huge breath and stuff the chloroform back into my pocket.

"What the fuck!" I hear behind me. Surprise and fear harpoon through me as I see him, in all his might, chest rounded and shoulders like boulders, consuming the door frame. I try to speak, but he is already upon me. He pushes me to the wall, his hands around my throat and punches me to the face. I see stars. Hell, the fucking milky way comes to the front of my mind. The taste of copper bursts into my mouth like a blood blister pressed under a vice.

I grab out at him, his turka teeth flashing in the moonlight. I kick him in the shin, but he doesn't flinch, his face that of rage, his veins pulsing at the side of his head and his tendons raised down the side of his neck. He reels his hand back once more for a piston punch, but I move my head, his hand colliding with the brick wall. He lets out a harsh grunt, releasing me, grabbing his wrist. I take out the rag and move behind him, grabbing the back of his shoulders, reaching my hand to his mouth. I latch on, but he back butts me, destroying my nose as it erupts in fire and crimson. Again, I see a wave of agony before my eyes and my mouth explodes with fury. Mark charges, a bull fuelled with fear, rage and steroids. He hooks me under his arms and we burst through the door and onto the landing, where we struggle, his hands gripping mine, my fist colliding with his jaw, his might overpowering mine. We fall then, hitting each step, the rough carpet burning into our skin as we crash to the bottom. I am on top now, and I move over to the counter. Mark panting behind me, clambering to his feet, getting to his feet drunkenly, and I smell it once more. The smashed bottle of chloroform next to his head. He is woozy, his gigantic body falling onto the table, collapsing it under his weight. I run over to the bottle and hold my breath. I take hold of the tub filled with syringes and fill them with the noxious liquid. I climb on top of him, the blood and swelling blurring my eyes. I think he tries to speak, but I don't wish to heat what he has to say. I jam the syringe into his neck and depress the plunger, sending the chloroform into his blood stream. I fill another, and then another, leaving the syringes in like a porcupine made of crystals.

Within seconds, Mark stops grabbing out at me, and I fill that cunt's body with every syringe I can find, pumping his veins with air, protein powder, chloroform and the filth found at the bottom of the sink.

I stand over him panting. I clean myself as best I can and put the bloodied rags in my pocket. Then, I take out your phone and take photos of his body. I leave the house quickly, stumbling, fumbling over myself. His father, if it was his father, would have heard the noise and would no doubt wake up to find his house destroyed and his son dead. By the time the police have gotten there and have done their investigation work, they will be coming for the killer. But that would be in a few hours or so I hoped, which would give me plenty of time to finish what I had started. Now, I had just one last stop to make.

16

Now

I checked the time. The night was drawing on. I stomp on the accelerator, flying through a red light to the sound of horns blaring in my ears. The second time I had put my life at risk for you today Lorna, but I doubt you noticed.

A few minutes later, I get to the waiting room, the receptionist eyeing me over her magazine.

"Lorna Withers?" I ask. The nurse gives me a nonchalant look, a sharp intake of breath and then wheels her overweight ass to the computer a few feet away. I stand there quietly like a well-behaved child waiting for the ice cream man to hand me my cone of Mr. Whippy. The receptionist taps her keys, staring at the screen tough ridiculously large glasses.

"You family?" She asks. I nod. "Name?"

"Christian Peters," I say. She taps the keys.

"You're not on the list," she says. I grip the bar of the reception desk.

"I'm her husband," I say through gritted teeth. *Let me the fuck in or I swear to god I will climb over this dark and stuff that damn magazine down your throat.* She taps on her computer.

"I have a Mark Wood down as her next of kin." The room shatters around me. *You bitch,* I think. *You have given his name instead of mine?*

"There must be some kind of mistake," I say, trying to keep as calm as possible whilst my stomach tears itself in two.

"Sorry," she says. "If you aren't listed, I can't let you through." She puts her nose back into her reading material and leaves me standing there, like I don't exist. I step back, my legs like air, and fall back onto a chair, the empty coffee cups still there on the ground by my feet. I put my head in my hands, trying to figure out why you would put him as your contact instead of me?

I get up and walk outside for some air. I check my watch once more as I breathe in the cool night air, my breath turning to mist as it disappears into the starless night above. To my right, an ambulance turns up and a patient is wheeled out on a gurney, a heavy-set man with a large beard racing next to them. He is broad, like a *sasquatch,* screaming the name "Jayne," over and over.

The paramedics open the emergency entrance, and as they move through, so do I. I slip in behind them, and checking nobody has noticed me, I move into one of the side rooms and wait a moment. A nurse moves past me, over worked and unable to keep her eyes open, she doesn't notice me standing there, thinking I am either a shadow in her imagination, or I am a visitor to the mound covered in a thin sheet laid on the bed next to me. I spot the fire alarm and grip it, pulling the plunger towards the ground.

The sound of the siren is deafening. Nurses drop their notes and doctors burst from their chairs and race to wards and grab their patients. I move to an unlocked computer and search your name. I find you there. Ward D4, room 3. I make my way there through the cries of patients and nurses that push trolleys and wheel chairs as they race out of the doors into the cold night.

I make it to your room and you are sleeping soundly, your arms patched up like a doll that has been re stuffed. You stir as I approach you, touching your face. I kiss you and hold you once more.

"I thought I had lost you," I whisper, your heat from your skin intoxicating, drawing me in. I hear the heart rate monitor pick up, and you scream in horror at the sight of me, as I put the chloroform over your mouth.

A few moments later you're on a wheel chair with a blanket over you. I have taken the precaution of strapping you to it by wrapping several pairs of rubber gloves tightly together, making sure you don't fall off. Thankfully the fumes have worked there way into your blood stream, and you're docile like a dog being put to sleep before surgery. We wouldn't want you to make a scene now would we? Oh sure you try to call out lazily to those passing by, but they're too busy running from the imaginary fire, and we're out the building and into the night air before we know it.

"Don't worry," I say as I put the key in the ignition. Your face is of terror, snot and tears falling from your face. "It will all be over soon."

We arrive a few minutes later at the warehouse. I have bundled you into the back seat. I didn't want to risk anyone seeing you in your hospital gown. Not with how much you continued to cry anyway. It was a real mood killer, and your tears had better not have stained the leather Lorna for fuck's sake. I know this isn't my car, but there's a lot to be said for people that respect things that aren't theirs, and those that happily leak their bodily fluids all over other people's shit. A clear distinction in morality and values. Some fuckers are just sadists.

I pull up to the front of the building where John is probably coming too by now. The bright beams from the car washing over the grey stone walls. I can't see Cara's car anywhere. Maybe she got lost? Traffic delayed? It made no difference anyway.

I open the back door and pull you out by your legs. Your eyes flash with tears and terror as they meet mine. I don't hold onto the gaze for very long though. I find you off putting.

"Stop fucking crying," I hiss, reeling my hand back and slap the tears away from your eyes. "This is all for you." Your eyes see the intent on my face and you take the hint and nod quietly. Look at you Lorna, your hair all matted and sticking to your face, your hands and arms bandaged up from when you pathetically tried to take your own life. "Why are you crying?" I whisper in the night. "I loved you so much, we had a connection, we are twin flames but you couldn't see it. You ran to Mark, ran into the arms of your husband." I spat in her face then, right in the eye. Grabbing her hair, I dragged her, bound and kicking, out of the car. Both hands buried into your scalp as you feebly kicked and pawed at the gravel, your whimpers like a triangle chime in an ensemble of chaos.

At the foot of the door, I push it open. John is lying where I left him, the fat fuck still bound to the chair, drooling on himself. I place you on a chair and take off your gag. In a moment, you breathe and heave huge gulps of air and begin to scream. I pull a bottle from the side of the work top and spray it in your mouth. Instantly you begin to cough, splutter and gag. "This is diluted bleach. Scream once more and you get another blast." You splutter some more, trying to fill those lungs with air that's thick with ammonia. "Now," I say, putting the bottle next to you. "If I may please continue?" I pull up a chair and sit opposite you. I see you're eyeing John, wondering if he's asleep or very fucking dead. Judging by the fluid leaking out of his ear, brown and translucent, I would say he is not far off the latter.

"Now," I begin, wiping my face with an alcohol-free wipe I had stuffed in my pocket. I take off my leather gloves and pull out a cigarette. You sit there half naked, the anaesthetic from the surgery still numbing your senses. I know you can hear me, that you can move your eyes and feel my touch, because you recoil once more when I place my hand on yours. "Hey," I whisper and shush you like a father would such a frightened child after a bad dream. "I don't want to hurt you baby," I whisper. "I don't want to cause you any pain. I just have to talk to you. I tried last night, I tried this morning, but you wouldn't listen." I stand then looking out of the frosted glass to the blurred grey and black of the car park, the single street light illuminating my face. "I love you. I have told you before, when we met a few days back, I didn't think you would understand, hell, I didn't think it was something I could really feel myself, after the shit I have been through. But you, you were different, are different, and

I know that you feel the same way. I just had to take care of a few distractions, a few things first, to make you think clearly, to make you see how much you really loved me, even if you didn't understand it just yet."

I walk to you and take your phone out of my pocket. I show you the pictures of your dead husband filled with syringes, lying cold on your kitchen floor. You begin to cry, and this upsets me. "Don't you see baby?" I say, "I did this for us? I did this for us both to be together." I look to John. "All of this is for you baby. I just have one thing left to do."

I move to my bag and take out a bottle of chloroform once more and douse the rag with it. I put your phone on the side of the counter and set a timer.

"This won't hurt," I whisper as I descend on you. You fight me, pulling your face away from the rag, but I can see it working, the fumes entering your blood stream. "I'm not going to kill you baby," I say. "I love you too much. I just want to help you, help you to love me. I know it is in there, you just need some assistance, and that's okay. I'll only do it for a little while I promise. I have done this before on a few animals: stray dogs, rats, cats. After a few minutes they wake up. They can't use their legs and the fumes kill the part of the brain for motor function, but the centre of the brain, for breathing and bodily functions still work. I want you to be comfortable, for me to take care of you," I press the timer on your phone and take the back of your head, and stuff the rag over your mouth and nose. "Forever."

"Leave her alone you sick fuck." The spluttering voice coming to my right startles me. I release the rag and you begin to cough and splutter onto the ground, retching so hard your eyes begin to redden. Something I thought only happened in the movies. You learn something new every day.

"John," I say, eyeing the big guy strapped so tight his fingers had turned purple. "How nice of you to join us for this wonderful moment." John's face is a dull grey, and the lump on his head had swelled to the size of a fist. I wonder how it would feel if I jammed my finger inside the wound? I wonder what would come out? I wonder how loud he would scream?

"What the fuck is wrong with you?" He stutters. The injury must have fucked his head up a little. I moved to him and slap him across the face.

"Don't you dare tell me that I am the problem you fat fuck! There, I fucking said it. You fat piece of shit! You fucking lowlife stupid bastard! How the hell can you of all people dictate to me what is right and wrong?" I grab his shoulders and stare him in those swollen eyes. "I am in love John. I am in love. Do you know what that feels like? Do you?" He begins to whimper then, the bravado quickly leaving him. I hear the sound of piss hitting the floor, and what little respect I had for him vanishes quicker than the smell of urine hitting my nostrils. "You think you know love? With Cara?" I begin to laugh. "Who do you think took the photos of her online slut profile John?" There, I see those eyes widen, rage pushing through the bruising.

"You're lying." I smile. No, fuck, I laugh. A roaring laughter that comes right from my stomach.

"You think *I'm* lying? You couldn't tell a liar if it was on the end of your tiny cock."

I hear a knock on the door. I snap my attention to the sound and quickly grab the bottle of ammonia before either of you have a chance to scream. The threat is enough, and another round of knocking prevails in the tense silence. I hold my finger over my mouth to Lorna, and she falls into a low whimper.

"Hello?" I hear her say, her voice confused, wanting. I smile to John. *Right on cue.*

"Invite her in," I whisper to him. He initially protests, shaking his head. I could punch him, jam my finger in that swelling mess of a head of his, hell, even cut off his balls with the scalpel I have inside my duffel bag. But I decide to be a little more tactful. I was never one for blood. I walk over to John and pull out the bottle of bleach and hold it an inch from his eyes. "Invite her in," I repeat. I can see the mental war happening inside his head, the choice literally paining him. "I'll kill her if you don't invite her in. I'll make you watch, and then I'll kill you too." I let the threat hang in the air for a moment, and then, one final time whisper, "invite her in."

"Come in baby," he says, fighting through the tears. Lorna buries her head into the floor and the handle depresses. As soon as her foot crosses the threshold, I grab hold of her and stuff the rag over her mouth.

17

Now

I take you by surprise, your eyes told me that. You scream as you try to fight back, seeing the hate in my eyes, seeing the pain that you have caused.

"Just like last time," I hiss. I can see your eyes moving to the back of your head, your strength fading. You claw my face and kick out at me, but I know that with every breath, you're falling further into my embrace. I can hear John's slurred cries screaming at me to let you go, Lorna, my darling, I'm sorry you had to see this part of me.

18

Now

"Wake up," I shout, splashing water in your face. You startle awake, your senses still out of it, your breathing still deep as you are shocked out of your slumber. "Good evening Mrs. Clarkson," I say, sitting on the chair in front of you, Lorna to your right, John to the left, *and here I am, stuck in the middle with you.* I had always loved that song. I always found it funny. Suddenly my mood has improved a little.

"What are you doing Chris?" You whisper. I lean back in my chair, folding my legs over, tensing my biceps as I interlace my fingers. I know you noticed I have put on some mass since you last saw me in this shirt. I wore it for a reason. It's the shirt I was wearing when you called the cops.

"Isn't it obvious?" I say, laughing. "I am showing my beautiful Lorna what terrible people she has in her life!" I gesture to John. "We have the glutton," I point to you Cara, "We have the lustful, the slut," and then I point to her mobile phone, the picture of her dead husband lying on the floor still lit up for her to see. She hasn't taken her eyes of it once. She would cry, scream, but I got tired of her doing that when I was tying you to the chair, so I gagged her. It was much better when she couldn't fucking speak. "And lying on the ground in his kitchen, the vain!" I stand, looking out of the window once more. "All of you are no good for her. I am here to show her that."

"You're a monster," Cara says, spitting onto the ground, the taste of the chemicals still lingering on her tongue. I turn, my face smiling from ear to ear.

"Me? Really?" I laugh and look at John who was just barely holding on. "Tell your husband how we met." Your eyes widen.

"It was you texting me? You planned this all along! What have you done to my husband!" You look at him with more love and pain than you ever showed me. Again, I feel my heart break a little, but then black cement and tar cover over the cracks, making it tougher and harder. The pain no longer allowed to seep out.

"Tell your husband what he needs to hear. He has seen your profile Cara." Your lip began to quiver then. You turned to me, those eyes filled with fury.

"That was a long time ago. I deleted that after you!" I laugh a little.

"I remembered your log in details. It was easy enough to make a new profile for John to see. I never did delete those photos. After you told me you had a husband, after we had *met each other*, you wondered why I was so fucking angry with you!" I raise my voice on the last word, swiping a small phone on the ground that lands on the floor next you from a desk top. "I mean, the audacity to make someone fall in love with you and then tell them that you're already taken! And you wonder why I got so pissed!"

"You tried to strangle me Christian!" You screamed, pulling at the binds. "I called the police to have you arrested!"

"Yes," I said, "But the thought of you telling your husband that you had been fucking a guy off the internet behind his back was something you couldn't bring yourself to do. Not to mention the amount you were drinking back then." Your face swelled with pain, it running onto the floor and pooling around your feet.

"I was a mess. I was depressed. I needed something, anything to make me numb."

"So I was just something to keep you numb then?" I said, my tone bitter, the cracks in my heart appearing once more. "Did you ever love me?" You turned your face to John.

"Baby, I'm sorry, baby, I didn't mean to, it was a long time ago, I promise, I...." Then you saw it, through your tears, through your pain and the haze surrounding it. Drowning in your own guilt, lost in a black sea of regret. His face was slumped low, his mouth foaming, his eyes open, just about anyway. His chest still, his skin turning bluer by the second. "No," you said, your voice stretching like an out of tune violin. "No! John! Baby!" The sound of your voice could never be captured in words. It was pure agony and pain, but then so much more. "John!" You turned to me, frantically pulling at the restraints. "Help him Chris! I'll do anything! I'll do anything you want! You want me to tell you I love you? Fine, I love you. I have always loved you, and I will be yours forever after this, I promise, just please! Help him!" You strain and you cry, you scream and you wail, as I sit there quietly listening to you beg, watching your husband, the man you treated so badly when he was alive, mourning him in front of me, the man you threw him away for. Your inconsolable tears turned into silent sobs, your chest rapid like turbulent waves in a shallow creek.

"And there you have it," I said. "Retribution for what you have done."

19

Now

Looking at the pair of you now, my old love verses my new love. Truth be told, I loved you both equally, but one was soiled, and one could be salvaged. I move to you Lorna, and I put my fingers at the bottom of your chin, your tears soaking into my fingertips. I lift your head, those eyes glistening in the dim light like still water overlooked by a fleeting lighthouse.

"How does it feel?" I say. "How does it feel to know that you have hurt me more than I knew possible, and yet I still want you. I still crave you." I lean in and kiss you on those quivering lips. "Does it feel good?" Your hands begin to tremble. You try to speak, but the drugs they pumped in you are still in your system. All you manage is a low murmur. "I thought as much," I say, deflated. I touch your wrists, the stitching that holds you together. "I find this in very bad taste." I run my fingers along them, bumpy like brail. Like I can read your shame. "I'll make sure you never leave me again."

I turn back to the bottle of chloroform and open up the timer on your phone. Three minutes, that should do it. To render your mind active but the brain damage so extensive, you can't ever leave me again.

"What has she ever done to you? You bastard!" Cara hissed. "What had she done? She had a husband, and you…" She looks to the floor for answers. "You are a monster." I smile. I love when people think they know me so well.

"When the police get here, they will find me unconscious, Lorna hardly breathing and you…. Well, you won't be able to tell them what happened, that's for sure." I turn back to you Lorna, and look you dead in the eye. "They will see the photos on your phone. They will see the bodies, the emails sent from your work, the suicide attempt. The notes left by the doctors of mental instability. They will blame you for all of this, and then when you are sectioned, unable to move or speak, I will be there by your side, forever." I put the rag to your mouth and start the timer. You heave heavy breaths as the toxins fill your blood once more. "That's it baby," I whimper in your ear. "Just a little longer."

The chair behind me topples over. I see you Cara, lying on the ground, face in the floor, struggling at the binds. I laugh to myself. "You're only going to hurt yourself doing that," I mock.

"I love you Christian." The words rock me to the bone. I turn to you, and I see the rag away from your mouth, and finally, you have spoken.

"What did you say?" I whisper, my mouth running dry.

"I said I love you. I know I have been bad, but I did it for the right reasons. I did it because when I met you, at the party, I knew I wanted you. I'm sorry I left you, I'm sorry I treated you so poorly. Me and Mark weren't doing well. That night, the night we met again, he was being his usual drunk self, and I grew tired of it. I saw you, I fell for you, I loved you from the moment I laid my eyes on you. I'm sorry I made you feel this way, I'm sorry I am such a horrible person. I'm sorry I said those things. I'm sorry I hurt myself to get away. I was confused. I'm so sorry. I love you baby." Your head dipped then, and tears, *real tears* came flowing from your eyes like a heavy rain over the arid dirt of my soul.

"Lorna," I said, touching your head tentatively. I looked at the rag. *Did I need to do this?* "Are you lying to me?" I begged, almost pleading with you to be truthful with me, that what I have sought from you, was finally in my grasp. You shake your head, and I believe you. Fuck, I believed you so much. I knew body language, and you held my eyes, no flinching, no blinking or looking away. No micro expressions. You held my gaze and you said those words that melted my soul like ice in a summer afternoon.

"I love you Christian. I always have. Do what you need to do, so we can be together." I leant in and hugged you then, tears running from my eyes, stinging them, filling my mouth and dampening the back of your neck. I moved back, on my knees, holding your face in my hands.

"I love you so much," I say. I didn't hear you Cara get up from the chair, or the sound of the bat dragging along the floor. I only felt it when you swung and cracked the top of my skull. I'm on the ground now, my head booming like a million cannon balls firing at the same time over and over. My vision is blurred, my mind wants to move but my body fails me as I grab out at your leg as you untie my love. The winter wind floods the room as I see you, both of you, leaving the unit into the night.

20

Forever

I crawl to my feet, stumble and catch myself on one of the counters. I try once more, my legs failing me, my head hot and my hands painted dark red like off jam. I steady myself, holding onto the wall as I fall out of the unit. I hear someone shouting, two figures in the distance running, one being dragged by the other. I see you both fumble, one of you falls. I step onto the gravel and I hit the ground again, the sting of the asphalt mixing with my wound.

I'm on my feet again now. I feel as though I am running, but my feet drag along the floor. I call out to you both. For you to stop, but your shapes continue to move, falling further into the darkness.

You are gone. The both of you are gone. Out of my life. I scan the night and find no shapes meet my eye. You were lost. I could chase you; I could find you. But I needed to do some cleaning up first. I had to recoup, rally myself and get better. Be more prepared. I would need to skip town. I had done it before. I was self-employed, nothing on credit, always paid with cash. It wouldn't be the first time I had changed identities. I could shave my head, lose a little more weight, maybe even get a killer tan. Move to that seaside town on the east coast. I had never been arrested, my DNA was on no police or hospital database. I was a ghost and I was good at it. Christian wasn't my real name, and I could move freely like a ghost, until I next found someone to love me, to care for me.

The next thing I saw was the light from the Range Rover hurtling towards me like two beams of a runaway train. I didn't feel the impact. Not fully anyway. I knew my ribs were broken, the sound of the fumes leaking from under the vehicle as the engine and head gasket crumpled in. I heard the screams and the blaring horns in my ears as I lay there on the floor, the world fading in and out of view, and then the sound of sirens in the distance, drawing closer to me. I felt heat leech from me, the stars above me finally emerge from the black cloudless sky, and for once in my life, I had found something truly beautiful to admire. The sky above me, twinkling in its majesty, me locked in its awe, as I felt myself leaving, drawing away to the night above. I saw you looking at me, that smile on your face, you know the one, the one that said *I know you're hurting and I like it.*

Love, it would seem, was indeed the cruellest, most mysterious mistress of all.

The Eyes

One

I awoke like I did most nights, pulled from my slumber by the sound of rattling on the bedroom window like long nails tapping at the glass. I trained myself to stay in my bed, to ignore the lure of looking out onto that dark lawn below, to see the Creeping Man smiling.

But tonight, more than other nights, the whispering, the darkness with teeth and tongues, spoke to me louder than it had before. Like an insect on the inside of my skull, unable to get out, impossible to ignore. I stood, sleep drunk but a familiar fear in my chest creeping like maggots burrowing inside a frozen carcus for warmth. I moved, legs heavy, drearily to the window.

The cloudless, star filled black that laced the heavens above watched over me as my eyes, no matter how hard I tried to resist, fell onto the dull lawn below. There it stood. A figure cloaked in black. It was its eyes that I always saw first: deep and red like the embers of a dying fire. Its hands as white as bone poking from under its flowing black coat. Its face hidden with shadow under a large top hat. I moved away, returning to my bed, not allowing the visions of monsters and devils to fill my head.

I push the eyes from my mind, forcing myself to detach from the waking world once more. I have quelled fear before, much worse than this, when the creature with the red eyes had made it up my stairs. If I don't give it heed, it will disintegrate with the dawn. If I give it attention, it will come closer. But it tries. Oh how it tries to make me weep, with its incessant whispers, wanting me, forsaking my will to sleep.

I snap my eyes open, the night still aloof, encased in a timeless box of dark. Had I been sleeping for a minute or more? The sky a still sheet of death, and the chittering and tapping of the spectre in my head.

As if hooked, I am on my feet, pulled to the windowsill beside my bed. There, like before, the creature with the red eyes is staring, its toothy smile alluring, caring, longing for me to join it on the dark lawn. I shake my head, like I always said, and quell its wishes once more.

Again in my bed, I rest my head, willing the being to vapour. But again I hear, the sinister sneer, of the rapping of knuckles on my door. It was inside, my heart began to pound. I hide under my covers, muting my sound.

Like air the thing moves, along my hallway into my room. It whispering even louder than before. Begging me to come with it, into the land of hell and fire, where I will be cloaked in shadow for ever more.

Inside my bed, shaking my head, my tiny hands, they tremble more. "Be gone you fiend," I hiss and scream, and shake my head once more. Its shadow grows, begging me to head through the door. I shake my head, like I always said, until the creature understands what I implore. But tonight, wrapped in fright, pull down the covers a slither more. I feel its might and in my sight, those reds my eyes doth bore.

It takes my hand and I scream and howl, the monster dragging me out my door. Out in the yard, I hit and shiver, scream and quiver, those red eyes staring into mine. The ground opens up and in my vision I see a world filled with spectres and horror. Withered souls and creatures of darkness, feasting on them as they clawed and clambered out of the hole. I pull away, the beings grip tight on my cuff. The wide grin of sharp teeth, its nose curved and pointed, red eyes and black fedora.

"Come," it says. Just one word and nothing more. Harrow fills my body and my blood turns to ice, the moon above no more. The stars are gone, and the world around me cloaked in shadow. A harvest of souls, the creature holds, a list in its hand to show. I am at the top, my name in black, my turn to be buried and rot.

The ground swells and the chasm grows, hell fire licking at my feet. Eyes sting with tears, and I see past those red eyes of death, the twilight breaking through the dark. The creature withers, turning to dust and ash, carried away by the wind. I lay on the wet grass, parents coming and holding me in their grasp.

I sleep then, the darkness gone to the land of Nether, for another day, I will wait, until the dark returns at late, and the rattling comes once more, rattling on my bedroom door.

There's Someone at the Door

One

The January snow came early as Ruth finished packing the rest of her and Simon's things. She hated the snow and knew that they would have to get up extra early to get to the airport in time for their flight. The smile hadn't left her face all evening as she packed her jumpers neatly into the suitcase, sealing them away with steel teeth. She hadn't been to Scotland to see her family all through the Christmas period due to work commitments.

"You work too hard!" Simon told her a few nights ago. A recurring rhetoric that repeated like a broken record.

"The book isn't going to write itself!" She scalded, three glasses of red wine deep as her thick rimmed glasses reflected the light from the laptop. She was so close to finishing her third Novel *Diamonds in The Night*, a story of three women that are sold into the slave trade of blood diamonds following a Safari trip in South Africa that turned deadly.

"I know." Simon resigned, getting up from his arm chair. The fire place crackled and popped as smoke pushed out of the chimney into the quiet street outside. They lived in a small cottage, nothing too fancy, but the old stones and the large meadow overlooking their home made it all the cosier, and even made the front page of the countryside brochures in their remote village in Devon.

Simon placed his aged hands on her shoulders. A carpenter for years who had long hung up his saw, but the hands told a story, and it was one of love and labour. "We need to go and see your mother in Fort William soon." He whispered tenderly, massaging the knots in her shoulders that had developed from the months of being hunched over a computer screen. "The publisher will understand. You are ahead of schedule anyway."

That had done it. The next day she got off the phone to the publishing house and she had a wry grin on her face.

"Well?" Simon spoke, lingering at the foot of the door like a nosey child. Ruth exhaled and Simon felt his aged heart begin to break. The look on her face told a story of sorrow. Her fair skin looking flustered. But then, like the melting January snow, a bright light emanated from her growing smile. One that said *I don't care what they say, everyone needs some time to themselves!*

The day was spent gathering last minute items and putting their belongings together into a couple of small suitcases. They would normally drive, but both comfortably in their sixties and with the thought of travelling so far in the snow, it just made more sense that they took the plane to Oban, hired a car and took the coastal route up to Fort William. Maybe even climb Ben Nevis in the Winter. Ruth had once been a keen hiker, and she felt like she still had some life left in her old bones.

Simon finished getting things sorted around the house: passports, climbing gear, maps. All the things he would *normally* leave to Ruth, he had taken care of, and placed them all in a duffel bag for the airport. As if knowing she was watching, he looked up to see her smiling in the doorway in her nightgown. Hair In rollers and supporting a Baileys on ice. Simon stood, moving to her, his silvered beard stretching into a wide smile. "Shouldn't you be getting some rest?" He joked. "We have a long day ahead of us tomorrow." A night cap later, he tucked her into bed and put on his coat.

"Where are you going?" She queried, a slight urgency to her voice. "It's late and the snow is falling. You should come to bed."

"I'm just stepping out to get some fuel." Simon said, sitting by her bedside and placing his hand on hers. "I looked earlier and the car is on fumes. We don't want to be rushed in the morning. I won't be long. I'll be right back." He gave her a small kiss on the lips. "Get some sleep." He stood and moved to the door, his hand lingering over the small lamp that sat near the doorway. Ruth watched wide eyed as his finger moved towards the switch. They held each other's gaze, and Simon nodded. His hand moved away from the lamp. And then he was gone.

Two

Ruth eyed the lamp that hummed lazily in the corner. The shadows of the bedside ornaments now stretching into long arms and mouths onto the walls. She cursed herself. "You're too old for horror stories Ruth come on." She scolded herself quietly, relinquishing the white knuckles that gripped the bed covers. Since Ruth had heard the stories as a young girl her grandmother told her about the house being haunted, it had always stuck with her. Things that crawl into your bed at night and wait for you to fall asleep before they eat you. She wasn't terrified of such monsters; she wasn't that ridiculous. She did however have nightmares when she was on her own, when the darkness seemed that little blacker, the wind howled that little louder, and the shapes in the night took on the forms of sinister apparitions. The light hummed quietly still, and her eye lids felt heavy. The Baileys kicking in now, making her gums and face numb. She let out a staggered breath before finally giving herself to the world of dreams.

She was walking. Her feet bare in the snow. Her nightgown flowing white. The sky was unloving and the morning sun struggled to get through the thick blanket of clouds above. The country road was cased in thick white and the wind fierce as it cut through her.

"I'll be right back." She heard those words again. An echo with no speaker. A sound with no source. Just bouncing, drawing closer then dragging away. Ruth was farther from home now, turning the corner onto

the bend where the road got busier on the way to the coast. Ahead, smoke pushed out of a car. A wrecked and crumpled shell with tyre tracks of black scarring the snow, like a toddler had drawn thick lines on paper with black marker. She felt dread strike her heart, and she ran towards the crumpled mesh of metal, howling his name.

Ruth reached the smouldering wreckage. He wasn't there. Where was he? She called out for help but only the wind heard her, and it answered back lowly, whistling through her clothing as the snow continued to fall. "I'll be right back." She heard his voice once more. The sound of heavy breathing behind her. She turned and a bolt of terror tore through her, as he stood there, face bloodied, eyes jellied and jaw hanging low.

Three

Ruth screamed, fighting away the ensnaring covers that wrapped around her, fighting away the monsters, the cold, the wind, the hell that plagued her mind. The vision lingered like the sound of a disappearing train in the distance, still able to feel the tremors of the rampaging wheels on the track rattle her bones. The black of night encased her. Consumed her like a wretched Viper that hadn't eaten in months. The snaking shadows that rushed to her. Apparitions in the dark closing in. Red eyes in the hellish night. Wind rattling the windows and deathly fingers nails rattling and *tap tap tapping* on the glass.

Hands took hold of her, took her into his. She pounded, called out, screamed for help. For release, until the breathing slowed and his voice, the voice she had known the for the last forty years brought her back to reality. Her eyes fell onto him, and he was with her. She could smell his aftershave, see the lines on his face in the darkness, his eyes through the light seeping through the bedroom window.

"It's okay, Ruth, its just a nightmare. I'm here." He soothed her like heat melting through dry ice. She lay back down on the bed, her head sweating and her body dampening the bed sheets. They held each other a moment as she recounted her nightmare. He laughed in that annoying way he did when she was feeling vulnerable, and a little silly herself. "You can't get rid of me that easy." He soothed.

"The light is off…" She croaked through her tears. "Why did you turn the light off?" You never turn the light off?" He didn't answer. He only kissed her and soothed her. She lay there still, her heart erratic. The night closing in. Until she felt the bristle of his stubble on her cheek, and like magic, the monsters lost their teeth. "It was so real," she cried, touching his face. He ran his fingers through her hair, took handfuls of her body and pulled her into him. She was soaked through and the smell of terror was strong. The love falling from him enveloped her, and she found the night seemed a little brighter, and the wind not as fierce in those sweet moments he held her.

She lay there awake for a few minutes, maybe longer, while she listened to him sleep. She thanked him silently for it as she got up out of bed, put on her nightgown and went down to the kitchen for a glass of water. The night was sheer black, and as she turned on the kitchen light and stepped into the cold, she paused. The heating wasn't on. Simon always put the heating on when it was the winter months. Maybe he had forgotten? Or maybe it was in between cycles? She would ask him in the morning about it.

Ruth poured a glass and watched the snow falling over their back garden, her reflection cast onto the sheet white ground that looked back at her. She knew they would have to dig the car out tomorrow morning before they set out. Another thing she had to do. The nightmare crept into her mind once more, like an echo from beyond, not quite done with her. She saw her reflection in the glass. Her mouth falling lower. Her eyes sinking to the back of her skull. She finished the glass of water quickly.

I shouldn't go. She thought. *I have too much to do. The weather is terrible, and the flights might be cancelled anyway, and that's even if we can get to the airports if they haven't cleared the snow from the roads! And what about Scotland?* The thought about how the weather was all the way up that far North made her blood run cold. She sighed heavily, her stomach in knots. Resounding to her anxiety and encroaching deadlines, she moved into the hallway next to the front door to use the landline.

Ruth dialled her literary agents' number to tell her she was going to cancel the trip to Scotland, that it could wait, that she needed to get things moving, that Simon would understand. That was what she wanted to do. But as she lifted the receiver and pressed the numbers and the phone began to ring, her eyes fell onto the front door window, and the figure she saw standing there.

Four

Ruth's fingers trembled and wrapped around the cord of the phone. She should shout for Simon, but if she did, *it* would know she was there... It didn't move, simply stood. A tall silhouette cast against the falling white. Shadows on the walls grew fingers that stretched out to her. The dark had its teeth back. A cold chill grew in her stomach like a burst sack of spider eggs which raced through her bones. "Hello?" The voice on the end of the line nearly made her scream. Tears pushed from her eyes as he held the receiver closely to her dry mouth, a shaking whisper staggering from her lips.

"There's someone outside the door...." Ruth hushed.

"What? Ruth? Is that you?"

"There's someone outside the door."

"Ruth, you're scaring me. What's going on? Do I need to call someone? Where's Simon?" Ruth stared in horror as the figure consumed the doorway. It's shadow bleeding through the glass and crept up the carpet to her feet, creeping into her home to consume her, to drag her into the abyssal black she had awoken from. A knock came then, three hard, long knocks which seemed to bounce and echo around the hall. Ruth screamed internally. The sight of it, the presence of it. The horror stories her Grandmother had told her about the creatures in the night. They were all true. They had come for her. Come to take her away.

"Ruth!" Her agent called at the end of the line. Unblinking, unbreathing, Ruth eyed the spectre. It was looking through the glass directly at her. She tried to call for Simon, but no words left her throat.

"There's some*thing* at the door..."

"That's it!" Her agent said urgently. "I'm calling the police. I'll call you right back. Do not answer that door!"

"Don't leave me alone with it!" Ruth urged, but the line cut off and a solid tone blared in her ear until the line began to bleep and stagger, before resounding to dead silence. The light switch for the porch was within arm's reach. She could, she must, she had to press it. To set the light on the creature of darkness and send it away. Another knock at the door. There was *two* of them now. Two figures at the door. Two shadows on the carpet. Two creatures wanting to come in and take her away. The sight of the two of them forced her body into a frenzy. "Go away!" She howled, finding the strength from somewhere. Forcing that frightened air out her trembling lungs. The shapes recoiled. They knocked once more, a booming sound which shattered the hellish howl of the marauding winter wind.

"Open up..." The fiend crackled through the glass, pushing its warped face to the frosted glass. Ruth turned to the stairway. She could run and get Simon, but this was her home, and that child inside her needed to fight away the monsters of the dark at some point.

She roused herself, roused her courage, like the three heroines in her novel when they break free of the slavers and head towards the sunset in a riot of valour and prowess. She took one step, the shadows watching her, not moving. She took another, the cold carpet pressing into her bare feet. She flicked the switched and heavenly light drowned the black figures in radiance and grace. The beating in her heart slowed for a moment. Then, the façade of hope melted, and she saw the high vis jackets and the hats of two policemen standing at the door.

Ruth's lips began to quiver. The worst of the worst of thoughts pushing into her mind like a rabble of uninvited guests. Suddenly, she wished for the demons to return. For the shadows to drag her away, for that would be a more welcomed visitor. She unlatched the door with shaking fingers. The night air struck her like a truck as she saw the two constables standing in front of her, their jackets dusted with ice and snow. Their noses red and hands wrapped in thick leather black gloves.

"Sorry to disturb you at this hour madam," one said, a tall, broad man. He took of his hat, revealing a bald head that shone in the porch light. "Can we come in? I'm afraid its bad news."

"What's going on?" Ruth said, the lump in her throat beginning to swell.

"I would like to discuss this inside please madam," the officer spoke. "It's about your husband, Simon." Ruth turned her head at the dark staircase leading to the bedroom. The night seemed darker once more. The walls moving with the shadows of falling snow, like they were constricting, breathing like a living creature.

"What about him?" Ruth quivered, her fingers turning numb from the cold on the frozen door. "He's upstairs in bed…" The words didn't feel real as they left her mouth. The two officers exchanged a grim look, both with faces of sorrow.

"No," the officer said firmly, shaking his head. "Simon was in a car accident tonight. On his way here, near the bend at the end of your road. The snow… He lost control. He was pronounced dead at the scene." A heavy breath fell from his mouth. "I am so very sorry." Ruth staggered back, every part of her breaking like a room of plates in a storm. She turned, running to the stairs, her legs failing her. She stumbled up the steps, shouting his name, calling for him, yelling at him at the disgusting joke he was playing. The door to the bedroom was ajar, and the bedroom window wide open. Wind howled through the open space. Ruth hit the light and the dark vanished revealing a bed filled with snow and mud. Bed covers strewn over. Black hand prints on the walls, on the floor and then as she found to her horror, on her arms and nightgown.

Aftershave bottles, Simon's aftershave bottles emptied and turned out onto the floor, soaking into the carpet. Ruth raced to the window and looked out into the meadow. A black figure stood there, unmoving, staring back at her with deep red eyes. It's features old, but not that of her husbands. His build much taller, slimmer and wiry, and the smell of aftershave carried by the wind into her nostrils, as the monsters from her dreams raced back into her mind. The creature waved to her, hands with razor fingernails, and teeth spread, long and white, then the black figure vanished in a blizzard of screams.

The Ghost in the Mist

And give no opportunity to the devil –

Ephesians 4:27

Part One

Chapter One

Catherine

Catherine held the hand of the patient who would soon stop breathing. "He's in a bad way love," she said, her hair tied up in a tight bun, her nurse pinnie stained in blood from the long shift she was only half way through. His wife was stricken with pain, and Catherine didn't need to see the tears in her eyes to know she knew she would be a widow by dawn. The man's wife didn't say anything. She didn't need too. She simply nodded, letting her tears paint the floor on the hospital ward. Catherine stood and relinquished the weak hand, before silently slipping out of the ward door. As she walked, she finally heard those heart shattering wails that the wife had been holding in for so long.

Catherine continued through the hospital hallways, passing rooms filled with broken souls. Most of them men, some women.

No children thankfully. They had been evacuated a few weeks prior, as news had reached the town that the Germans would soon be performing raids on the denser populated parts of the country. Catherine found a small room that had been left unused since the cleaners had relocated to the entrance to the hospital, and she slipped into the quiet and closed the door. She sat a moment in the dark and held her face in her hands, letting her own pain seep through her fingertips and fall to the ground. A moment passed, then another. Catherine dried her tears and released a deep breath, before getting back to work.

Silent bodies on trolleys glided past her like ships through a midnight stream. The casualties had gone up since England had moved across the channel into France to stop the war machine of Adolf Hitler. And as she looked around the wards filled with bodies, sleep deprived doctors and nurses, and more blood than she could imagine, she never knew that she could truly hate someone.

Catherine showered and tied her hair up before waving goodbye to her Ward Matron Susan, a heavy-set woman whose husband worked down the mine. Some had shunned her for her husband being a coward, some even suggested in the whispers of sewing rooms and church benches, that Susan had encouraged her husband to drop the trolley of coal on his hand so he couldn't fight in the war.

Catherine never joined in the gossips and whispers of the town though. Her Franklin wasn't away fighting, not while his father was still alive. But as the days drew on and his health deteriorated, she knew that he would soon enlist to join the war effort. The mocking, leering and sniggers from the other townsfolk of her husband were mere noises in the wind to her, but it was the nights of crying and self-loathing which her husband committed in the midnight hours when he thought she was slumbering, that was where the real torture in Catherine's mind burrowed deep. How he would sit at the breakfast table, looking at the newspapers, his teeth bared and fists clenched. That was what really made her fear awaken. He would get angry, and she would have to beg him from walking out the house and marching to the town hall to enlist. *But the day will* come she thought as she spilled out into the cold night. *And that will be the worst day of my life.*

Chapter Two

Catherine

Dawn kissed the horizon over the Mountains that were topped with winter snow. If you were lucky, you might get to see a deer stretching its hind legs as it trotted elegantly across the tree line, darting between the ferns and hopping over the small creek that ran along the road. Catherine eyed the cloudless blue dawn as she walked home. Sleep drunk, the smile on her face not to be confused with one of contentment or glee. Her heart was heavy, and although she had scrubbed her hands until they were raw, she could still feel the sticking of dried blood that gathered under her finger nails. It had been a rough one, but all she could do was smile, because should she let the front break, she would collapse to the ground, unable to bring herself back.

The morning parade of steel workers, miners and trades men were walking in droves past her towards their work stations. Normally they would ride bicycles, however the mayor had requested that all metal that was not essential was to be taken and melted down. This thought made her laugh internally, as she watched the men walk past, their eyes heavy and skin forever blackened with coal dust, that somewhere in the world a soldier was fighting the enemy with bullets made from a children's tricycle. The sight of a window cleaner made her pause. Who had the money these days to pay for someone to wash the dust and grime from their homes? Let alone the cost of the soap. That was hard to come by these days.

Catherine continued on for a few more miles until she reached the end of her street. A terrace road that had a small children's park at the end of the road in the middle of a fenced off park. You could climb through a hole in the gate that the local children had created so they didn't have to walk a half a mile to the 'official' entrance. One child had gotten stuck there a few weeks back and cut a deep gash into his thigh. The mother, worried about her child being deemed as 'a trouble maker,' didn't take him to the hospital and instead washed his wound with vinegar and lemon juice, before wrapping it in a hand towel. Catherine remembered the boy arriving in the emergency room when she was on shift, bacteria completely devouring his leg, before sepsis took the rest of him. A few days later, the police were seen dragging the mother's bloated body out of the pond on the very same park, and the childhood memories Catherine had of playing on those swings and skipping rocks on the bright summer waters were taken from her. She hadn't been onto there since.

She approached the front door of her home and found the living room light to still be on. Catherine felt a bolt of fear shoot through her. Thank Christ the Germans hadn't found their town yet, or Franklin would have given them a target. Catherine looked through the window and tried to peer through the dirtied glass. She couldn't make out anything, other than the chair in the corner of the room facing the radio, and shape slumped over the side. Brian must have been difficult last night because Franklin wouldn't ever leave the light on through the night. He must be exhausted, or was too tired to notice that he had nearly destroyed a whole town. Catherine was surprised that the neighbours hadn't banged on the door, however as she looked around the silent street, she saw all the blackout curtains were drawn. No one else had even noticed that one of them was waving a big red bullseye to the enemy whilst they slept in their beds. She needed to get in quick before someone saw.

She put her key in the door and turned the lock. Inside was the familiar stench of stale tobacco and mould. The walls, once bright and white, had been ravaged by damp. Since the local plasterer had gone to fight, she just had to sit and wait until the walls caved in around her. The longer the war went on, the more the black devoured the white, like the darkness was closing in around her. The carpet was dull and she heard the sound of pans cluttering around the kitchen. Catherine moved to the living room and shut off the light and shadow drenched the walls. Brian was passed out in his chair. His mouth drooling, the psoriasis eating away at his face and his hands under his faded beige jumper. The coal fire had been left to burn out, only small glowing embers fighting through ash and soot behind the iron doors of the mouth of the fire. The poker lay along the base.

A touch of Brian's face confirmed he was still alive and he would burden them for another day. She scolded herself at the thought of such a thing and shook the feelings of contemptment away. She was just tired, and not tired in the ordinary sense. She was tired through to her soul. Her heart was so heavy she was amazed it still beat. Her bones ached; her legs dragged the rest of her wherever she needed to be. Her cloth pinnie filthy and her hair a dishevelled mess. She wanted a rest that sleep would not satisfy, and watching the slumbering mound in front of her, his chest rising and falling, she afforded herself a small tear. That's all she could manage right now.

In the kitchen, Franklin was standing cooking a couple of eggs. He was using grease from the oven on the frying pan so they didn't stick. No bread, but dry crackers along with a few slices of bacon he had managed to trade for an old pair of gloves with the local farmer. The smell ignited Catherine's dry mouth with saliva.

He heard her presence and he turned to her, his square jaw beaming a bright smile, his long black hair like a dark stallion, tied up in a pony tail. He was shirtless, his body hard and chizzled through his years as a rugby player. Blue veins pushing out of his biceps and his tree trunk legs supporting the god like physique above them.

"Morning baby," Franklin said, his teeth bright and his hands wrapping around her tiny frame.

"I stink." Catherine protested, aware of the dried blood on her clothes and her desperate need of a bath. Franklin ran his fingers through her hair, catching on knots and dirt, but if he noticed them, he didn't show it. Those piercing eyes finding hers, and the memory of death and severed limbs, the sound of blood hitting the floor, the faces of loved ones who were told that their father, mother, son, daughter, wouldn't be going home with them again, faded away in those emeralds of jade. His breath had a lingering smell of coffee and mint, and the touch of his lips made the night of horrors she had walked away from fade away.

"How was your night?" He asked tentatively, running his rough hands along her cheek.

"Awful," Catherine whispered, finding her words. "Four arrests, a few infections and managed to patch a few bodies back together."

"Sounds like a hell of a night," Franklin said. "Dad had a rough one. I haven't had much sleep. I need to get him up for his breakfast shortly." Franklin gave her a tight hug that lifted her from her feet a few inches from the dirtied floor, like the beast was taking his beauty back to his castle for the evening. He let her go and Catherine moved to the food.

"I'll sort this, you go wake your dad up," she said with an undertone of bitterness. She didn't want him to wake up, their lives had been more about caring for *him* than caring for each other. But she didn't mention it. She didn't want to revive the argument again. Franklin left the room and she prepared the food. The smell intoxicating and her empty stomach that yearned to be fed. But not with this meal. This food was for *him*. Franklin and her were to have rations again. Dried oats with a blot of jam, no milk. Dried crackers and dehydrated apricots, washed down with water from the sink that had gotten a funny taste recently. Those large hands landed on her tight shoulders once more, and finger tips like hard rocks broke through the tenseness.

"You go to bed baby," Franklin whispered, kissing her neck. "I'll sort this. You get some rest." She turned and met his eyes once more, before falling into his chest.

"You left the light on."

"Does this mean we're dead?" Franklin joked darkly. She eyed him once more, a look of vex in her spheres of red rimmed blue. "Not funny?" He said, his smile wavering. She shook her head. He sighed and took the spatula, turning over the bacon. "I'm sorry. Nobody came to tell me so I doubt they would have noticed. Dad had a rough night with his chest. I didn't realise what time it was." Catherine felt the warmth of his body as she fell into his strong back, tracing it with her lips.

"It's okay," she said, burying her face into him. "If we were killed, then I would find you in heaven." He turned and held her once more.

"I love you," he said, and she responded in kind, and they let his father sleep a few moments longer whilst they held each other on borrowed time..

Chapter Three

Franklin

The days turned into weeks, and weeks became months. News came over the wireless that Hitler and his war machine had taken over France completely, and that the enemy was on the border of England's shores. London had been bombed for weeks straight, and almost all children in densely populated cities had been evacuated to quieter fields afar, away from the scars of death and fire brough by a foreign army. Rations had been cut by the government, and the telling ribs on Catherine's small frame were testament. She had forgotten what it felt like to eat a full meal, and water was used as a substitute to keep the pains of hunger away for a little longer.

The conscriptions had begun, and despite the government promising that the war would be over by Christmas, that promise grew thinner with each passing day. And as the nights grew darker, the fingers of winter stretched further along their home town, dusting the barren trees with snow and the bite of the wind grew fiercer, the news of Stalingrad, the last stronghold of the Russian Federation, had fallen into the hands of the Germans. Europe was growing desperate, and there was news that in the west, the Japanese had begun their own attack on America. Hatred and hunger for power it would seem, is like a fast-spreading cancer. When the blood is flowing, mankind dives in for the softest parts to take what they can, when they can.

Pressure had been building in the town for the local steel workers and miners to join the war effort. Droves of women taking to the streets screaming that could do the work themselves, that their men needn't stay home and support them, but instead run into the hell across the seas to fight a monster with an endless appetite for life.

Franklin had seen the eyes on him as he wandered the streets to pick his father up fresh bandages and clothing, ointments to sooth his chest and scarred lungs from the gas of the last 'Great War.' He remembered the sound of the elderly chemist, his glasses thickly rimmed and his nose hair touching the top of his upper lip.

"Why are you collecting these?" He said accusingly, almost spitting on Franklin's presence. "Your wife is a nurse. Why are *you* not going fighting for your country?" Franklin didn't get the bandages that day, or any other day afterwards. He had to ask Catherine to steal them from the hospital, of which was risking both of them even more.

But today, on the coldest morning he could remember, and the darkest one he had seen of late; Franklin knew there would be no more delaying the inevitable. Franklin awoke at 05:30 as usual, got dressed and made his father breakfast, only to find him slumped more awkwardly with his eyes vacant and the blood pooling under the skin, his dead eyes bulging like rotten yokes on jellied egg whites. Franklin called the hospital for assistance, and Catherine finished her shift immediately to come to his aid. They held each other until the undertakers left, and he didn't utter a word until the sun fell below the horizon that night. For the first night since the first bullet had been fired, Franklin felt the weight of the War now on his shoulders. The sounds of bombs and bullets flying through the air, the stuff he had thought and imagined in his dreams, of being in a trench up to his knees in mud and human filth, rats running over his feet that rested on the dead, shivering in tight garments with a helmet that didn't fit properly. The smell of gun powder stinging his nostrils, watching a landscape of death that didn't move, and when it did, someone else fell to the ground. It was real, and Catherine held him throughout the night, and neither slept a wink.

Dawn broke over the high mountains yet the birds made no sound. The wind was still and the trees did not rustle themselves awake. The local cockerel at the farm down the road did not make its morning call, and the world outside seemed that little stiller, greyer than usual. The streets were silent, destitute, as news of the war finally coming to England's shores, to Franklin's home town. He sat up in bed, sweat pouring from his back and sticking his long hair to his brow, the realisation of what he must do came pushing through his head like a runaway train.

This morning, with a fire burning inside his stomach like a furnace under dry wood, he dressed quickly. With the burial of his father nay a few days ago; a small ceremony at the local church, the eyes of widows that visited the empty graves of their husbands that had given their lives to the war effort overseas, scowling at him, whispering under their breath whilst sobbing into their handkerchiefs, he knew that there would be more tears to flow in his own home in the hours to come.

He showered quickly and dressed smartly, putting on his best shirt and tie and a pair of beige trousers, long hair in a pony tail. The bedroom mirror was chipped and cracked and had flakes from the fallen paint that had rattled loose from when the blitzkrieg had finally found their sleepy town, descending death, hell fire and fury on the silent houses in the night. Catherine had gotten dressed and raced to work in the depths of the night, despite Franklin pleading for her not to go.

"They need me!" She raged, fighting to get through the door as he clung to her scrubs. She left in the night then, and Franklin listened to the bombs fall. A few minutes later, he was dressed himself and racing out the door. Whilst others cowered in their homes and said their prayers to their God from under their dining room table, Franklin ran, hands interlocked with Catherine to the hospital where she was thrust into a circus of horrors and blood. There, he raced to help those fleeing burning buildings where flames so fierce sprouted fingers and fiery teeth, devouring everything and anyone they could, their screams mixing with the popping of burning wood and crumbling of brick.

When dawn broke above the mountains, the town had changed forever, and those in it. War had come to their front doors. It was no longer on the lips of the radio presenters, in the ears of the local townspeople or in the eyes of the those that read about it in the newspapers. It was in their hearts, the stench of it on their skin and the ash of it in their hair. The tears of death staining the cheeks of childless mothers and fathers, husbands with no wives, mothers with no sons, and Franklin who could no longer hide from the truth he had been running from so long: he had to fight, and with his father's passing, no more excuses could be fathomed, no more reasons to stay home could leave his lips. He had a duty, and as he did up his tie he took one long stare at himself in the mirror, pursing his lips, and wondered if this would be the last time he would see himself this way.

He sat in the kitchen with a cup of black tea. The water was not much more than room temperature as the bombings had disrupted the gas supply and he had to use the canister from the outhouse. He was sparing with the fuel however, not letting it burn for more than a minute. He stared at the cup of bitter fluid, his mouth dry but no desire to drink, the sound of the night before dancing around his mind. The sight of the silhouettes on fire in those windows. War had come to his home, and he was to go straight to the heart of it and tear it out. He checked the clock. It was just before seven in the morning. He doubted Catherine would be home soon, she would no doubt work straight through until the following morning, grabbing what little sleep she could on the floor of the office in the Accident and Emergency department or even one of the wards. Franklin's heart heavy with woe, but he tried to fight back the fear rising in his stomach. Not as the prospect of being away from home for so long, or stepping into the unknown on unknown soil a thousand miles away to an enemy he had only heard about on the wireless. The real fear was if he was strong enough to come back alive, and if he did come back at all, would his wife recognise the man who walked back through the door to be the same man who walked out of it.

Chapter Four

Catherine

"I need more bandages!" The nurse cried. Catherine eyed her, despair in her eyes.

"Leave him," she said flatly. "He's already dead. Give him some morphine and move onto the next one." Catherine moved away, leaving the red headed nurse whose name she couldn't remember, staring at a man whose arm and leg were missing and more of his blood was on the hospital floor than in his body. His lips had turned blue and his skin fading into grey, and the blood drained from the nurses face all the same, as she swallowed hard and moved quickly to another body in a bed that was painted red, hoping to save this one instead.

The day was a blur. The casualties came in by the droves, and the night time onslaught from the Germans did not discriminate: old, young, black, white, men, women, paupers and doctors. Anyone the bombs touched came into the hospital, and if they lasted the journey in the ambulance or by being carried on the shoulders of their family members or people on the street, then they could get some form of treatment. Most of them didn't make it to surgery. All of them would never be the same again.

"They left the lights on at the Samson's place," the ward sister said to Catherine as she touched the face of an elderly woman with most of her body blackened by flames. "They are responsible for this. They should have known better!" The pain in her voice. The frustration, the anger that laced her words was felt by every sister, doctor and nurse on the ward. But they kept their frustrations away from the ears and eyes of those that sat in the waiting room and the wards, screaming in pain until the morphine took effect, or falling into a slumber when it just wasn't enough, one that they would never wake up from. The porters had abandoned trying to keep up with cleaning the blood, and instead used their cleaning trolleys to help transport medication, bandages and supplies to whoever shouted the loudest for it. Dawn came and went, and the night descended again, and as Catherine walked outside in the night air, the sound of planes overhead made a fresh blanket of terror wrap around her. It was, however, the sound of a passing car. She lit a cigarette and began her walk to her home, where she would collapse into a sleep filled with the sounds of the dying.

Catherine got to her home and touched the handle. Something felt off. She hesitated and eyed the empty street. She couldn't put her finger on it, maybe it the exhaustion, pure muscle memory being the only thing that had gotten her from the hospital to her front door. But something inside her, a feeling of dread that swelled and grew like a straining balloon filled with rattle snakes shook inside her stomach. She buckled over and hurled out her insides onto the grass. She steadied herself on the door step and she hurled and strained until nothing else came out, and then Catherine dry heaved for a few more minutes, pulling out the back of her throat. Her bones began to rattle first, then her fingers and hands, soon followed by all of her body, like she was filled with a million ants trying to break out from her skin. Her body flushed red hot and freezing cold, and above her she saw the moon once more, swollen and red glaring down on her, telling her that the worst was yet to come.

She lay there for a moment, her hair matted to her face and her stomach knotting. "Frank..." She cried, holding herself. "Frank..." Each breath, each movement an effort, a pain, like her lungs had been filled with burning coals. Catherine felt the night air cooling her, and her uniform, drenched in strangers' blood. The shivering began once more, and she pawed at the door. Her uniform had crept up to the top of her thighs, and her shoes were soiled in mud and grass. "Frank..." She tried once more, pawing at the front door. Catherine waited for the sound of the door opening, the key turning, but it never came. Moments passed that felt like hours, as she lay there in the wet and cold on the door step, the blood moon still above her watching her writhe in pain and fatigue.

She felt the stomach turning once more, and she prayed to her god for release.

She didn't want to throw up again, she didn't think her body could take it. She could still hear the screams of the patients, but now they were fully inside her mind, like before they had just been the background noise of the radio, and now they were a full orchestra playing just for her. High pitched wails and low gargles. Blood hitting the ward floors and body fluids leaking, children crying and terrified. Bandages ripping, scissors cutting, matrons howling and wheels of carts squeaking. She had it all in her head with her on that lonely step, the wind biting at her, cutting through her like ice exterminating a dying ember. Her eyes began to feel heavy as the shock gripped her, and she tried all she could to stay awake. She thought of her parents who were no longer with her. She thought of Franklin and her life with him. She saw the child they had never had the chance to have, or the home they had never had the money to buy. She saw it all in her mind's eye, and the terrifying moon above her began to turn brighter, glaring down at her in the night until it shone like a bright star, and she felt its warmth on her. The sky became blue and fluffy white clouds glided along lazily and the sound of birds she had forgotten, bird song she had never heard but knew all the same played in her ears as the green leaves fell from the swollen trees. She began to smile and her heart began to slow, and then her eyes closed, and the sound of screaming disappeared, replaced by the familiar sounds of distant plane engines.

Catherine's eyelids flickered to the touch of water, warm, scented, dripped down her cheeks. She opened her eyes to see Franklin's large hands touching her head with a wet cloth. She was lying in her bed, the blankets heavy on her limbs.

"Hey baby," he said, his voice low. The room was dark, lit only by a small gas lamp in the corner of the room. Shadows rising and flickering, stretching towards her like beasts of the night, teeth and claws ready to sink into her.

"What happened?" Catherine struggled. Her throat was so dry, she could hardly rasp a whisper, let alone a full sentence. She cough and her chest exploded in agony. Franklin put his hand on her chest as she tried to sit up.

"Don't," he said quietly, but firmly. "You were found outside. I had gone to the hospital to bring you home but you had already left. We must have missed each other. I came home to find you lying on the wet grass. I got you inside and changed you, wrapped you up warm and nursed you." Catherine tried to piece her mind together. She eyed him through one eye, her mind trying not to fall back to a dreamless sleep.

"How long was I asleep for?"

"A day. You slept all yesterday. I haven't left your side in case you needed me. She saw on the ground two towels, one on the floor as a make shift bed, the other wrapped tightly for a pillow. Bandages coated in red and soaked with sweat littered the ground. A bucket, silvered and chipped, filled with bile.

"Too much work at the hospital. Not enough rest. No food." She began drifting back to sleep. Franklin watched her as she slipped out of consciousness once more, and held her hand by the bedside until the morning sun broke through the thick clouds over the mountains.

In the morning, Franklin showered while Catherine slumbered away her nightmares. He eyed himself in the cracked mirror, noticing his hair was longer, sticking together, the lice since relinquishing his scalp for more desirable pastures. He would need to cut his hair before enlisting, but that didn't matter right now. As he tied the cuffs of his uniform, tied his neckerchief and threaded his belt through his trousers, he stared once more in the mirror, wondering how he would break his wife's fragile heart.

He returned to the bedroom to find Catherine awake, the colour returning to her face. She smiled warmly as he entered the room, but then those pink cheeks drained of colour once more as her eyes fell onto his attire. He drew closer, his head low. He knelt at her bedside, neither saying a word. She reached in, grabbing handfuls of his hair, pulling him into her breast. Her head resting on his crown, he traced her bare thighs and held those large hands around his wife's hips, where they sat a moment, listening to the wireless speak of war, death in the South, and government tearing itself apart.

She lifted his head and stared into those eyes she had woken up to for as long as she could remember. She touched his face and kissed his lips. That silence held in the air and said more than either of them could. Tears welled in both of their eyes, and they held each other a long moment, wondered if they would ever hold each other again.

Part Two

One

Franklin

The day when the world went away, Franklin was the sickest he had been in his entire life. It couldn't have been something he had eaten; he hadn't put anything other than water and cigarettes past his lips since the night he had said goodbye to Catherine at the train station nearly three days ago. The ride had been long, and every time he closed his eyes, all he could see was the look of pain in her face, etched into his memory like a nightmare he couldn't forget. His heart was haemorrhaging woe, and he found himself falling into the memory of the red eyes of his wife as he waved her goodbye.

The thought of him returning home to an empty shell, his wife not there, and the local policeman telling him that his wife had been killed by the Germans, disease or even by her own hand. The feeling of fear prickled his skin. Fear was much more primal than sadness, as sadness is conditional, circumstantial. Sadness could be rationalised, thought through and objective thinking. But Fear on the other hand, walking blind into a world filled with death and fire, a million miles away from everyone and anyone you have ever met, cared for or hated. Even a hated face was a familiar one. Moving to a place and a time where death is waiting for you, brought to you by an enemy that doesn't know your name, nor cares about your life or your family or your dreams and wishes. Doesn't think about your struggles or your reasons for being there. Only one thing in their mind keeps them going, and that is the simple task of killing you before you kill them.

There are no winners here, he thought to himself as the train trudged through the country side of an alien land where the street signs didn't make sense. *There were no winners here, only those that lose the least.*

The train was rickety and old, with hardly anywhere to sit other than a few hard wooden chairs. Most of those around Franklin had taken to sleeping on the floor, holes opening under the brittle wood revealing the blur of train wheels and gravel below them. The men that lay around him, dead men whose hearts still beat, most of whom he hadn't even looked at, let alone spoken to in more than a brief grunt, were eyeing the ceiling above them with terror in their eyes. They were mainly young, maybe around nineteen to twenty, but he guessed that some were younger than that, lying to have a chance to fight for their country against the Nazi war machine that threatened to take everything from them.

He doubted those fresh-faced boys had ever seen a dead man before, ever had a fight or heard the earth-shattering cries of a widow as you pull their husband still ablaze out of a burning building. They were chasing the stories of glory that they heard on the wireless and in the newspapers, stories of soldiers, Allied and heroes alike, conquering mountains of machine gun trenches, single handily dismantling the murderous devils that were the enemy.

Franklin saw one of the young men laughing with his friend and smoking a cigarette, both of them lying on the ground with their duffel bags as pillows, a pack of cards and cigarettes spread onto the dirtied floor beneath them. A third boy, a little older than the other two, a dusting of puberty above his top lip, clutched a bunch of rosary beads in his hands and was counting them quietly to himself. Him lost in prayers for hope, happiness, love and safety, as well as a few Hail Mary's thrown in there for good measure.

"What's he doing?" Franklin said, addressing the group, eyeing the boy with the beads. His voice was barely audible over the drone of the train tracks, the shadows of passing trees slipping along his face. The world disappeared as they moved through a tunnel, and when it reappeared, the boys were looking at him, faces tightly bunched.

"What did you say long hair?" The smoking one said. He sounded educated, pronouncing the T's and stretching the vowels a little too much for Franklin's liking.

"I said, what is he doing?" He repeated. The three boys eyed each other and stood, their legs stiff from lying on the ground for nearly a full day.

"What's it look like he's doing?" The educated one said, his hair waxed and dark, combed over to one side like a stud from a black and white romance movie. His voice was slightly high and the remnants of acne still marred his chin. Franklin tried not to laugh at how hard this little pompous punk would no doubt piss his pants the first time a German pointed a rifle in his direction. "He's praying!" He said. Franklin leant forward in his seat and put his hands together like a steeple.

"To God?" The educated boy looked to his pals, one was stocky with a little facial hair, his uniform crisp and no doubt fully ironed and pressed by his mother before he had come to war. The other, the one that had been praying, remained silent. He was much smaller, slim and was balding early, however Franklin imagined him to be the older of the three. "Well then," Franklin continued, sitting back in his chair. He took out a pack of cigarettes from his pocket and lit one, taking in a long drag and exhaled the plume of smoke into the cabin. One guy next to him, an older guy with a bald head and bags around his eyes, maybe in his early forties, noticed the smoke dancing around his nostrils, and appearing still half asleep, almost out of unconscious habit, took out his own cigarettes and lit one up with a match, the potent hit of sulphur stinging the air and the nostrils of those around him. "If your boy is praying to God," Franklin continued, knocking the ash on the ground and then crushing it with his large black boots. "Then who are the Germans praying to?" The three boys gave themselves a worried and somewhat bemused look between themselves, before scoffing and sitting back down, continuing to thumb their playing cards, their faces much less jovial than before. The older one continued to pray, after Franklin saw a moment of contemplation in his mind.

Franklin sat back in his seat that dug into his back and ribs, his reflection in the dirtied window that of a grimace, watching the world pass by in washed out grey. The man next to him, began to laugh to himself quietly. Franklin looked to him with bemusement.

"What's so funny?" He asked. The man craned his neck and eyed him ever so slightly with those restless pits of brown.

"You don't get many people on a train to war, questioning who someone is praying to." He continued to laugh, a rattling laugh like air burbling through thick tar and phlegm.

"I guess not." Franklin said, returning his gaze to the outside world. The bald man took out another smoke from his pocket and lit it with a match, the familiar scent of sulphur hitting the air.

"Where are you from?" the man said. Franklin pondered a response, but having nothing to look at other than the fields and mountains of an alien land, and the sickness of missing his wife in his stomach, he whispered.

"Manchester."

"I have a cousin in Manchester," the bald man chuckled, that chest rattling once more. I'm from Redditch, just outside of Birmingham."

"Never heard of it," Franklin said, still staring out the window. "I'm from a small town outside of the city named Leigh. They say it's not part of Greater Manchester, but it really is. Just silly pride of the locals demanding we're part of Lancashire." The three boys looked up from their game, cussed to themselves and then continued. A second later, the leader, the toff, began an adult tantrum when his high queen lost to two pair, and he had to give up a few coins to his friend. Franklin doubted his friend would keep the winnings in the end, the toff's tantrum screaming *'I have never been told no in my life.'* He looked like he was used to getting his own way. He wouldn't last very long on the front. The bald man extended his hand.

"Colne." Franklin turned, eyeing the hand of this stranger. He saw his nails were filthy, probably a miner whose skin was so engrained with soot they would never come clean again.

"Franklin," he said, taking the man's hand. He was freezing, like he had been dead for years. Franklin returned his hand and placed it inside his jacket. Colne spoke a little more about his home town, his Irish father and Scottish mother, and how he had been named after the town his father was born in. He spoke about his lack of family, and that he had been taking care of his father before he passed, meaning he had to join the war. Franklin didn't share such information with the man with the sunken eyes. Eventually, Colne stopped making small talk, and he smoked himself stupid as the cabin filled with thick smoke and burning ash. Franklin saw on the horizon the sky lighting up with flashes of whites and oranges, and he knew that he was venturing into hell with a bunch of lost souls that wouldn't pull him from the fire should he fall into it, and he had never felt more alone in his life.

"You got a wife then? Kids?" Colne said.

"Look," Franklin said, turning, nearly choking on the stench of the smoke that pushed from Colne's mouth. "I'm tired, and I don't want to talk, no offence."

"Well we got nothing else to do," Colne said, taking another drag of his smoke. He pointed out of the train window. "Looks like were getting close," he said, his voice solid, like he was pointing out a landmark on a family trip.

"Does this not scare you?" Franklin said. "Being here, now, doing this? Are you not a little worried?" He realised when he said it he was showing weakness to a man who was just as likely to bash his skull in with a rock rather than give him a meal.

"Why?" Colne said, breathing in deeply. "Does it scare you?" Franklin shook his head and took out a smoke and lit it, the blue ethereal fingers slipping down his lungs and soothing his nerves.

"I have seen my share of death," Franklin said, exhaling.

"Then you'll be welcoming to shake its hand!" Colne said, a long smile etched along his face.

"What did you say?" Franklin said, taken back by the comment. Those eyes looked a little darker to him, and his skin grew greyer."

"Your wife will die alone in her bed Franklin. Die alone without you, screaming your name until she goes mad from heartbreak." Franklin eyed Colne with terror in his eyes, mixing with fury. He felt his hands tense up, his shoulders harden. The cigarette burning to the end and scolding his fingers, but he didn't care, didn't feel the pain. The pain was right there, in his chest, and this fucker and unlocked the door.

He went to speak, to shout, to beat this bastard's face into the ground, but as he stood, he found himself alone in the carriage, the outside world sheathed in black, and the rain rattling dulled.

"What the?" He whispered to himself, the smoke that lingered in the air spinning, circling back into the ends of the discarded cigarettes laid on the floor. He was alone, and fear gripped him, dancing along his heart as the confusion did in his mind. He turned once more to where he had been sitting, and there, in front of him, was Catherine laying on a bed, white sheets draped over her face, a box of empty pills lay next to the bedside table.

"Catherine?" Franklin said, his face reverbing from the walls that yawned and bended with the sound. He fell to his knees, touching the mound under the sheets. Franklin held his breath as he let out staggered sobs that fell onto the blanket, turning to embers, smouldering and burning swelling black rings, before setting a light, flames sprouting before him, consuming the one he loved, eating her alive. He dove on her, thrashing at the spreading furious vicious flames that spread from her to him, eating his flesh, crawling down his throat and bubbling his lungs. She rose then, her eyes jellied, her skin bubbling and stripped away, revealing a half toothy smile behind one of her cheeks. She took him into her embrace, those fingers bones scrapping along his scalp, as she consumed him.

Two

Franklin

"Hey!" A voice pushed through Franklin's mind. A rough hand on his shoulder as he began to shake. "Wake up!" The voice said. Franklin lurched forward, his brow wet and clothes sticking to him. He saw all eyes in the carriage on him, and he felt a chill run through his bones. "You okay?" The voice said again. Franklin eyed the dirty hand on his shoulder. It was Colne, looking as weary as ever.

"Yeah," Franklin whispered, rubbing his hands over his face. The curious eyes of the carriage returned to what they were doing. The Carriage had sunk into darkness, only the small light from cigarette embers and the occasional flash of the moon in the night sky permeated the darkness. "Had a nightmare."

"Whose Catherine?" Colne said. The sound of her name struck Franklin in the face like a brick through glass.

"What did you say?" He said, his eyes narrowing.

"You were saying her name in your sleep," Colne said, in a relaxed tone. "Your wife?" Franklin again felt a wave of embarrassment pulse through him.

"She's my wife yeah," he said.

"Is that why you haven't joined up earlier?" Colne said. "You look older than the rest of them in here. Mid-twenties, if I may assume. The last lot of bombings do it? I heard your end got hit pretty bad."

"It did," Franklin said. "But that's not the reason. My dad was ill, needed taking care of."

"Could your wife not have done it?"

"She works at the hospital. She's there most of the time these days. I had to take care of him." The realisation that Franklin no longer needed to be at home to look after his dying father sank into Colne's mind.

"I see," he said. "I'm sorry kid." Franklin waved the comment away.

"Thanks. He was dead a long time ago, it just took a while for the body to realise. He died a few days before the last lot of bombings. Catherine worked for two days straight and I was pulling people out of burning buildings all night. I enlisted the next day. What about you?" Colne didn't answer straight away. Instead, he let the words absorb into him, thinking about how to respond.

"That's brave of you kid," Colne said, "Your mum would be proud." A small silence fell between them then, the sound of the train rumbling around them on the track that led to where they didn't want to be. "I'm a miner," Colne said, holding up his hands that were the same size as two shovel heads, the dirt and soot engrained into his skin, confirming Franklin's earlier suspicions. "Have been since being a teenager. I hurt my leg a few years back so I was put on light duties, which is just as well, because when the Germans hit Birmingham a month back, they destroyed the mine whilst it was in operation. Forty-eight souls gone in a blink of an eye. They pulled a few out, but they died in the hospital."

"Jesus," Franklin said, his eyes widened. "I am so sorry." Colne put his hand up.

"It's okay," he said. "I figured that I should have died with them if I am honest. My leg has been much better for a good year or so now. Still a bit of a limp, but nothing to keep me from the fight. I should have been down in those mines with them when the bombs fell. So now, I'm bringing the fire of what they did right to their front door." His voice was low, bitter and carved with malice. "And I'm going to enjoy watching each one of those fuckers die."

Three

Franklin

The air was hot when he landed on the coast of France. He couldn't remember getting there, other that it had been periled by either a dreamless sleep or a nightmare in his waking hours. He saw the bodies of those that had fallen as he moved into the camp, moved through them. The carcasses of the dead, draped over on gurneys in white sheets like flat ghosts. Him, Colne, and the others had stopped their chatter, pissing or eating, whatever they might have been doing at the time when death permeated the air.

They passed through those places quickly, but each time the men found themselves moving through one of those camps where the dead were to be laid in their final resting place, they felt like a piece of them remained, like it leeched part of their soul and fed the dead grass with it.

One of the soldiers had been unfortunate enough to have some of the local fish in a small village flanking a great river. Franklin was unsure of where this had happened as he didn't recognise the languages anymore, the faces and the landscapes now blurring into one. The next couple of days were bereft with cholera, yellow fever and other insidious diseases. Two men had been put into isolation, lest the rest of them become ill. The two men however, didn't make it to the next station alive, and they quickly became one of those ghosts on a gurney. Their time at war over before they had had a chance to shoot their weapon or feel the pain of seeing another man die at your hand, or to bite down on your own tongue so hard it bled, whilst pulling the shrapnel of an exploding grenade out of your skin.

The day was grey now, as it had been since the day Franklin had left home. She was all he thought about. His love, his only, his all. The woman he wanted to return to. He couldn't afford to get sick, as he promised her a safe return. He wasn't a religious man, but he felt that someone, something, was watching over him, willing him to return back to his beloved, as she willed him to return back to her. Call it God or the Devil himself, he felt those eyes of something beyond watching over him, and that courage, no matter how ill placed, kept that will to live alive in his heart, the only thing keeping him going in those despairing nights filled with the sounds of screaming men who held their stomachs as they shit, sweated and vomited out their insides. If it wasn't the pain of illness that struck the men, then it was the fucking fear that turned their insides inside and out, painting the train decking in what little lining they had left on their stomachs.

The landscape turned to either be never-ending forests or complete frozen wastelands. He passed through broken cities, smouldering buildings flanking the landscape like ghosts of which they once were. Chipped paint and broken homes and withered bodies.

As the train continued on, Franklin saw more soldiers and stern faces. Less smiles meeting their passing, but more pain and dirt, more children with soot on their faces. More animals with missing limbs. More men and women draped in baggy clothing. More destroyed cars. More grey. More aching in his bones, wishing for the sun to break through the smoke that seemed to gather more on the horizon with each break of the reluctant dawn.

After what seemed to be a never ending journey through the wasteland of nothingness on a train ride that appeared to harbour no end, the tracks finally ran out, the train wheels abated for more than a few minutes for a leg stretch, and the soldiers were ordered off the train, marching hastily to the sound of gunfire in the distance.

Four

Franklin

The stench of gun powder forced its way into Franklin's nostrils as he fumbled and willed his tired stiff legs out of the carriage. The town name, he couldn't pronounce, but he knew this was where he was meant to be. Where he was to stay and train to be a soldier, to push the enemy back from the neighbouring towns and cities. This was supposed to be their safe haven, their place of refuge. But here, he saw nothing but death and hellfire raining down on him. Men a clumped against shanty's and make shift bases made of trampled tents and overturned carriages. Soldiers holding their stomachs as more of their insides were on the outside than in. People wailing, howling and screaming for help. The destruction above, angry birds that soared above him, roaring, spitting fire to the ground and against other mechanical monsters that flew and buzzed overhead. The sound of men screaming for their mothers, begging for death, begging for life, some screamed and held themselves in a foetal position. Some stared blankly, their faces vacant in the fog of war until they were met by a fist from either his comrades or a bullet from the enemy.

Franklin hurried, the thick mud consuming his boots, his mind unable to process anything more than the fear that pushed into his soul. He felt like he couldn't move, shocked and in horror at the sight of the bloodshed, the deafening sound of mortar fire and the rattling of gun fire, casings hitting the ground like iron rain.

He felt a tug on his shirt and looked to the sight of a man covered in dirt. He was young, fresh faced. One of the boys from the train. He had been right behind him, and yet here he was, laying on the ground. Franklin tried to process what was going on, but as he tried to search his mind, search it for answers like *how the hell to stay alive*, an explosion rattled his bones to his left. The sight of shrapnel hurtling through the air, smashing into the side of the carriage and the ground. Franklin felt hot and cold at the same time, and an ear-piercing ring rattled through his mind. He eyed the boy shouting at him, his lips moving but nothing could penetrate the sound of the ringing in Franklin's ears. After a moment, his screams and cries came back into focus, and so did the sound of engines roaring, men screaming, and weapons firing. Franklin screamed as he felt hands around the collar of his shirt. He turned, ready to swing, fight, bite and thrash. It was Colne, his face animated, taking fistfuls of his clothing and dragging him away. Franklin turned to tell him about the boy who needed help, but as he turned, he saw that same boy lying face down in the mud, his legs no longer there, but instead what looked like the contents of a meat grinder spilling onto the ground.

Colne dragged Franklin like a terrified child to the side of a concrete building where several others were stood, taking cover from the bullets and hellfire that appeared to be coming from every direction. Poofs of smoke and dust dancing around his feet and face like the air itself was exploding. The sound of commands, a returning of fire, and the angry tongues in an unknown language yelling orders Franklin didn't understand. He knew those tones though, he had heard his father scream them in his sleep when the booze hadn't quite knocked him out. The screams of war, the screams of *Kill those bastards before they kill you!*

Colne gripped hold of him, the faces of the soldiers that took cover the sight of a thousand childhood nightmares, a million dreams, and a lifetime of worry, all thrust into one moment.

"Take this and fire!" Colne commanded. Franklin took the rifle from his hand. It was much heavier than he expected, even with his strength and his working out, he found it to be much bulkier. You never really knew the weight of something before you held it in your hands. Both a child, something so light, but so heavy, in the sense that to drop the child would carry such a heavy price, and the weight of a weapon designed to kill another man, another human being just like you. Who really fought in the wars other than brothers of separate tongues? Nations declare war, but soldiers and families pay for it.

Franklin stood in horror as he saw fighter jets fly over the horizon, dropping liquid fire on the ground. Over the hill, the sky was painted red, with bellows of thick black smoke pushing from the ground into the air. The landscape of cars that had been mauled and spat out by a giant set of jaws. Soldiers in alien uniforms lying dead, face down in the ground, and the hum of tanks and the roar of heavy engines speeding towards him. His legs began to tremble. He wasn't cut out for this. His family and the village were right, he was a coward. He was trying hard to fight it, putting his father's illness off as an excuse not to go and fight in the war, but here he was, standing face to face with his patriotic duty with his pants quickly filling with piss. He gripped the rifle again, then went to put it down, tears gathering on his eyelids.

"No," Cole shouted. "We go together!" He screamed. From the far side, behind the train that had been sliced and peppered with lead, the insides of its engine sticking out from its hood, the back carriage ablaze, soldiers began to run and charge towards the horizon of death. Heavy boots and screams of war filled the air. Colne gripped Franklin, taking him by the arm and eyed him with wild fury. "You ready?!" Franklin didn't know how to respond, or what to say or even how to say it, but he was running now, heavy boots slapping the muddied ground, his trousers soaking in the mud, stepping over maggot filled bodies, hurtling towards the enemy line. He saw the ground around him bubble as bullets and speeding balls of metal carved up his path in explosions of water, grass and shit. He ran faster, digging deep, his thighs burning, keeping his head low, his heart rampaging in his chest, lungs on fire. Finally, he found a large metal wreck of what used to be a four by four, the smell of petrol piercing the air. The war machine all around him, Colne looking at Franklin with murderous intent in his eyes. "Shoot them Frankie," he said. Franklin eyed him, worry bleeding through the haze of adrenaline.

"What did you say?" He mouthed, unable to shout over the rattling of machine guns and roar of engines in his ears. Colne eyes flashed with fire as an explosion erupted above them. A world of hell and destruction encased in those white spheres of brown.

"Kill them all." Franklin peered around the hunk of metal, seeing the enemy close to him. He could almost smell them, he could see the whiskers of their beards, the marks on their faces from acne scars, the wrinkles in their skin from long nights of no sleep. Franklin tucked into the side of the vehicle, clenching his eyes shut, breathing heavily, his fingers digging into the wood and steel of the rifle. His eyes snapped open and he turned to speak, to call to arms, to shout *Let's fucking go!* But as he turned, he saw he was alone. Colne was gone. Fear wrapped him then, ravaging his bones, marred with confusion. Had Colne made a run for it without him? Had he retreated? What was going on?

An enemy soldier crossed the threshold, and turned to see Franklin standing there with the rifle. In an alien tongue, he pointed and screamed at Franklin. Two others appeared by his side, their faces flushed, hurried, fumbling with their rifles. Franklin pulled back the hammer and aimed clumsily, his fingers trembling, hands shaking. He squoze the trigger, aiming at anything he could. A round left the barrel in a flash of light, the rifle slamming back into Franklin's shoulder, connecting with a German's thigh, a puff of blood and fat bursting into the air, the soldier falling to the ground, holding the thigh which had a bone sticking out of it. Screams of agony all sounded the same no matter what language you spoke. A bullet slammed into the overturned car next to Franklin's head, and a hot splatter of steel and petrol splashed into his face, stinging his eyes mercilessly. Frantically he wiped an eye whilst stepping back, fumbling his pocket to reload the rifle with another round. His feet met something and he fell onto his back in the dirt and grime. There, staring at him, was the pale face and vacant eyes of the oxford boy, the life long left those eyes.

Franklin fumbled the weapon, slamming two more rounds into the chamber. He held the barrel up as a German dressed in grey took aim at him. He pulled back the hammer once more and fired both rounds, a flash of light and ear-splitting boom that rattled his jaw. One round went wide but another blew a hole through one of their chests. The soldier that still stood, a tall slim man with most of his teeth missing, stood over him and quickly cocked his rifle. Franklin saw the end of his life staring him in the face in that barrel of black hot smouldering death. The German pulled the trigger but the weapon didn't fire. Panic slapped the German's face, and he pulled the trigger again and again, each click of the gun stabbing Franklin's nerves.

Franklin lept to his feet and slammed into the tall man, pushing them both onto the ground, fumbling in the mud, fingertips finding whatever part of flesh they could. Franklin pulled back, reeling his boulder fists back and slamming them into the German's face, teeth cracking, nose popping and bursting, hot thick jam falling from his broken face. The German went for something, pulling it up for the world to see, the setting sun catching the end of the blade. Franklin straddled him, gripping hold of the man's arm, the two of them ensnared in a will of desperation. Locking eyes, grunting heavily, pushing and twisting, the knife blade long and pointed with a serrated edge. Designed to bleed, to carve flesh, to kill. Franklin punched the German once more, dazing him enough to let the tip of the blade meet the top of the German's chest. Franklin pushed hard on the knife handle, the popping of the blade as it ruptured the sternum, sliding through soft tissue, cutting arteries and piercing the heart, the light going out of the soldiers face as his eyes fell into Franklin's. Sweat pouring from his brow, blood soaking into his pants, as the last ember of life vanished from the soldiers' eyes. In that moment, they were not enemies, but two boys that had grown up on the same earth, separated by two languages and land, both trying to do the best for their own families. Franklin reeled up, dislodging the knife, throwing it to the ground beside him. He outstretched his hands like a giant bird of war, heaving a huge breath in, the scream of agony and hatred ready to leave his lungs.

His body flashed hot. The air in his lungs no more. He looked to the ground, seeing bones and blood splattered on the dead German's paling face. Franklin touched his stomach and his fingers found soft flesh. It was hot to touch, the steam of the gun shot pushing into the cold air. The wind felt sharper, and as Franklin fell to the ground, all life fleeting from him, he found himself swirling in thick black.

Part Three

One

Catherine

Catherine shot up in the night. Her heart hammering in her chest, her body quivering, the clothing sticking to her body. She searched the room trying to find where she was. Her fear spiking, ripping her nerves apart like razor blades danced on the thinning strings of her soul. Hands on her, large, big and rough touched her, something whispering in the darkness. She tried to scream but no sound came, those hands over her mouth, telling her to be quiet, she's having another nightmare, telling her she'll wake the baby.

Two

Franklin

Franklin stood in a large white room. He saw men around him, doused in white light. Their clothing no longer burned and bloodied, but instead fresh and well dressed. Their wounds had healed, men that had their eyes blown out the black of their skull or their legs ravaged by gangrene were now fit, well and running around in their new found health. The floor was marble, and the air smelt cleaner than any time he could remember. At the end of the hallway, men, women and children ran around together, stepping onto huge boats that sat atop a giant lake of crystal water, overlooking a horizon of mountains that seemed to carve into the sky. The day was warm and the sun shone on Franklin's skin like being kissed by the angels themselves. His own wounds were gone, and where as he may have felt fear as such a peculiarity, he felt nothing but a deep calm. He saw a familiar face, standing at the edge of the large white hospital and was smoking a cigarette. It was *Colne*.

"Hey!" Franklin shouted. He ran to Colne and he greeted him with a warm smile. "What are you doing here?" Franklin said, then looked around him. "Wherever *here* is?..." Colne took another drag of his smoke and flicked some of the ash onto the lush green grass that were below their feet.

"You know where you are kid," he said. "You know where you are."

"Are we still in France?" Franklin asked. Colne shrugged.

"Somewhere nice I know that. I just know that I'm not being shot at anymore, the worst part of my job I say. So I don't care if this is France, America, hell even fucking Glasgow. That's fine by me." He let out a small laugh and took another drag of his cigarette.

"I have to get back to France," Franklin said. "I need to finish the fight against the Germans. I have to get home to my wife Catherine."

"Ahh, yeah," Colne said. "You said you have a girl. Kids?" Franklin shook his head.

"No, we tried but it never happened. Then my dad got ill and it went on the back seat." More and more people raced out of the white building and boarded the ships and were ferried off to the land beyond the horizon. To the place under the mountains. "Where are they going?" Franklin asked.

"Somewhere nice," Colne said, then cleared his throat and

spat on the floor. "But its better than here, that's for sure. Look how happy they seem to be getting on that boat."

"Are you going?"

"Me?" Colne said, eyeing Franklin with a grin. "No, not me. I won't be going. I have somethings I need to take care of first."

"Like what?"

"Personal stuff. Like, making sure you get on that boat and do what's best for you." This peeked Franklin's interest.

"What's best for *me?*" Colne dropped the end of the smoke on the ground, reached in his pocket and pulled out a fresh one.

"You heard me. You need to get on that boat, and stop worrying about getting back to your wife. Aint nothing you can do about that now. You gotta wait for her on the other side of the river." Franklin eyed Colne with confusion.

"I need to stay here and get back to Catherine," he said, worry creeping into his voice. Colne shook his head.

"Nope, that isn't going to happen."

"What are you talking about?" Franklin said. "I just get another train home and go see her when the war is done?" Colne laughed loudly at that one.

"The war *is* done," he said, throwing his smoke onto the ground and stomping on it. "You're dead," he said, taking out another smoke. "You've been dead for three years."

Three

Franklin

His mind shattered, breaking into pieces right in front of his own eyes. The ground began to change. No longer a lush green and vibrant carpet, but instead it was muddy and filled with water. Bones and flies and clothing sank into the thick sludge. Colne stood above him, Franklin falling to his knees. The sky above them turned grey, the mountains in the distance shrouded in mist. The sky above them thick with darkened clouds, as rain pelting from the dark sky above and lightning slammed into the river which had gone from a calm oasis to a tyrannical abyss of death, huge gusts of wind smashing waves along the coast line.

"What is happening? What is this place?" Franklin screamed through the rain and the wind.

"This is your purgatory kid," Colne said, his features turning grey. "This is where you choose what you want eternity to look like. There are those that can accept it, or those that cannot. Those that get on the boat, and those that want to go back." He outstretched his hand, his finger tips pointed, his knuckles prominent and his flesh and dull brown. "I am the one who collects those that wish to go back."

"You could take me back? Take me back to my wife? You could take me home again?"

"That I could kid," Colne snarled. Franklin stared at the ground and screamed, falling back onto the floor, his face fixated in terror. In the sludge in front of him lay a man, hair pitch black, eyes missing and filled with maggots and face pasty and white. The dog tags read FRANKLIN WARBURTON. He got to his feet, forcing himself to look away at his own body. Around him he heard gun fire, the sound of mortars slamming into the ground. The smell of gunpowder pushing up his nose. The revving of engines and the popping of gun barrels.

"Make your choice kid," Colne said, crouching down. "You want to stay here? Or do you want to go home?"

"What do I have to do? What do you need?"

"Well that depends on what you want," Colne said. Franklin took a deep breath.

"I promised my wife I would go back to her. I promised I would come home when the war was finished. I want that. I want to see her again." Colne smiled, his tongue pointed and long. His teeth serrated. His eyes a deep red, head bald. He rose higher, him growing taller, wider, more muscular. His skin fading into complete blackness. The crown of his head spouting horns thick and sharp like a goat. He picked up Franklin and hauled him off his feet by his throat.

"So be it," the Devil snarled. "You may go back to your wife and be with her for the remainder of her life. Go back to the life you knew, return from the war to find her again, but in return, when she takes her last breath on earth, you return to me." Franklin coughed and spluttered.

"Okay," he said breathlessly. "It's a deal." Franklin watched the world around him blur, the trees turning to ash, the ground opening up and the creature that held his throat disappear in front of his eyes as he was dropped through the earth. Stretching arms of bodies sewn into the mantle of the earth reaching out to him, calling for his help, screaming for him to free them, to take them back to the boat. Deeper and deeper he fell, the abyssal black below him glowing a deep red, and above him, the sky fractured and chunks of sky fell to the earth like the shattering of a huge pane of glass, mountain faces crumbling into the ground as the wind spiralled around his face as he tumbled through endless blackness, screaming the name of his wife, that he would be with her soon, that he would fulfil his promise.

Part Four

One

Franklin

It was morning when he awoke. The sound of the train docking at the station brought him out of the realm of nightmares. Franklin looked around him. He was the last one still on the train. Outside, people milled around like a time he had not known before. Franklin got from his seat and stepped from the train onto the platform. He was still in his army uniform, but to his surprise, no one seemed to bat an eyelid at him, them all focused on their own worries and journeys that morning. Franklin looked at a news stand and saw the headline of the paper –

GERMANY SIGN DECLARATION OF IMMEDIATE SURRENDER.

They had done it, he thought. They had won the war! A surge of euphoria rushed through him. He jumped for joy, screamed to the heavens that they had won! Finally! The date on the paper,

MAY 7th 1945. He had been away from home for three years. He didn't know what was going on, or what had happened to Catherine in his absence, but he knew he wanted to see her, to hold her, to walk through that front door and wrap is hands around her. To make love to her, to touch her flesh to his, to have children with her and to move away to somewhere greener and open.

The dream, or the creature in his mind, whatever it was, he didn't know. He felt amazing, his body not broken, damaged. He had read somewhere that the mind can block out whole memories of something traumatic. On the fields of France, when he was shot, he must have been in a coma for some time, plagued by vivid nightmares. He could figure out the details later, but right now, he had his life back, and he had a wife to return to. The clerk at the news stand was cashing up and filling a jar with sweets. Franklin checked his pockets and found him to not have any money anyway, so he was thankful when the clerk took no notice of him. That would have been embarrassing.

The spring morning was cold, and the dawn was lazily breaking over the mountains, a layer of mist blanketed the surrounding fields, bleeding into the street. Franklin walked through the thick fog, the house coming into view. It was the way he had left it, albeit the lawn needed to be mowed and the tree in the front garden had begun to bloom. The windows were cleaner, and an air of life and vitality emanated from the building. It was not the sad wreck and empty shell of a home he had left before going to fight in the war. Instead, it was a home, not a house. It was a building where love was to be grown, built and shared for many years. It was a happy home, with freshly painted walls and the new front door, which he saw was open. He took a deep breath, standing at the foot of the door. His fingers felt numb and he held his breath, his excitement begging for release. The hallway smelt of fresh flowers as he entered. He could hear something in the kitchen. The sound of cutlery being put away. He could smell her perfume now, already remembering the beautiful tone of her voice.

He stepped into the kitchen, his body rigid with anxiety. He didn't want to scare her, but he knew the sight of him would be a shock. He turned the corner and there she was, as beautiful as she had ever been, long brown hair that curled at the bottom, a red bandana around her forehead. Her dress flowing and black with white polka dots, and her lips in coated in bright red.

"Hey baby," Franklin said. Catherine stopped putting her things away, plates and the sorts, and hesitated a moment. She lifted her head, and looked right at Franklin. He stood there, his arms out, a smile on his face as wide as it could go. She smiled back at him, moving to him. His arms out, wanting to hug her, to hold her, to love her.

She passed right through him, and in stunned shock, he turned and saw her moving to the front door, like he was made of air, him invisible to her. The sound of a car door closing and little feet patting along the floor. *A daughter, they had a daughter.* She reached down and scooped her up into her arms, the girl's hair long and brown like her mothers, wearing a small pink dress. Catherine kissed her on the lips and then the head. They had managed to have a child after all. Franklin's body was a pit of emotion, spiralling and turning over from unbearable glee to crippling sadness.

He moved to speak once more, but then someone else walked through the door. Another man wearing a suit and tie, smile wrapped around his face, kicking the door closed with his heel and taking the girl and Franklin's wife into his arms.

Two

Franklin

Franklin felt rage like he had never before. He raced to Catherine, lunging for the man whose lips were firmly planted on hers. He screamed and dove at him, and like Catherine had done before him, Franklin passed through the body like he was smoke passing through an open window. He landed on the floor, rolling and getting to his feet. Franklin raced to the man once more, screaming to him to get out his house, to leave his family, swinging his fists, screaming for his death. He knelt in front of Catherine who spoke to the child in happy, fuzzy tones, whilst Franklin broke his heart, crying, tears streaming down his face as to why she could have done this to him? That he was back, back to be with her, to fulfil his promise to her.

The night drew in, and Franklin stood in the corner of the room whilst he watched his wife put her child to bed, and as she got into bed with another man and made love to him. Franklin stood in the corner of the room, silently as they both slept. He sobbed more than he knew was possible, but the tears no longer came. He whimpered, whispering her name as to why she could do this to him, that he was able to come back and witness this, and what kind of sick trick was being played on him. There was no God in Franklin's mind. Not anymore. No god could allow such misery to befall a man of faith. Whatever God's plan was and Franklin's part in it, he didn't care. He wanted nothing more to do with it.

He moved outside, and standing there on the edge of the kerb, was Colne. Franklin felt the rage return, and he raced to Colne who didn't move. Franklin punched him to the face, his knuckles connecting with bone and flesh. It felt good, really fucking good to hit something, to hurt something. Colne stood, unmoving. Franklin punched him repeatedly in the face, stomach, kicked and elbowed him wherever they would connect. He let his fury out on the unmoving man until his lungs burned and his throat was on fire. When Franklin was drenched in sweat, he fell onto the cold ground and stared at the starless black sky above.

"Are you going to stay? Or are you coming with me?" Franklin eyed the dark sky above him.

"You lied to me." He said, pushing through the pain in his throat. "You told me I could return back to her."

"And you have!" Colne said, moving to Franklin. "I said you could come back home and spend the rest of your wife's life by her side."

"But she can't see me!" He cried, that pain forcing its way through the ball of razor wire in his throat. "I promised I would come back to her but she can't see me." His face flushed with red, drowning in his own tears. Colne reeled down to him, putting a hand on his shoulder. "Don't touch me!" Franklin screamed, throwing Colne's hand off him.

"You're dead Franklin. You died on the fields of France, June 11th, 1942. Your body is buried over there, your wife was made aware one month later, and she mourned your death viciously. But she has since found happiness, and you need to stop torturing yourself. I brought you back, I have completed my side of the bargain, but I am not a miracle worker, only the big man upstairs has that power. I would have given you another chance, a real chance, if I could, but I am not allowed. It is your God that has allowed you to suffer, not me. I am just the one who tries to make the best out of a bad situation. Give me better tools I say. Give me tools to make those that have served their Lord be more rewarded." The words, the trickery and the realisation cut through Franklin like knives through wool. "So, your choice is this: stay, and watch your wife grow old and die in the arms of another man and watch her daughter mourn her mother and father, and not you, as you become a memory in the wind on the tongues of those that never knew you. Or, come with me, live in my palace until the day your wife must make the decision to step onto the boat or not. What do you say?" Franklin's mouth tightened, his heart splitting in two.

"I will stay," he croaked. Colne's eyes widened; his lips tight.

"When I leave Franklin, there is no calling me back. If you choose to stay, you will be here, a shadow in the corner of the room, a ghost in the mist, until your wife's dying day."

"I made my wife a promise. I will keep my promise. I will stay, and I will watch over her until she takes her dying breath. I will be by her side until her heart stops beating and she leaves this world, because then, when she is standing on the banks of the river to the mountains, I can look her in the eye and tell her I came back, that I was with her through every day of it all, and that I love her, have always loved her, and will always love her, until I am no more." Franklin stood and righted himself, wiping the tears and snot from his face. He looked at his clothing, he was in the war-torn uniform once more, coated in blood and mud. "I never left that field," he said. "My body is lost to the war machine, but my soul, my love, was sworn to my wife Catherine on the day we wed. I am hers in whatever form I may be, and I choose to stay, forever."

"When she takes her final breath, you will return to me. You may be with her at the docks of the river, but not a moment longer.

And that, is the price you pay for love." The Devil said, before he faded away into the surrounding mist. Franklin watched as the glowing sun climbed from behind the mountains. He took a breath, turned, and walked back into the grey house of happiness and smiles.

The Strain

One

"Got another one for you," Jesse said, dragging a bloodied faced adolescent to the front desk. Alice eyed the boy from behind her computer screen. Around nineteen years old, reeking of cheap booze and wearing a white vest top that was way too small for him. Not to mention the blood stains. She couldn't overlook those.

"You're having a laugh aren't you Jesse?" She barked, rolling her eyes and looking at her third spent cup of coffee. "I'm going to have to close the suite if you carry on bringing me every dickhead that calls you a pig in the town centre."

"Who you calling a dick head?" The bloodied boy said, almost incoherently. His eyes glazed over like he was a walking zombie, the cheap vodka in his system the only thing stopping him from completely dying and rising again as an upstanding member of society. We wouldn't want that now would we? Jesse tugged on his handcuffs and the boy howled way too dramatically, "Ouch! My wrists! My wrists!" Alice rolled her eyes and gave him a once over.

"You can't be much older than eighteen, am I close?"

"Fuck off!" The whelp barked. Alison laughed to herself. The boy's face contorted, scoffing and tutting. "What you laughing at?" He whined. "Fucking pigs the lotta ya. I haven't done anything wrong." Jesse tugged at his cuffs once more and told him to *Calm the fuck down.* Alison sat back and let the two have a colourful exchange of words. She checked her watch. *Six hours and counting before home time.*

"Okay," Alison barked. The boy silenced himself. "What is your name?"

"Fuck you."

"Okay 'fuck you,'" Alison said, "how old are you?"

"As old as your pussy," the whelp laughed. Jesse barked at him once more, but Alison quickly quietened him with a raise of her hand.

"Okay Fuck you," she continued, putting her glasses to her face and began typing on the computer in front of her. "What is your address? Or are you going to come out with some other slur for that too?" The boy didn't answer, only looked down at his trainers.

"You've ruined my fucking shoes!" He protested, lifting them up for all to see at how badly his shoes had been 'Fucked up.' They were Adidas, not the most expensive shoes the two cops had ever seen, but they imagined they would have cost a few quid. "You better pay for these you bunch of pigs!"

"Want me to take him to the cell Sarge?" Jesse said through clenched teeth. Alison imagined the whelp had been a pain in the arse since he had been first locked up. Jesse had brought many prisoners to Alison in his 23-year career, all spent on the streets. The slow decline in humanities braincells clearly getting to him tonight. He wasn't usually this touchy. Most had called him mad for never leaving the streets, but he said he loved driving fast cars with blue lights and breaking down people's doors too much to sit behind a desk. Alison however, didn't mind the slower pace of policing, even if that did mean dealing with the product of testosterone, puberty and hormones, mixed with poor parenting, a culture of entitlement and of course, drugs and alcohol.

"Is he known PNC?" She asked.

"No. Nothing."

"So this is your first time being arrested?" Alison said, leaning over the desk once more, her hair pulled so far back in an attempt to force her eyes open. It had been working so far. That, and the fact that it had been a busy night and there were three other nut cases in the drunk tank and fourteen other prisoners in their individual cells ranging from rape and murder. It would seem, contrary to popular belief, the police were out catching rapists and murders after all. You just don't get to hear about it very often.

"I've been arrested before," The boy laughed. "My girlfriend puts me in handcuffs all the time. I bet you would like me to handcuff you wouldn't you? You old bitch!" Jesse again asked if he should be put in a cell, hogtied and stripped down to his birthday suit and placed in safety clothing and be allowed to sleep it off until the morning. Alison didn't entertain the request, although she figured teaching this little shit a lesson in manners and respect wouldn't be a bad thing. Alison stood and moved to the other side of the desk, down the small step and onto the custody suite floor. She walked to the boy who suddenly didn't look so fucking brave. A sergeant for over twenty years, she knew how to instil the fear of God into the little terrors that walked into her suite with but a single look. *If hell had eyes*, the cops that knew her would often say. *If hell had eyes indeed,* she would joke back.

"Listen," she said, somewhat tenderly to the boy. "You have two options." He looked right at her, leaning in, the smell of the booze knocking her sick. "You can either answer my questions, go to your cell with a cup of tea and get your head down and get a ticket in the morning, my personal and most favourite option..." She turned her eyes hard and glared at the punk. "Or," she continued, "we can drag you too your cell, strip you down and put you in safety clothing. Your choice." Alison stared hard at the boy. She saw that glint in his eye, one which came when he wasn't used to getting his own way.

"Sort your face out lady," he sneered. He coked his head back and Alison saw the foam gathering around his lips. A big ball of spit. He puckered his lips, aiming for her face. She dodged the projectile, it smacking on the floor in a lump of green and white. In an instant, Alison took him under the arm and pulled him to the ground where he met the linoleum hard. He howled in pain, the blood from his nose cracking and flowing again. "Get the fuck off me!" He howled, tears falling from his eyes. "I haven't fucking done anything! Fucking pigs! Police brutality! Help!"

"On your feet," Jesse commanded. The two cops pulled the wailing brat to his feet and dragged the boy kicking and screaming to the cell which a detention officer had kindly prepared for him: safety blanket, safety clothing and a roll of toilet tissue in case nature called. He was placed on the blue plastic mattress and stripped down and searched, before his cuffs were removed and Jesse and the other officers left the cell to the sound of him howling and crying, threatening to sew, telling them they didn't know who he was, that his dad worked for the BBC, his sister was the prime minister and his brother was Jesus Christ himself.

"Fucking Friday night," Alison said, readjusting her hair. "Is it a full moon out there?"

"Isn't it always?" Jesse said, panting and sweating.

"You're getting old mate," Alison goaded, before returning to her perch behind the desk. "You need a desk job; need to slow down." Jesse shook his head, taking out his pocket note book and then putting his handcuffs back in their holder, not before dousing them with a healthy amount of sanitiser.

"Nah," he said. "I'd end up hating the world and being a miserable fucker like you if I did that." The two of them laughed. Not many people could get away with speaking to Sargent Alison Hawthorn like that, but her and Jesse had been in the force together since day one. She went for the promotion route, he just liked being a big kid and playing cops and robbers. Both were happy, and that's all there was too it. *Misery is the nature of the job*, Jesse often said. Which was true. Nobody ever calls the cops when they're having a good day.

"So," Alison said, loading back up her computer screen. "What's this delightful young man's name?"

"Lucas Jones," Jesse said, reading from the rough scribbles in his note book. "Age 19."

"Let me guess, he's been locked up for drunk and disorderly?" Jesse shook his head.

"Surprisingly no," he laughed, leaning on the desk and touching his face. "The idiot decided that on the police car rear wheel would be the best place to take a piss," he started to laugh. "While we were all stood there." Alison nearly choked on her coffee.

"You're joking?" She laughed. Jesse shook his head. Alison rolled her eyes and sat back in her seat sniggering to herself. "What an absolute grade A bell end. Where the fuck do these people get their brains from?"

"YouTube and Instagram. Apparently it's 'Trending,' they call it *Hog Washing*."

"Outraging public decency it is then!" Alison said, typing onto her system. "Shame being born without a fucking brain cell isn't a recordable crime."

Two

Jesse left the custody suite following the blaring of his radio. Someone was shouting for assistance, and it didn't sound good. He raced through the heavy custody doors, stabbed the key in the ignition and drove like a mad man, sirens and lights blaring.

The night was still young and the cells were filling up quickly. Sargent Hawthorn was the queen of the suite tonight. Normally there should be three sergeants on in the evening and five detention officers. Tonight however, she was left to fly solo with only two pairs of helping hands, sickness striking most of her team down. There was a hell of a flu going around. It had been all over the news, the new 'strain' of some unknown illness was working its way through Europe, spreading to the United States and even reports of it in Australia. The government had toyed with the idea of a national lockdown, but they didn't want to infringe civil liberties like that, not to mention it being electoral suicide. So the night clubs were allowed to stay open, and the pubs and bars were still in full swing, and Alison was at the receiving end of natures whelps and law breakers, and she happily sealed them away from the rest of society. She had stopped caring about the people she booked into the custody suite a long time ago, since Ronald Freeman had walked into the cells, screaming that he needs help with his drug addiction, which is why he steals so much. Alison helped him, sat with him for hours, giving him the best fucking advice you could ever hope to get, put him on rehabilitation courses and addiction recovery programs. She could have sent him to prison for a minor offence, albeit a prolific offender. But she didn't. She saw the light in a lost man's eyes, and she let him off, against all advice from her superiors, putting her neck on the line. That night, Ronald Freeman was booked right back into custody. He had robbed a supermarket with a firearm and had shot and killed a mother of two who couldn't undo her seat belt fast enough to get out of her car he was trying to steal with his stolen £46.32 in his pocket. Alison never gave someone the benefit of the doubt again.

The clock stuck three and the buzzer went again. A van this time, on the CCTV camera overlooking the custody yard. It was Jesse once more, with another prisoner for her.

"What've you got for me this time Jesse?" She said on the intercom. A loud revving of the engine burst through the microphone, followed by shouting.

"Open the doors Alison!" Jesse hollered. "This lad is going fucking nuts!" Alison's heart began to bounce. She pressed the buzzer and the heavy custody gates crept open. Jesse drove into the holding area and the iron doors closed around the van. Several cops spilled out of the back, followed by the passenger, then Jesse. They pulled opened the back doors of the van and yanked out a writhing figure that was bound in limb restrains, handcuffs and a headguard. Its face, she couldn't tell the sex, was bloodied and marred. Arms and legs pulling at the binds and cuffs, blood and flesh tearing as it did.

"Go open the doors!" Alison commanded a detention officer,

Joanne, a small plump woman with shaved hair, ran through the heavy metal doors and propped them open. "Fred," she said, addressing the remaining detention officer who looked like he just wanted the night to end, an elderly gentleman with short receding grey hair and more wrinkles than you could shake a stick at. "Go get a cell ready: safety clothing, put the matt on the floor and turn off the water to the cell for now!" Fred did just that. Alison could hear the howling and screeching from the prisoner as they were carried out of the van and through the hallway, past the holding cells that were now thankfully empty, cops on each limb, holding the head, and one red faced officer running behind them trying to catch whatever equipment fell from the bustling bobbies. "Straight to cell nineteen!" Alison Hawthorn barked. The cops eyed her thankfully, their faces a state, blood marring their uniform, the howling creature in their arms thrashing, trying to bite, scratch and fight. Incoherent noises pressed through the thing's vocal chords. She didn't know someone could make such sounds, like a hyena amped up on cocaine while fucking a giraffe. The cops vanished into the open cell. Alison took her glasses off and tightened her boots, ready for a fight. She threw on her belt: Captor spray, baton, limb restraints, spit hood and cuffs, and ran to the aid of her colleagues.

Inside the cell, the prisoner was placed on their stomach, handcuffs riding all the way up to their forearms which were bloodied and purple, the cuffs on as tight as they could go, the beast still straining against them, close to breaking either the cuffs or it's forearms. One cop lay on the prisoner's ankles while another on their knees. One supported the head, and Jesse laid out the commands, standing with his baton drawn.

"Take the limb restrains off!" Alison ordered. The one on their legs began to peel the tight black Velcro away. The more he did, the more the thing within them kicked and struggled. They came off and Alison threw them out the cell. The thing bucked and kicked, nearly throwing the cops off of it. The prisoner was frail, thin, vascular, but fucking hell it was throwing the cops around like squirrels holding onto a gorilla. Next came the restrains off the ankles, and a cop hogtied its legs and leant on them, tying them into a figure of four. One cop leant down to the fucker's face and tried to talk them round, telling them to relax, to calm down, to stop being a cunt. Didn't work. The prisoner continued to howl and fight like possessed by a banshee. It lashed out, going for the cop's hand with snapping teeth. The cop recoiled, just missing the snapping jaws.

"Take the cuffs off," Jesse said, baton primed and ready.

"Get your gas out," Alison ordered. Jesse shot her a look of pain.

"He's been gassed three times Ali," he said. "No effect. Coked out of his tree or something." One cuff came off and the prisoners' hands flew around like snakes on fire, the cuffs still attached at the wrist. The snapping snatching mound of emaciated flesh, doused in captor, sweat and blood, slipped from the fingers of the officers. That flailing wrist caught one officer on the forehead, the rungs of the open cuff slashing her skin, leaving a huge gash in her face. She screamed, falling back, holding her face as blood poured through her finger tips. Hands grabbed her collar, hauling her out of the cell. Alison jumped and took her place, grabbing the prisoners flailing arm tight. He pulled her around like a rag doll. He was strong, whatever he had taken had make him into the skinny hulk. She forced the prisoners' hands into its back, kneeling against its legs.

"Get out!" She barked to the remaining officers. They raced for the exit, picking up anything that fell from their belts, stumbling over each other. Jesse was the last to leave, grabbing Alison's belt from behind and ejecting her from the mound and yanking her out the cell. The being dove to its feet, its eyes wild, jaw swinging, arms outstretched like a bouncing ball with teeth. Alison slammed the door of the cell shut, the prisoner meeting the hard steel with its fists and face, banging furiously, manically, over and over, howling and screaming.

Two cops stood at the cell doors panting heavily. One disappeared into the bathroom and was heard throwing up. The one with the head wound was being seen to by the nurse, her face draining of colour, uniform doused in bright red. Jesse stood at the sergeant's desk with Alison, looking at the monitor of the prisoner that continued to go completely postal, the sounds escaping its throat echoing around the custody suite.

"We need to get them to a secure unit," Jesse said. "Clearly a mental health job. You need us on level fours? Constant observation?" Alison thought about this.

"They can't stay here in this condition," Alison said, holding her face in her hands, the thing continuing to hit its head on the door. "Going to need someone to sit at the cell with him if he doesn't calm down." She wiped the sweat from her brow, the sting of the captor spray on her skin. Jesse's heart skipped a beat.

"Maybe he'll calm down," Jesse said with trepidation. "If not, the nurse might have to give him a shot to put him under." Alison eyed Jesse, then the monitor.

"Maybe." Alison looked around for her coffee, but it was nowhere to be seen. "Have you ever seen anything like this before?" She said.

"No," Jesse said, eyeing the screen with worry on his face. "I have seen some shit Alison, even a few cases of ABD, but nothing like this."

"Who are they?" Alison queried.

"I have no idea," Jesse rebuked, taking a drink of water from a bottle in his trouser pocket. "That's how the job came in. Cops went to a report of someone attacking people in the town centre. They turn up and there this guy," Jesse pointed to the monitor for clarity, "running around, diving on people, pummelling them, screaming to the heavens. The cops rock up, press their emergency button, we fly down there and can't believe what we're seeing." Jesse sat down, his breathing heavy. "This guy. He was tasered, gassed, clubbed, cuffed, punched, taken to the floor, everything you can think of. Two cops are currently in the emergency room and the rest of them with paramedics that are helping those that were attacked." He let that last part hang in the air, the face of a man who can't process what has just happened, sitting, leaning forward with his hands together. A man who has witnessed the world tear itself apart.

"Never seen anything like it."

"Drugs?" Alison said. Jesse shook his head.

"No. I have seen people coked off their eyeballs. I've seen violent fuckers go at it. I have seen PCP, Crystal meth and every cocktail of amphetamine, mental health and all sorts of other crazy. Nothing like this guy. Something isn't right with him." The two watched on the monitor as the prisoner circled the cell like some kind of wild animal, twitching, thrashing out like struck with sudden jolts of lightning. Eventually, the rest of the crew watched on the monitor too. Alison, dare she admit it, felt something which she hadn't felt in over twenty years of the job since her first day lacing up her boots and hitting the streets.

Fear.

"Right," she said, breaking the tense silence of eyeballs glaring at the bloodied mess on the screen. "I'm gonna put him on level threes. I want someone watching on the monitor at all times until the morning shift comes on. Then it's their problem. I want someone on the phone to the local hospitals, psych wards, see if they've had anyone get loose. I want people doing checks, to try and find out who the hell this guy is." The team nodded.

"Sarge," one of the cops said. It was the woman with the gash to the top of her skull, a bandage wrapped around her head.

"What?" Alison snapped, turning to her. As soon as she saw the colour of her skin, she knew things were going to go from bad, to worse.

The cops' eyes had sunk into her head, her skin a dull grey, veins thick and purple creeping across her face. She was holding her right arm for the world to see. The nurse stood next to them in shocked horror.

"You didn't tell me about that?" The nurse stuttered, her lips turning dry. Everyone stood in shock and watched the cop roll up her sleeve to the wound of matted flesh that looked to be turning black before their eyes. In the centre of her forearm, where the skin is the thinnest and the veins the juiciest.

A bite.

Three

Things went from bad, to really bad, to utter horse shit diarrhoea on your wedding dress bad real fucking fast. The cop began to convulse, shake and fit, hitting the deck and flapping on the floor like a live salmon thrown on the grill and stabbed with forks.

"What's wrong with her!" Alison barked to the nurse who stood there flabbergasted, holding her hands out and shaking her head. The officers watched as the woman's face turned pale, her hair matting with the blood and froth that foamed around her mouth and sank into the blue carpet. A dark patch appearing in the centre of her crotch as the smell of piss pierced the air, pushing its way into the nostrils of the terrified onlookers. As fast as it had begun, the shaking and fitting stopped. All hearts were in throats. Jesse pressed his radio, trying to get a signal.

"No signal Sargent," he whispered. "I can't radio for an ambulance from in here, I'll go outside." He went to move but Alison tugged his coat. Her eyes begging him to stay while her face stayed stern. He nodded, stepping back. Turning to the screen, eyeing the bloodied prisoner on the monitor. Still stalking around the empty cell, sniffing the air, waiting to find something moving.

"Is she okay?" Freddy, the older detention officer said warily. The nurse moved cautiously, treading lightly on the bile-soaked carpet. She drew closer, getting on her knees and pulling out a pair of blue rubber gloves, snapping them tight on her hands. She leant in, pushing the hair and foam away from the cop's face, listening to the sound of breathing.

"I can't feel anything," she said. No sooner had the words left her mouth, did the cop's head rear up and sink her teeth into the nurse's cheek, biting down and pulling a chunk of meat away with her. The nurse howled, screaming in pain as she recoiled, holding her face, blood pissing between her fingers. All shrieked and stumbled backwards, the bloodied cop on her feet, eyes wild, racing to the closest body to her. She lept at Alison who dodged out the way like she was a big dose of herpes flying to a virgin on her wedding night. The bloodied bitch slammed against the monitors that lined the sergeant's desk. She turned, teeth snapping, wanting more of that flesh, more of that muscle.

A nameless cop, new to the force, Alison hadn't seen him before, was too slow to react. The wretched bitch ran through him, knocking him off his feet like a bowling ball through sugar paper. She dove onto him, his hands jamming into her face, shouting for help, trying to get her off. Alison moved and grabbed the woman's shoulders, but she turned and slapped her away, knocking her back. Jesse dove into action, his baton drawn, laying fourteen inches and eight pounds of holy hell across her back. She didn't flinch, her body shaking, twitching. He struck again, the baton snapping across her back. The thing turned, her face marred with thick black sludge, her eyes bloodshot. She howled something unnatural, sending a blast of fear through the remaining cop's hearts. She turned back to the body in her hands, reeled her head back and drove her teeth into him, tearing his throat out. Red flashed and splattered on the ground, thick spurts drenching the monitors and the faces of horrified onlookers as the wretch began to hammer fist the haemorrhaging officers face, his howls of horror pitching to the air.

Alison grabbed her baton and along with Jesse and another brave bobby, they pummelled the holy fuck out of the wretched bitches back: snapping vertebrae, breaking rips, knocking her from the quivering writhing bloodied rookie. The creature fell to the floor, jumping to her feet, running at Alison with murder in her eyes. Alison moved once more, but this time, swung the baton low with both hands like a baseball player hitting for home. The cop's left shin cracked against the steel and her face ricocheted from the counter of the sergeant's desk, smearing blood and teeth along the monitors of the prisoners on CCTV.

That bitch hit the floor hard, her toe touching east and her knee pointing west. The nurse was still howling, crying in pain, being ushered into the medical room by a detention officer. The rookie cop staring vacantly at the ceiling, skin pale, chest still. The bitch on the ground still tried to get to her feet. Alison punched her to the face and she fell limp once more, her fingers grabbing at Alison's boots.

"Freddy, what cells are free?" Alison called. Freddy looked at the list of prisoners.

"Seventeen, four, nine, thirty, eight —"

"Fucking hell Freddy just one will do!" She grabbed the cops' shattered legs. "Jesse, a hand?" The two of them dragged the girl writhing and screaming into a vacant cell before slamming the door shut. Not a second to catch her breath, Alison raced back to the sergeant's desk and dove onto the dying officer, wrapping a cloth around his neck, ordering someone start CPR, another get an adrenalin shot, another call for an ambulance, and a million other things that flew from her mouth in a rampaging word salad of orders.

"I can't get through!" Freddy called, holding the phone to the control room. Alison jumped to her feet, barking more orders to keep going with the CPR. She hauled ass and snatched the phone from Freddy's quivering hands.

"Sargent Alison Hawthorn to —" No dial tone on the other side. She tried again, hitting the reset button, just dead air meeting her ear. She unplugged the phone and tried again. "Hello? Anyone?" She tried to usual extensions: upstairs, the back office, the main station a few miles down the road, a hotline to Jesus Christ himself. Nothing. They were cut off. No signal. No phones. Just her, a bunch of terrified cops, a madman, a mad woman, a dying officer and a building full of convicts that want to tear you limb from limb. Alison slammed the phone to the receiver repeatedly until it chipped and splintered. "I fucking hate Fridays."

Four

Sweat pushed from the brow of Jesse as he continued CPR on the rookie. His short hair sticking to his forehead, the gel since relinquished and staining the top of his stab vest. His body rigid, another officer, a younger looking woman with more wrinkles than allowed for a girl of her age, took it in turns. Alison had flinched when she heard the sound of ribs cracking, blood spurting from the rookie's mouth like a quaking volcano, staining her scuffed boots. CPR was common place with her, but you never got used to the sound of someone's bones breaking, like the sound of an engine misfiring.

"That's enough," she had said, after instructing the detention officers to try and get through to someone that could help. They had a defibrillator on site, but you needed the code to access it, of which no one knew. Not to mention more of the boy's blood was soaking into the carpet than was left in his body. "He's gone. I'm calling it."

"You can't call it," the young officer said. "You don't have the authority." Alison sighed heavily.

"I know I can't," she said, sitting down in her swivel chair, leaning over the two exhausted bodies in front of her. "But I need everyone at full strength. The boy is dead. I'm calling it." Reluctantly, Jesse and the other officer stopped with the compressions, the rookie's eyes never changing, forever staring blankly at the stained pale ceiling above them, into the eye of the CCTV camera, his face reflected in a warped orb. Freddy arrived after a moment and placed a blanket over the rookie's face, saving the rest of them from those dead fish eyes. "Put him in the back room," Alison said. "We can't do much more with him now."

"What?" The female officer said, taking her hair out of her bun and tying it back up again. "You can't just put him in the storage room like he's a piece of furniture in the way." Her voice was hard, and her eyes harder.

"Look," Alison said, getting to her feet. "I am sorry for your colleague. He was part of our family, I know, and what happened was awful," her face turned hard too. *If hell had eyes.* "But the fact of the matter is, we need to keep this space clear. We don't know what we're dealing with and we don't know when help is going to come, if it comes at all. We need to stop anything else from complicating the situation."

"So Sam is just a complication?" The officer said, holding back the tears, her fingers trembling. Alison let that hard glare slip a moment.

"What is your name?" She asked, touching the lip of sincerity.

"Hannah," Hannah said, wrapped in venom.

"Okay Hannah," Alison began, "let me put it this way. I am your sergeant, and you will do what I fucking say in my custody suite."

"Easy," Jesse said, stepping in. "Let's not lose our heads here." The two women shot Jesse a look of pain, and his face dropped like walking into a fancy restaurant on a date and finding it filled with all your ex-girlfriends.

"I need you to put him in the back room. He can stay there until we get some help," Alison said calmly. Hannah glared at Jesse a moment, and without returning her gaze to Alison, uttered –

"Fine. I'll take his legs."

Hannah sparked up a cigarette. She was watching the prisoner from the town centre on the monitor, a full cup of fresh coffee next to her that had since turned cold. She wasn't allowed to smoke in here, but if she didn't get a hit of nicotine soon, she would kill someone herself.

"Where are we up to?" Alison said, stepping from the back room onto the custody desk after checking on Sam's body, then double checking the door was locked as she left. Jesse sat playing with his handcuffs. The two detention officers doing the rounds of the suite.

"Stephanie is pacing around her cell like the other guy," Hannah said, the wrinkles in her face getting deeper by the second. She turned to Alison. "Sam?" Her eyes were bloodshot, a thick cloud of smoke surrounding her. Alison put her hand on her shoulder and she shook it off like she had placed a hot coal on her bare skin, Hannah's eyes fixed on the large blood stain on the carpet.

"I covered him over. Like I said, we'll get him to where he needs to be, his family will be made aware as soon as possible." Alison put her hand back to her waist. "I'm sorry."

"Thanks," Hannah said, her voice beginning to break. She couldn't have been much older than twenty. Probably never lost a loved one. Definitely never saw someone she knew die before her eyes, something the more seasoned officers had grown too used to. *You turn on job mode,* Alison often thought. *The mode that puts emotions to the back of your mind and you get the task done, and grieve later.*

"What about the other one?" Alison said, pointing to the prisoner from the town.

"He's..." Hannah said, leaning into the monitor, "still." She pulled out the pack of smokes a lit a fresh one. Alison went to protest, old habits dying hard, but then held out her hand.

"May I?"

"You smoke?" Hannah said, the pack open. Alison shook her head.

"Not for years." Hannah eyed her wrinkled palm, then took out a straight and put it In Alison's hand. She sparked it up, and those tense shoulders dropped quickly, relaxing with an exhale of blue. Alison coughed and laughed to herself. "Still tastes as good as I remember." The two women sat together and Alison pointed to the prisoner from the town. "He's just standing there," she said. The prisoner was rigid, his arms bleeding, badly bruised, staring at the door of the cell. Unmoving, just gently swaying on the ball of its bare feet. The two women shared a look, and neither needed to say it, but they were both freaked the hell out.

"What's going on?" Hannah said, more of a statement than a real question. Alison shrugged.

"I don't know, but the main thing is he is in there, and we are out here. It will be time for the morning shift to come in in a couple of hours. For now, we should be okay." She turned to Jesse. "Anything on the radio?" Jesse pressed the talk button on his radio but a solid tone met his ears.

"Nothing. No signal, no transmissions. Nothing coming in or out. Like the whole things gone down." That sent a wave of worry through the hearts of all in the suite.

"Let's just get through the night. Help will come," Alison said, returning to the CCTV monitor, eyeing the cop who had now began sinking her teeth into her own arm, and the prisoner who swayed, his eyes vacant, mouth bloodied, and fingers clicking and jittering. *I hope.* "Where is the nurse?" Alison said, noticing her absence.

"We put her in one of the cells too." Jesse said. "I didn't want to take any chances. She's on a camera." Alison moved to another rig of screens. She saw the nurse sitting on a blue mat and holding her face. They had put some bandages in there with her to clean herself up.

"Okay," Alison said. "At least we can keep an eye on them. We know where they are."

"Want me to go out and try and get some signal to radio for an ambulance or some back up?" Jesse said.

"No," Alison snapped. "It's too dangerous. We aren't going anywhere until either the phones come back on, the early shift come in, or we get some kind of indication of what the hell we're dealing with." All agreed. Safety in numbers, even if you were in a pit of snakes. "We still have power, so the cameras work, and the cells are locked with keys. Only the entrance to the suite is controlled by power and key cards. At least if the power goes out, we can leave here and the prisoners remain secure. Alison turned to Hannah, who was sitting there turning more and more pale by the second. "You okay?" Hannah snapped to attention.

"Yeah, just scared is all."

"We're all scared," Alison said. "Why don't you go in the back and make us all a brew. Something we could all do with." Nobody hesitated in throwing their orders out as Hannah walked into the back office and fired up the kettle, the sound of clinking mugs and cutlery dancing in the air. Suddenly, the thought of coffee and a cup of tea made everyone feel that little better. "Freddy," Alison said, him returning from his rounds. "Go check the drunk tank. They've been more relaxed than normal." Freddy stood and grabbed a set of keys from the board. "No," Alison barked. Freddy looked at her with surprise. She shook her head. "Don't open the doors, only use the hatch to talk to them."

"What if they aren't breathing? If they don't wake up and I need to go in?" Freddy sounded worried. He was trying to hide it, but Alison knew the sound of tremors in a man's voice when she heard it, no matter how light.

"That's a chance I'm willing to take. If they move, you leave them, if they don't move, you shout their name and if they still don't move, you shut the hatch and move on. There's been enough happen here tonight. Let's not get brave." Freddy put the rung of keys back on their hangers and moved down the various wings, sliding down prisoner hatches, being given a range of responses from *'go fuck yourself,' 'What was all that shouting?'* and *'When is my solicitor getting here?'* Alison smiled. Even when the world was falling apart, the boys in blue tried to hold the tape together as best they could.

The kettle popped and the hot beverages of calm were quickly brought to the cops whose mouths were drier than they could ever remember. Freddy returned from the checks and began inputting them on the computer.

"Well none of them are dead," he joked, and a chorus of laughter broke through the office. A much-needed break in the macabre. The laughter died a few seconds later, like a small fire caught in a winter wind.

"What the hell is going on Ali?" Jesse said, speaking for the group. "First the guy we brought in, then Steph, the nurse is gonna be next, and Sam…" He pointed to the backroom where the boy lay dead and covered. "What the fuck is happening? I can't get a signal; the phones aren't working?" A wave of fear spread through the room. "It's like it's the end of the fucking world or something." Alison tried not to laugh.

"You watch too many horror movies Jesse," she said sourly. "It's more than likely a fuck tonne of kids taking a shit tonne of drugs and having a tough time with them."

"No Alison it doesn't work that way. The way that guy was, still *is*... It's nothing I have seen before. And why would Steph turn like that if it was just drugs? Its more than that."

"What're you trying to say Jesse?" Alison queried once more. He ran his hand through his hair.

"I'm saying we all need to get out of here whilst we can and make sure our families are okay. I don't give a shit about these guys in these cells."

"We can't do that Jesse," Alison said. "We can't leave these people to rot in a cell. They aren't model citizens, but we can't leave them."

"Alison," Jesse started.

"Jesse, no. I know you're worried about your family, your son, but he'll be okay. I can't have you venturing out into the chaos when we don't know what's happening. The phones will be back online soon, the early shift will come on and we can make or calls and visits then. But until then, we need to stay safe." Jesse squirmed in his seat.

"You can't seriously expect me to sit here whilst the worlds going mad and my boy is sat home wondering what the hell is going on," he appeared breathless, flabbergasted. "Have you no heart? I know you don't have a family, but...."

"That's out of line Jesse," Alison bit. "My personal circumstances are irrelevant. Your son is fine. You have a job to do."

"You're so sure about that?" Jesse bit. "Same as you were sure about Ronald Freeman? How did the husband of the woman he murdered feel about that?" As soon as Jesse finished talking, his heart hammered in his chest. He had crossed the line, dancing on a raw nerve with ice skates. Alison held her gaze, hands trembling. The room got that little smaller, and that much hotter. "I'm sorry Alison, I –"

"It's Sargent Hawthorn," she snapped, flexing her muscles. Jesse eyed her stunned. Never in all their time of knowing each other, had she ever pulled rank on him. Not once, and she saw the hurt in his eyes, but her fury hid the agony in hers.

"Fuck you Sargent Hawthorn." Jesse spat, standing to his feet.

"How fucking dare you Jesse!" Alison roared. "I am your superior officer and you will listen to my orders!"

"Oh fuck your orders Alison. I don't give a shit about this fucking job or the pieces of shits that are in those cells right now. I am going home to my boy to make sure he is okay. Something I don't expect you to understand." Alison felt fury raise in her then, like the overflowing of lava, ready to blow.

"In all my years as a sergeant here I have never abandoned those in my care. Not once. Not when the terrorist attacks happened, not when the Fed told us to stay home from work, not when there was the pandemic and people couldn't come in. I value what I have and I will not abandon it." She moved and grabbed a set of keys.

"What're they for?" He queried, puzzled.

"For the cell your son is being held in."

Five

Jesse walked with Sargent Hawthorn to the end of the suite, the sound of a huge rung of keys rattling in her hands. The walk was silent, only their footsteps on the cold linoleum flooring meeting their ears. Hawthorn was furious, her body tort and her hands trembling with fury. She wanted to scream, to cry, to howl her frustration, but she knew that Jesse was right. There were more things at stake here than the peoples lives who have decided to ruin others. But that wasn't the point. She had a job to do, and whether she liked to admit it, she had nobody to go back home too anyway. Maybe she didn't understand what love really was? Maybe years of seeing human beings tear each other apart had destroyed what little empathy she had left? She both envied and pitied Jesse. He had all the love, but all the stress and worry that came with it. That didn't make her better than him, it just made them two very different people.

As they drew closer to the drunk tank, they heard the sound of the rabble and the commotion. This wasn't unusual; throw eight drunk people in a room together with one toilet and no way out, people are going to get a little heated. But this was different, and despite the reservation of pride and stubbornness she held in her chest, she began to move quickly, thankful Jesse wasn't far behind her.

The sounds turned from muffled groans to loud shouting, screaming and cries for help. Alison got to the tank, the sounds inside like a hundred jackals running around the place. She dropped the hatch. The boy formally known as 'Fuck you,' was on the floor convulsing, throwing up thick white foam mixed with bile and black blood. He was shivering, shaking, his body rampaging, every muscle twitching, sweating heavily, bones cracking and popping. The others pinned themselves against the wall as close as they could, like the boy was a gaping hole into hell that was growing at their feet.

"Fuck," Alison called, getting the keys out. Jesse pushed her out of the way, grabbing hold of the keys and fumbling the lock. Jesse stole a look through the dropped hatch, his eyes widened.

"Trevor!" He shouted. "Trevor, you in there?" His heart in his throat, scanning the room for his son. In the corner, his eyes fell on him, right next to the fitting boy. Huddled in a corner, his hood pulled over his head, the stamp of a night club on his hand and the remnants of blood and vomit on his shirt. "Trevor! The fuck are you doing in there!?" Trevor didn't hear him, instead he sat huddled in the corner, gone to the world in a drunken stupor.

"Open the fucking door!" One prisoner shouted, a young guy, 'Craig,' Alison thought his name was. He had pulled his pants down in the custody cell and urinated on the charging desk. "Hurry!" Jesse found the right key and Alison stood behind him, her gas drawn.

"We can't open the door Jesse, not with one of those things in there!" Alison shouted, trying to grab the keys from Jesse. "What about the rest of them?" Alison said.

"Fuck the rest of them Alison, I have to get my son!" He was frantic, turning the key. Alison tried to move, to stop him, knowing he would be rushed. They needed to control the room first and get what they needed then sort out the rest, but Jesse pushed her away. Her feet slipped and she went down, hitting the wall behind her with a hard crack, her head spinning as she slumped on the floor. Jesse hauled the door open. "Trevor!" He called. The crowd rushed him, drunken terrified criminals running through the custody suite towards the front door. The sound of cops struggling, fighting with the rabble pushing through the haze in Alison's ears. Jesse ran into the cell, stepped over the twitching boy and grabbed his son. He screamed when he saw his face under the hood. His face was dull, eyes vacant and white, blood smeared around his mouth. Trevor lunged for Jesse, tearing into his throat, fingers finding eyes, cheeks, mouth. The twitching boy joined him, sinking teeth into whatever fleshy part he could find. In the suite, the prisoners banged on the cell doors, the drunks with their new found freedom grabbing keys, unlocking the cell doors that kept the murderous creatures contained. Screams permeated the air and blood painted the light green walls. Gurgling, bubbling of blood and bile, as infected tore into the living, eating their insides while they screamed in agony. The rookie in the back room banged on the door to be set free, to join the meal. One infected found the fuse box, enraged and murderous, smashing it to pieces, killing the lights and opening the suite doors, as the infected raced into the howling night, to the cities that were aflame.

The Nightshift

From the author -

Back in 2010, I spent a short time living in an old terrace house in my town of Wigan. I always had the feeling of eyes on me, heard noises and had doors close when I left them open. One night, I heard the sound of a woman scream and race up the stairs. I woke up and found the house to be empty and the bedroom next to mines door closed when I had left it open. Inside the room, all the wardrobe doors were open and the once neatly made bed covers were on the floor. I later found out that a previous occupant, a young woman, had hung herself in that same room.

I left that house that night and never went back, but I will hear the scream of that dead woman for the rest of my life.

- Jay Darkmoore

1

Welcome to Welch Mill

"Have you ever seen a man die?" Carl said, a rugged faced man with skin darker than the coffee he was drinking. His eyes were bulging, veiny, like he had forgotten what sleep felt like.

"On the rigs." Tom said, touching the cuffs of his moth bitten suit jacket. "He was a friend of mine. It's the reason I left. Made me think about the dangers of being out on the sea." Tom leant back in his chair, the smell of salt water tingling his nostrils, then the smell of the extra strong coffee permeating the small office.

"I see." Carl said in his rasping voice. The interview had been going on for just over fifteen minutes, and neither man had said very much at all. Long stares, like Carl was trying to weigh Tom up, figure him out. See what he was made of. "You ever done security work before Mr. Mackenzie?" Tom shook his head.

"No," he said, a little too quickly. "But," he rebuked, remembering he couldn't afford to fuck up the job opportunity. He had medical bills to pay. "But it can't be that hard can it?" Again, Tom slapped himself mentally, digging himself an even bigger hole he was trying to claw out of. Carl leaned back and layered those tobacco-stained fingers within each other. His suit jacket was clean, crisp, tailored even.

"It's okay," Carl smiled, his missing teeth pushing through those dry lips like missing tombstones in a graveyard. "Most people say that. The work is easy yes, but the solitude is something you have to be wary of. It's not something to be snuffed at. Long nights alone can play tricks on a man's mind. You're the fifth person I have interviewed for this position in the last six months." Tom raised a brow.

"Why so many?" Carl held his stare. There was something lingering behind those bulging eyes, like a poker player not wanting to let it slip after going all in. But what cards was he holding? Was it a single three or a full house? Tom shook away the feeling of ice creeping under his skin. "I'll be okay. I'm used to being on my own. I'm not scared of the dark." He laughed, but the jovial tone fell dead. Carl's eyes stayed unmoved and his lips remained pursed together.

"I asked you if you have ever seen someone die," Carl said with a heavy tone. Tom again felt the cold return. The touch of the arctic wind on his face carrying the screams of a drowning man. He pulled open a drawer and took out some paper work. "We have spoken to your last employer, Atlantic Oil LTD. They say you had a drinking problem on the rig?"

"I don't know what that has to do with anything?" Tom said, leaning back once more, his hands folding together.

"Is it still a problem?" Carl enquired. Tom's face contorted; his lips tight behind his bushy beard.

"I haven't touched a drop in just under a year." Carl nodded.

"The reason I bring it up Mr. Mackenzie," Carl leaned forward, clearing his throat. "The Night," he said, "The shadows. They can bring things from your mind back to life. Have you ever spoken to a professional about what happened on the rig?" Tom scrunched his face like biting into a rotten apple.

"With all due respect sir, that's none of your business."

"My apologies" Carl rasped, leaning back into his chair again. "The reason I ask is we have had past workers fall under great stress whilst on the shifts. We are a long way from another town and is very solitary. Now you'll be starting this job in the darkest part of the year, not to mention the coldest. I just need to know you're up for the task."

"I can handle it," Tom said. Carl smirked again, that toothy grin peering at him. "What do you mean *great stress?*" Tom asked, more thinking out loud than expecting a real answer. Carl shifted in his seat.

"They have reported strange goings on. I don't believe in any of it of course, but then again, you are the fifth person I have interviewed for this position in a few months. The last employee was found by the morning cleaner with his hand down to his elbow in the mail sorter. He died en route to hospital." Tom's eyes widened.

"He lose his fuckin keys or something?" Carl laughed quietly.

"Perhaps." Tom let the story fade from his mind. This was obviously some kind of practical joke they play. He had worked on an oil rig where all people did was scare each other and play jokes on each other all the time. It was the boredom. Play games or go crazy.

Or drink. And drink a lot.

"I'm just making sure your welfare is in check," Carl said.

"Thanks," Tom sighed. "But I'll be fine." Carl nodded and took out some paperwork.

"I don't mean to scare you."

"You can't scare me." A thick silence fell between the men then. The ticking clock in the corner of the room irking Tom's patience. The large window from the main office next to him was showed lots of cars leaving the parking lot of the warehouse of the

Welch Mill Delivery Company. The sun lazily dipped behind the forest that encroached across the road. The streets were going to be busy soon, and he didn't have a time to listen to ghost stories. "Sorry to be rude," Tom said, shifting in his chair. "But I have somewhere to be soon. Somewhere important. Have I got the job or not?" Carl took another long drink of his coffee. He checked the clock behind Tom and checked the long shadows creeping from the woods onto the asphalt. He stood, stretching out like a stiff piece of wood and moved to the window. The sun painting the sky pink and red, bleeding into each other as the day light died. Carl stood silently a few moments, touching his face and running his hand through his short greying hair. He mustn't have been much older than Tom, maybe mid-fifties, but his face was aged. Deep wrinkles on his neck and cheeks. Finally, at the end of Tom's patience, Carl moved to his desk and took out a small bundle of papers with a pen and pushed them to Tom who began filling them out roughly, signing where the little paper arrows told him to. He handed the paperwork back to him and they shook hands.

"You start tomorrow night." Carl said. Tom nodded a slight smile and began putting on his coat over the faded suit jacket. Carl thumbed the paperwork, a faraway look in his eyes. He took one last look at Tom as he went for the door, like he was saying farewell to man heading off to war. A man whose memory would haunt his dreams forever.

2

Later

The traffic heading into the city was anything but ideal. As Tom eyed the rows and rows of solid red brake lights in front of him, he felt his blood pressure begin to rise. He turned on the radio of his pick up and let the sound of classic rock pelt his ears for a few moments, before plugging in his phone into the centre console and clicking open his music library. A hit of the shuffle button and the melodic sounds of Indie music came flooding into his ears. His mood felt that little bit better, albeit the taunting digital clock on the dashboard flickered at him, telling him he was very late indeed.

The interview had gone well, but Tom felt a little uneasy about it. Not the stories which the manager had told him, he was used to horror stories and things that go bump in the night. You don't spend eight months isolated form the world on an Arctic rig and not see a few strange things after all. Tom saw the phone buzzing and connected it to his bluetooth. He already had nine points on his driver's licence for speeding to late appointments. He didn't need any more for being on his mobile phone, which is why Jayne had bought him the adaptor for the damn thing in the first place.

"I'd rather you get here late than never," she had said one day when he had been pulled over by the police for doing 57 in a 30. Thankfully the officer had a heart and let him off with a warning when Tom explained 'Why he was going so fast Sir." Most of his points had come from static speed cameras he hadn't noticed since moving in the area. The heartless robotic fuckers. He answered the phone, swiping along the screen with his finger tip.

"Hey babe," Tom said, the frustration in his heart melting away at the sight of her name.

"Hey," she sounded calm which was always a good thing. Happy to speak to him, which was even better. "How did it go?"

"I got the job," Tom said, a little more flatly than would be expected.

"That's great!" Jayne spoke with what little strength she could muster. "How do you feel about it?"

"Happy."

"You don't sound too happy about it?" She said, a little worried.

"You know why Jayne. You know I don't like this kind of work anymore. The only reason I'm taking it is because the money is okay, they aren't too strict on the background checks, and I can start quickly. Didn't even mention my record."

"That's good," she said. "It was long time ago anyway."

"I know," he said. "The interviewer was a real stiff though!" Tom let his hard lips crack a smile. Jayne giggled. He imagined her standing against the wall, cradling the phone in her ear and twiddling the cable around her fingertips. But he knew she would still be in her bed, the credit on the call soon to run out.

"Oh really? I can't wait to see you and you tell me about it!" She laughed again, and that sweet sound cut Tom into pieces. His ran his rough tongue along his lips, his beard leaving a taste of tobacco in his mouth that had stained his facial hair a dirty yellow. He hadn't smoked since Jayne had come home from the doctors, but that craving had never left him. He just got better at ignoring it.

"I don't have to take the job you know," Tom said with a sigh. "I would rather stay at home and take care of you myself. We can take the hit on the money. We can live off what I got from the Rig. We can..." Jayne cut him off.

"Don't be saying things like that Sash." *Sash. He hated that nickname but she loved it. "Sasquatch" Aka Big hairy bastard.* "You were going nuts being at home with me, and the carers help so much. We can't just 'survive' off the little money we have left. I wouldn't want that for you, or for me. I feel like a burden enough." The traffic began to move, but Tom was focused on the feeling of his throat being sewed up. A blaring horn snapped his attention back to the road and he waved to the animated prick in a Porsche behind him. "You aren't a burden baby." A small silence then. "How're you feeling today?"

"Oh you know me, I keep going." He could tell she was smiling, and again, his throat sewed shut that little tighter. "The job will be good for you."

"I don't want it Jayne. I don't do well for long periods of time in the night. Messes with my head." The two went quiet again. Then she spoke.

"I know Sash. Since what happened with Brad, I..." *Brad.* The name cut through him.

"Sorry I have to go," he said bluntly. "I'll be there soon." Tom hung up the phone. He didn't need to think about that. He didn't need to think about the sound of screams in the midnight sea. He was reminded of them enough.

3

Evening

He pulled up to their house and let the engine idle a few moments so the heating stayed on. It was winter, and the snow was due to fall any day now, and the bite of the wind was a constant reminder that the hot summer and picnics in the park were a faded memory. The large trees that lined their street, once so vibrant and green and teaming with birds and squirrels and all kinds of other critters, was now stripped and barren, like lonely skeletons standing by the road side, trying to lean down and touch those living underneath it with its wooden finger tips. He pushed the door open and brought in Jayne's bags and placed them in the living room next to her bed. He put the fire on, lighting it with a couple of matches and then putting on a low setting whilst the logs burned and popped in a growing glow of red, like pulsing veins of lava pushing through the wood giving way to thousands of tiny dancers dressed in blue and yellow.

Back outside, Jayne sat bundled up in her coat with her scarf around her head. She had asked the nurse draw her eyebrows on for her, which Tom thought to be strange. He thought a moment of rubbing them off and re doing them, making her look constantly surprised, but he didn't think that would be appropriate. He opened the door, trying to shield Jayne as much as possible from the cold breeze.

The sun had fully dropped below the horizon now, painting the sky in dark reds and yellows, bleeding away from a dull blue. The moon in its full phase, looking over them. Tom eyed the sky line as he carried Jayne into the house. It reminded him of those long nights at sea, where the night sky was bursting with billions of tiny lights like a black canvas left in the hands of a toddler armed with glitter and glue.

He got her in and carried her onto the bed. Undressing her, he wiped her down with wet wipes and re dressed her in her nightgown. She had been sleeping most of the journey back home, and even him carrying her didn't wake her fully. She stirred a little and cracked him a small smile, but then sleep took her once more. He tucked her in the metal framed bed, got her bed pan and her crutches next to the railings should she need to get out for some reason. He fluffed her pillows and put some lavender oil on the duvet. She always loved the smell of lavender. That, and roses, but he was fresh out of that one. Finally, he placed her slippers over her feet and tucked them under the covers, and hooked up the IV drip and the heart monitors to her. She looked a little like a robot; wires poking out here, there and everywhere, and the sight of her made his stone face begin to weep. He never cried when she was awake. He wouldn't let her see him like that, so he bottled it up for moments like this, when he could allow himself to grieve for his wife that still breathed. Only a few tears though, never anything more than that. He couldn't open the dam fully or he might not be able to close it again. Carl's voice pushed into his mind.

"The shadows. They can bring things from your mind back to life. Have you ever spoken to a professional about what happened?" Tom shook the sound of him away and stuck something on the TV. He listened quietly to the sound of the heart monitor beeping and took out his journal from the side of the bed. He had always written down his thoughts. Something that helped him get through the months at sea. Something that stopped him diving in it at times too.

Sunday 22:03

Home

Jayne is in bed now. I'm glad she didn't have too much of a bad time at the hospital. She's such a strong woman. God knows I would be telling everyone how much that fucking camera hurt. There must be a better way of finding tumours in the stomach right? Rather than a damn camera?

The chemo is kicking her ass. She hasn't been sick much, but her hair has finally gone, and she is so weak and sleeps most of the time.

She wants me to go for this job. I don't want too really; I want to stay with her. What if something happens and I'm not here? I know her sister is only a few minutes away, but still.

She does want me to get out the house though. And to be honest, the break would be nice.

Tom looked at this last line. "The break would be nice?" He scalded himself, almost disgusted at what he had written. He tore the page out and threw it on the fire. He called himself a prick and wrote something new -

Sunday 22:09

Home

I got the job. Jayne's doing as well as she can. Some shit on Tv. I could kill for a drink. Goodnight.

- Sash

4

Welcome To Welch Mill

"Coffee machine is busted." Jerry said, his unbuttoned shirt giving way to his flabby neck. Tom looked at him with amazement. There was no way someone as 'big boned,' as Jerry should be wearing a shirt that tight. Let alone walking around the warehouse on the night shift.

"Got it." Tom said, looking at the broken machine.

"So if you want some, you'll have to bring your own."

"Gotcha," Tom laughed, remembering the pack of supplies in his car.

"I'm sure I will," Tom eyed up the cupboards, seeing if he could salvage a beverage, courtesy of the company. He began pulling doors open, looking through the tea-stained cupboards in the warehouse canteen. He pulled old cardboard boxes out of different styled tea bags. Most of them empty: regular, extra strong. The De Caff teabags were still in their plastic wrapping, and Tom wasn't that desperate yet. His fingers reached all the way to the back and he pulled out a small box of green tea. He gave them a glance and took one out, then flipped on the kettle that looked more used than a £5 whore in Amsterdam. Jimmy eyed the green tea bag sitting in the cup. Tom sensed the glare. "What?" He said, a little more defensively than he intended. He didn't want to come off as a dick on his first job. Especially not to his new boss.

"Nothing." Jimmy said. "The last guy we had doing the night watch security shift was into the herbal stuff too. He was a little..." Jimmy made a circle with his finger around his temple. "Squirrely." Tom tried to hold back the smile beginning to crack behind his thick brown beard. Jimmy's face stayed stoic and flat, so Tom buried the smirk behind the bush of tight whiskers.

"Squirrely?" He said.

"Yeah." Jimmy nodded. "But, working a shift like this? Alone in your post watching the monitors? It can get to a person sometimes."

"Really?" Tom said. His skin beginning to flush. He thought again about the bullshit interview he had the day before. How they were trying to pull his leg. It seemed everyone was in on the gag. "How so?" Jimmy went to speak, his large belly rising as he struggled to take in a full breath. The man must have easily weighed close to thirty stone, and if Tom smelt as bad as he did, he wouldn't want to take a breath too deep either.

"Well, you're the fifth guy we've had in the past few months doing this work. I don't get it," Jimmy said. "The money is decent, the hours are long, yeah, but you get the radio, the canteen and get to relax. Just, for some reason, no one seems to want to stay very long. It's annoying actually. Finding new staff all the time." Tom felt the room grow a little warmer.

"Why does nobody seem to want the job? Is it the isolation? I worked away for years on the oil rigs in the Atlantic. My own company is what I prefer. People are arseholes. No disrespect."

"None taken," Jimmy said, resting his sausage fingers on the stained counter. "Two guys left without giving notice, and the last guy, the one who liked the herbal tea, was found in a bad way." Tom's ears pricked.

"A bad way?" Tom eyed Jimmy who shrugged.

"He was always a little odd. Was found trying to pull something out of Gretta."

"Gretta?"

"The mail feeder." Jimmy said. "Big fucking rattling thing in the middle of the warehouse in between the mail racks. Can sort and spit out over one thousand envelopes sizes A4 to A6 in less than a minute," Jimmy said almost proudly. "Poor bastard was found by the cleaner in the morning with his arm up to his elbow in the mouth of Gretta. She had almost chewed it off."

"That sounds terrible." Tom said coldly. Jimmy shrugged once more. Maybe getting his exercise in for the day.

"He was a weird guy. Was still alive too when the cleaner found him. Taken away in the ambulance. Kept on talking about 'The Night.' Fuck if I know. Guy was a freak. Ex junkie. Been in prison for armed robbery a few years back. Was found with LSD in his bloodstream. Go figure."

"You normally hire ex-cons?" Tom asked.

"Most of the time in fact," Jerry said. "The company is part of some government scheme. We hire those trying to get their shit together, and the government pays seventy five percent of the wages."

"That's good," Tom said. "What were the others like?"

"The employees? One was an ex-coke dealer, the other, a woman, was into fraud." Tom smiled slightly.

"Giving people a second chance. I like that. But the LSD thing? I knew a guy once that fell into a bush and thought he was time itself. Spent three hours masturbating until the police got hold of him." Both men laughed loudly. "What was the guy's name? The one who decided to feed his arm to Gretta?"

"Fuck if I remember," Jimmy snorted. "Wallace? Walter? Willy? We have that many different staff here, nobody can keep track of the new faces." Jerry eyed him and smiled slightly. "Speaking of convictions," Jerry said, eyeing him. Tom felt the room grow a little warmer. "Don't worry about it. I know you've got your shit together," he said, almost condescendingly. Tom went to speak but the kettle clicked off. "Your water is ready." Jimmy said, quickly changing the subject, exhaling a steady blow breath smelling of takeaways and cigarettes.

5

Welcome To Welch Mill

They walked from the canteen through the corridor. It wasn't well lit, and the only light coming from a few single lonely bulbs suspended from the ceiling by thick wiring like glow in the dark spiders. Portraits of employees and message boards hung on the walls. Tom noticed a fundraiser was happening for a local cancer charity. *'Race for life.'*

"You got a pen?" Tom said, holding his hand out. Jimmy turned with a grunt. He was panting. He must be sweating his back out now in the fifteen feet they've walked from the canteen.

"What?" He said. He looked upon it with horror. "You don't want to go running do you?" He gasped.

"I like being outdoors, doing some exercise. Like I said, I was on the Oil Rigs. Only dead men stay idle."

"True," Jimmy said, scratching his large chin, digging his fingers between the acne and patches of unshaven stubble. "Not for me though." *I've noticed,* Tom thought. Jimmy studied the board a little closer. His big eyes bulging under his heavy rimmed glasses.

"Well if you want to join, you gotta put your name down."
He handed Tom a pen. "It's a good cause though. I usually join them
afterwards for a couple of drinks down the pub." Tom wrote his
name on the A4 paper underneath the flyer.

"I want to book that night off," Tom said, handing the pen
back. Jimmy laughed.

"Jesus, not even done your first night and you're making
demands. You'll be after my job next." Tom didn't share the big
man's laughter. He tapped the date with his pen, holding Jimmy's
gaze. His smile faded.

"September 8th. I 'm taking that day off," he said stoically.

"Remind me in the morning okay? I'll see what I can do for
you." The two continued on through the corridor. It wasn't very
long, maybe a hundred feet or so, and they passed a few offices
which still had their monitors still on standby with big sticky notes
with big black ink saying 'LOG OFF DON'T SWITCH OFF,' in good
passive aggressive office fashion, the screensavers light pushing
through the darkened windows. They got to the opening at the end
and Jimmy pushed open the double doors. Both stepped through
and he held out his hand at the large open space in front of him. His
face painted in a wide grin under the dull light, like a slave trader
telling his new arrivals they were going to work in the land of milk

and honey, the look of pride slapped across his face.

"This is *my* baby. *My* creation." Jimmy let out a satisfied grin, and Tom half expected him to either burst into tears, break into song, or touch Tom's shoulder with a solemn look in his eye. None of which Tom particularly welcomed.

"It's big," Tom said flatly, looking into the warehouse filled with rows upon rows of shelves of different boxes and bundles of paper. A sleeping forklift truck sat alone in the far corner under a florescent light strip which flickered and blinked. Tom eyed the small bar to the left. It was waist height and made of white chipped wood. Behind it, several large panes of glass and a door leading into the room behind. Through the glass, a chair and several monitors propped up. The view of the security stream visible from where he was standing.

"I'm guessing that's where I'm going to be calling home for the rest of the night?" Tom queried, nodding to his nocturnal palace with his cap.

"Indeed. That's gonna be you." Jimmy stood back up right after taking a rest against the wall. "Some more things I gotta show you first." The two men meandered through the warehouse shop floor. Jimmy taking pleasure in showing him the alphabetised freight, mail, optics and sorting panels. "This is where the magic really happens," he said, gesturing to a bunch of yellow and white sacks made of rough woven plastic, dangling from metal hooks like dismembered ball sacks. "The sorters get mail from all over the country, and it all comes out of this machine right here." He tapped on a large metal machine with a huge open mouth, baskets and mesh wiring at the bottom, loose letters and documents clinging for dear life on the edge, less they fall onto the ground.

"I'm guessing this is Gretta?" Tom said, inspecting the machine for remnants of bone and finger nails. Jimmy nodded.

"You guess correctly. She may look gentle, but she can bite. As well as the last weirdo you're taking over from, we've had another couple of guys loose a finger or two in this thing. One guy mangled his hand up really bad. Nothing a nice redundancy package can't fix though." Jimmy slapped Tom's shoulder. Tom's boulder like shoulders didn't budge, nor did his stern face.

"Was he okay?"

"Of a fashion," he said. "He had to learn to jerk off with the other hand, if that makes you feel any better." It didn't make Tom feel any better. Considering the state-of-the-art machinery and set up of the place, and how reputable the company was, it seemed like a little circus show of horrors. He had been here for less than an hour and already learned of several accidents. Tom wondered how they hadn't been sued or closed down, but he didn't figure he should bring up such things on his first shift. He wondered what else had gone on and why the manager was being so coy about the whole thing.

"This place pays weekly right?" He said as Jimmy continued to show him the wonderers of the warehouse.

"It sure does. Or monthly if you prefer."

"Weekly is fine." Tom stopped and sighed. "Look, I'm gonna need a week up front if that's okay? I hate to ask but, the wife..." Jimmy stopped mid shelf fingering and turned to Tom. Tom stood stoic, trying not to look too desperate. He never asked for money, ever. But a time comes when a man has to swallow his pride and ask for help, and here he was, swallowing it up by the spoonful. "I'm sorry," Tom said after a moment of silence. "I just..."

"No, that's completely okay Tom," Jimmy said. "I understand. I'll see what I can do for you." Tom felt his heart beat a little slower. A feeling of warmth pushed through him and for the first time in a while, he felt a blanket of genuine warmth wrap around him, and dare he think, he cracked a smile under those dim lights.

"Thanks Boss. It'll help a lot."

"You've got a big heart Tom. I can see that. Nothing wrong

with sharing a little kindness. Not enough of that these days." He moved in a little closer and gripped Tom's hand, tightly. "You'll do really well here my man." He surveyed the racking and boxes. "Yeah, you'll fit *right* in here."

The two continued to the last part of the warehouse. A small door set at the back which was locked. It looked as though the room had been thrown up in a haste; the walls were thin and made of plywood. Roughly painted and had no windows. Jimmy pulled out a set of keys and unlocked the door. Inside was the loneliest damn toilet Tom had ever seen. The thing looked so cold Tom thought if he went on it for too long the base would strip off the top layer of ass hair and skin. Tom figured he would not be using the shitter tonight. The last thing he wanted was to be sat frozen to the bowl mid shit, unable to run and stop intruders from ransacking the safe in the boss's office. How the hell would he explain *that* mess when he got home?

"I personally like to use this when the place is quiet," Jimmy said. "It's small, secluded and is locked. It isn't much, but it's more solitary than the others you'll find near the canteen on the hallway we came through to get here. Most of the workers use it too. Let's face it, no one likes others hearing them shit." The idea wasn't appealing to Tom, like him going to the cheap whore all the guys had already ran through, but he smiled and nodded anyway. Jimmy closed the door. "Now, the part you have been waiting for." Jimmy

began walking, the smell of sweat stinging Tom's nose. "Your

office!"

6

Welcome To Welch Mill

The skin around Tom's ball sack tightened and his breath pushed from his mouth in a puff of smoke. He zipped up his thick jacket up tight and dipped his cap down. He was thankful he wore extra layers before coming out, the winter air biting his skin.

"Cold?" Jimmy said, hulking his huge feet along the ground.

"Freezing."

"You get used to it. Trust me." *Easy for you to say walking around with all that blubber.*

"Don't you have the heating on or anything?" Tom asked, pressing his beard down into his neck. Jimmy shook his head.

"Sorry kid." Tom's nostrils flared. *Kid. Don't call me a fucking kid.* "Thermostat's been busted for a little while. Just in time for December. Merry Christmas to us hey? There's a small heater in your security room. Nothing fancy, but should stop the icicles from forming in your nostrils." They walked around the wooden bar and through a singular door in between the large glass panes. Tom saw filing cabinets lining the walls, an old ticking clock that seemed to be busted, to his delight. A couple of desks with dead monitors, reflecting his etched ghostly silhouette back at him. On one of desks bore a small placard that read 'YOU DON'T NEED TO BE MAD TO WORK HERE, BUT IT HELPS!' and another, more macabre one 'LEAVE YOUR SOUL AT THE DOOR. YOU WON'T NEED IT HERE.' How to sell a place to a guy. At the back of the office stood another door, brown and looked like it wouldn't hold back a pissed off mouse, let alone an intruder, with the word 'SEC RITY' written on the front. The 'U' was missing.

"Where's the rest of the sign?" Tom pointed out. Jimmy, who had pulled put a bar of chocolate from fuck knows where, studied the sign under the harsh UV strip lighting. He shrugged.

"No 'U'. I suppose the 'U' isn't important. As long as someone sits in that room and watches the monitors, it doesn't matter what the sign reads." Tom felt a little offended, like he wasn't needed. But he had a point. It could have easily read 'Secretary,' which he supposed when there's nobody home and he's the only one there, it's pretty much the same thing.

His mind wandered back to Jayne. She had been a secretary in her old job before she had gotten too sick. Tom had finished at the rig and was working as a mechanic. The hours were long and he was often exhausted when he got home and stinking of motor oil. Jayne's doctors had said it was just fatigue, stress, maybe even a little bit of the flu. But when the 'flu' got didn't go away, it turned out to be much worse, and Tom hung up his tools to be at home for her in the day time hours. He didn't need sleep. He never had. A couple of hours and a powernap through the day had been what he was used to when working those long months out at sea. His doctor said he was heading towards a heart attack through stress and his nervous system at risk of burning out. But he never listened to the advice of the doctors. Jayne's illness was a prime example, but it started earlier than that from how his mother had believed in them so avidly. Until a Tuesday afternoon check-up turned into something sinister growing inside of her, missed over and over, until she vanished into herself, Gin her new best friend.

He shook the memory of his mother from his mind. Why had she popped into his head? He hadn't thought of her in months, longer even. God had it been *that* long? It must have been close to five years this coming Christmas, when she sank half a bottle of *Gordons Dry* and got behind the wheel of her car –

"Are you listening?" Jimmy scowled.

"Yeah," Tom hurried, scratching the back of his head, letting the memory of mangled metal and broken headlights fade from his mind. Jimmy eyed him with those reddening eyes and those puffy sacks hanging underneath them. He gestured to the single chair propped up against a wooden desk with three monitors with split screens in front of it. They were black and white, except for the canteen which was in colour, the lights still on.

"This is the epicentre of security of my warehouse," he enunciated the last part like he was speaking about a prized possession, a child, a lover or the last bag of Doritos. "Here," he made a sweeping motion with his hands, like he had discovered the lost treasure of Horus in the Valley of Kings, "is where you will spend your shift, looking over these monitors with explicit attention. Anything moves, you check it out. There's a flashlight in the drawer with a tonne of batteries, and there's a kettle and sink over there," he pointed to a small fridge and wash basin. "We don't keep it stocked though, so I imagine you brought your own things?"

"I did. It's in my car out back. I'll get my bag before you leave."

"Wonderful news. Don't want you falling asleep on me. Gotta keep my baby in check."

"Yes Sir." Tom said bluntly.

"Sir was my dad and he was a prick. Call me Jimmy." He said, puffing out his chest.

"Thanks," Tom said sourly, "but I prefer Sir. I think familiarity breeds contemptment, and I'm not into letting myself get too close. No offence." Jimmy was taken back. He obviously wasn't used to being told *no.*

"I see. Any reason for that?" Jimmy waited for an answer. Tom took in a breath. He heard the swooping of waves and thunder. The wild air against his hair and the calls of a drowning man in the black tirading sea.

"Experience."

7

The Shadow on the Monitor

Tom walked alone out of the SEC RITY office and through the warehouse. He meandered down the hallways past the empty offices of Payroll, Human Resources, Witch Craft, and into the main lobby, where customers came to collect missed parcels, mail, lost children, and pressed his lanyard against the small black box at the entrance and pushed open the set of double glass doors. The night air hit him like a truck, and he could see the night sky suffocated by black clouds, the last remnants of the evening sun disappearing behind a snaking black claw in the night sky. Considering he had the cloud coverage, the night air bit his balls worse than foreplay gone wrong. He walked along the walk way lined with dull grass, the sound of his boots clicking on the asphalt. He reached his numbing fingers into his pocket and pulled out his car keys towards his truck. He clicked the button and the machine's headlights lit up.

Hello again. That was a quick shift? Did you miss me.

The sound of his wife in his ear. He shook her away. He didn't need any distractions right now. The first night away from her, leaving her alone in bed, against all his morality. But when you have wolves knocking at your door asking for bills to be paid and there no more 'Just one more month' chances left, you gotta ignore the pain in your chest and do what makes sense. Tom pulled at the door handle and the gathering frost crunched, relinquishing its icy grip before popping open where he climbed into the driver's seat.

"Don't feel bad," Jayne had said as he was leaving earlier that night. *"I know you don't want to go, but you're going crazy being at home with me all the time. You'll be fine, and so will I. If I need anything, I can call my sister. You get out for a while and enjoy the first shift at the new job. You'll love it. You need it. I love you."*

He bit down on his lip hard, trying to stop the rawness creeping in. He slammed his hand on the steering wheel and gripped it tightly, pressing his head into the leather. He breathed long and hard, remembering what his councillor had said. *Breathe, and breathe a little more until it passes.* So he did just that, and after a few moments, the pain subsided, the thought of his wife being without him, or more likely, him being without her.

He reached in and took out his rucksack from the passenger seat. It was filled with snacks, a metal flask of coffee and a couple of tea bags and a bottle of milk just to be safe. He had his journal too, to make notes of interesting things he would see on the cameras. Conversation topics for when he got home. God knows they needed something new to talk about *other* than the Cancer. He threw the bag over his shoulder and shut the door. He checked for his mobile phone and battery pack, fingers pushing past the packet of biscuits and chicken bites, he found it there tucked at the bottom and breathed a sigh of relief, a plume of ghostly smoke clinging to the inside of the wind shield.

Tom walked back to the entrance of the building. It stood in front of his home for the night, taking it all in as the night air numbed his face. The building was big and made of iron cladding, like a mountain of black obscuring anything and everything the closer you got to it. Thankfully it was only one story. There was the lower deck, which you needed to take a ride in a rickety elevator to get too, but that was where the uncollected parcels without a return address was kept. After six months they were either destroyed, or if it was something good, auctioned off at the annual Christmas party. He's been told by Jimmy that someone got a Rolex last year. Work all year in a job you hate for the chance of something good at the end. And people called *him* crazy for picking the night shift. The money wasn't terrible however, so he convinced himself anyway. It was a little over minimum wage, but the option for overtime was always there, and the work wasn't hard. Watch a bunch of monitors for a few hours, read a book, watch a movie. How hard could it be? He felt the baseball bat in his carryall digging into his shoulder. *Just in case,* He thought, and the feel of that metallic hitting stick made him feel that little bit safer. He took out his lanyard as he got to the front entrance. It was wrapped awkwardly around his neck and arm, so he dropped the ruck sack to the ground to stop him garrotting himself as he took out his pass.

He heard footsteps quickly behind him. He span around on the spot, his heart jackhammering. Nothing in the darkness moved, the night air seeming a little warmer as his face started to flush with blood. He didn't call out to the darkness. Only fucking morons did that. He'd seen his share of horror movies, and he wasn't in the habit of walking into the woods alone because he heard something moving.   He waited a moment. Something moved in the distance in the tree line behind the car park. It was small, dimly lit by the street lighting of the car park. A moment later, he saw it emerge from the distance.

A dog.

Tom meandered back to the SEC RITY room where he found Jimmy looking over the monitors.

"Do you see it?" Tom asked, gesturing to the screens. Jimmy moved next to him, his heavy weight creaking the table.

"See what?"

"The dog on the monitor, in the distance. Little thing. Thin too." Jimmy eyed the screens again. He shook his head.

"No," he said, "I don't see anything." Tom queried the big man.

"You sure? It was right there." Tom pointed to where the dog had been. Jimmy again looked at him for longer than was comfortable.

"You probably did see one," he said. "We get them from time to time, all sorts actually: badgers, deer, foxes. All kinds of critters. If they come to the building, do me a favour and don't feed them. You'll end up like the last guy, screaming to high hell about the damn dogs he kept feeding on shift."

"Like the last guy?" Tom scrunched his face a little. "You mean Wallace?"

"Something like that." Jimmy scratched his receding hairline. "The guy was seen coming into work in his last few shifts with bags and bags of fresh meat for the damn things. He was warned about it a few times." He put a sausage finger on the monitor. "They're fucking huge those woods. Go on for miles in all sorts of directions. All sorts of things go on in there." Jimmy pulled out a bundle of papers in a binder and began flicking through them on the desk. Tom wanted to pry further, but held his tongue. Didn't want him thinking he was turning squirrely on his first night.

The two went over some more of the checks, the HR Policy and the fire evacuation procedure. Who to call if the cameras go off? Who *not* to call should anything else go wrong? "I have had the pleasure of being on call for your first week. Carl, the guy who interviewed you, doesn't like to be pestered every five minutes by the newbies. I'm not happy about it, but I get paid for it. Anything you need to ask about: questions, queries, where the toilet paper is kept, give me a call." He looked up from the bundle of paperwork and gave a slight smile. "But don't take the piss."

"I'll be fine Sir."

"Wonderful." Jimmy packed the papers up. "I'll see you in the morning. Have a good shift."

8

The First Night

Monday 21:30

SEC RITY ROOM

I honestly thought I thought I was going to throw up at the smell of that fat bastard's body odour. I mean, I don't shower every day or use deodorant all the time, but Jesus, that guy needs Febreze lined clothing.

Anyway. First night is underway. Got the game on my phone. England are winning, which is surprising. Thankfully I remembered my charger, because it would have been a long night otherwise. The monitors are pretty quiet at the moment. I saw a dog too. It was a skinny thing, maybe a Rottie or something, but still I saw it sniffing around the truck. Maybe I dropped something on my way in. It had gone by the time Jimmy had come around though. Little bugger probably took a quick shit and ran away. I'll have to watch my step when I leave in the morning. Place is a little cold but nothing I can't handle. But I gotta remember to bring some extra layers with the weather set to change.

I keep thinking about you babe. I'm watching the clock and trying to resist the urge to call you and check in. I know you'll be alright. It's just a few hours and I'll be home again to make you some breakfast.

I did hear something strange before though, and to be honest, I don't really want to write it down, but I will anyway so we can talk about it when I get *home. I could have sworn when I was getting out of my car and walking to the building earlier, that I heard footsteps behind me. I turned around, ready to beat the fuck out of some little punk who thought I'd be an easy target, but only the wind met me. The wind, and the trees in the distance. Either I imagined it, or they have some big fucking squirrels around here.*

He put the pen down and giggled to the thought of a squirrel running around the car park in a pair of size twelve steel toe capped boots. He sat back and watched England play the last few minutes of the game against Switzerland from the iPlayer. He hadn't watched it as he needed some sleep earlier in the day, and had avoided all social media, not like he went on much anyway, to not risk seeing the result. They were winning one nil so far, and a few moments later, as Tom had cracked open his Thermos and poured himself a cup of coffee, the game ended and Tom turned it off and put the phone on standby mode, before checking if he had any missed calls. He saw there were none, and checked his voicemail just to be sure, before putting it away in his jacket pocket.

Tom had experienced the quiet before when he was out at sea. He had been in the middle of nowhere: no wind, no stars and just the slightest lick of the gentle sea touching the foundations of the rig. But as he sat there in his chair, coffee in hand, he could hear the sound of his heart beating in his ears. He looked over the monitors, the grey static picture looking back at him. Tom remembered something else he wanted to write in the journal, to say something about the game. He pulled it open and got to work.

Also,

The game was pretty good, E gla d play we

"Fuck," he hissed as the pen ran out of ink. He hoped he had brought another one and rummaged through his bag to fish another biro or hell, a damn pencil would do. He fingered through the bottom past the array of snacks and goodies he had with him, but there was no pen. He wasn't desperate enough to write about England not playing terrible to use a sachet of tomato sauce, however the thought did cross his mind. Instead, he sat back and looked around the desk for something to write with. He cracked open the drawer on the cabinet and smiled. To his heart's content, there was a nice crisp biro in black to write down his thoughts. He picked it up and went to write. As he closed the draw, the pen slipped from his fingers and he crouched to get it. He mustn't have been concentrating, because he lifted his head and banged it on the bottom of the protruding drawer, a small cut appearing at the top of his skull. He bit down and hissed, then let out a long, seething "Motherfucker," before leaning back in the chair. Tom leant to close the drawer when he saw his colossal head had dislodged the bottom. Again, he called himself a fucking idiot, knowing this would no doubt come out of his pay cheque, but as he looked further, he saw something-

The drawer had a false bottom, and under it was what looked to be a small stack of papers. Tom put his hand in and fished out the bundle. It was coated in a light dust, and he blew on it, sending particles across the monitors. The wedges were frayed and browned, and the spine of the book was well worn.

"The Space Between," he mouthed the name of the story. The cover was like the old readers digest books you could order. No picture, just a leather dust jacket with the title on the front. No author either. Tom opened it, the smell of damp and moth balls pushing into his nostrils.

"As I wandered through the howling night under the midnight sun, I found myself in a precarious position. One not of

contemptment, but of fear. A primal fear that one doesn't inherently understand, but is all too familiar when its icy fingernails trace up your spine.

"Alone I wander through this wood. Dark and void of life. Like the winter hath stripped all its delights and warmth, leaving only a skeleton of its former self. A shell, if you will. A shell of its former glory."

What Tom could surmise; it was the story of a boy who had lost his friend in a large forest. Either lost, or he had been abandoned and was trying to find his way home. It was macabre at best. He put the book down a moment and gave a quick look over the monitors. All still on that black and white screen. He flicked through the cameras: the basement, the offices, the warehouse and then finally the car park. Nothing of note.

Tom dug into his duffel bag and pulled out a couple of small snacks. More out of boredom than hunger, and dug into some biscuits.   He opened up his journal, touching the cut at the top of his head. He wouldn't need stitches, but the morning shower would hurt like a bitch. He moved over to a fresh page, after crossing out the shit about England playing well. *Not meant to be* boys he thought to himself with a small smile. He took out a pack of Nicotine gum from his pocket and started to chew.

He held his hand steady a moment, unable to bring himself to mark it. The blank page eyeing him like it had teeth. His pen hesitated over the first line, like about to step into freshly laid snow. You want the first imprint to be good, and he didn't want to fuck it up on the first word. *How the hell do writers do this*? He thought to himself, thinking of all the books he had read, amazed how they all started out as empty space.

Only a few hours in. Not long left to go now.

P.S. I hit my head. It fucking hurt, but I found a book which I might give a read. Seems to have been written by some pretentious bastard, but I don't know why it was there? Maybe one of the old workers had left it there. Maybe it's actually filled with nude pictures and it was his hiding place for them?

He put the pen down. That would do for now. He would come back to it when he thought of something else to say to himself, or more, to make notes to tell Jayne later.

9

Dawn

"How was the first night?" Jerry said, opening the door at 7am sharp. Tom was a little further into the book he found, so engrossed in it that he didn't hear the big man come in. The boss eyed him annoyed. "You should be watching the monitors, not a book." Again, Tom didn't stir, staring at the book, like he was sleeping with his eyes open. Jerry moved to him, half wondering if he was dead with his eyes open. He looked over his shoulder to see if there were some nudie photos hidden in there which Tom didn't feel like sharing. "What you got there?" He said, moving closer. Tom could feel the breath on his neck, but he still didn't pull his attention from the pages, his knuckles turning white, digging into the leather cover. Jerry's eyes licked the pages, and his heart skipped a beat. "Hey!" He bolstered, kicking the chair Tom was in. Tom flinched, rubbing his eyes, breathing quickly like he had been shocked by a raw wire when putting up the Christmas tree.

"Hey boss," he said, running his hand through his hair and beard. "You been there long?"

The drive home was as shit as you could imagine. The first night shift, the busy roads that kept you from your bed, and the fumes you were running on, trying to stay awake before the copious amounts of caffeine in your system began to drop. A red light, then another red light. Tom beeped his horn at a slow motorist and revved the beast's engine loudly, digging the needle into the red. The car in front waved him a *fuck you* then took off. Tom continued quickly behind it, before turning off the junction before the motorway. He didn't need to go on that in rush hour, so he took the longer route. It would be faster, less well known. He never used a sat nav, he found them to be lazy. So many people got caught in unnecessary traffic because they relied on a computer to tell you where to go. Tom however knew this part of town like the back of his hand; the back routes always got him where he needed to be without being stuck behind Miss fucking Daisy.

He got onto the long stretch of dirt road that ran parallel to the motorway where he could see hundreds of parked cars. The morning was still pretty dark, so the motorway looked like a million red eyes blaring into the morning twilight. Tom pulled out his phone and quickly checked if there was any missed calls. Nothing. No messages either. He checked the road in front of him, cruising with one hand on the wheel, his attention elsewhere. He punched in the number for his voicemail and looked up, raising the phone to his ear.

A dog! A fucking dog!

Tom stomped on the brakes of the beast as hard as he could, sending his mobile flying along the ground and slamming into the side of the passenger door footwell. The back end of the beast slid as the wheels locked, the dashboard lighting up with the ABS sensor, the brakes releasing and tightening quicker than a virgins first orgasm. The dog in his headlights didn't move, it only stood there as the giant hunk of metal corralled towards it. Tom bit down, his arms straight, his body tight, twisting the steering wheel, banking a hard right to the wrong side of the road, just narrowly missing the animal. The engine began to stall, heading straight for a farmer's brick wall that lined a huge empty field filled with low mist. He slammed his foot on the clutch, threw the beast into first and pulled the clutch back up and revved the engine, forcing the rev counter right into the red for the second time that morning, the hood of the pick-up stopping inches from the brick wall. Tom held his gaze on the wall lit up by the bright lights for a second, panting heavily. Once he caught his breath and was sure he hadn't shit himself, he looked in the rear-view mirror. The dog was gone.

He arrived home around twenty minutes later, his feet crunching on the fallen snow as he made his way to the front door. The lights were still off which was a good thing. It meant that Jayne hadn't been getting up during the night, or if she had, she had been strong enough to turn the lights on and off. Tom put his key in the lock and stepped inside. The house was quiet, the small sound of the television set still on in the background. The smell of the gas fire in the air, the heat making the home a cosy little number. He stepped into the living room, knocking the snow from his boots which gathered on his heels. Jayne was still in bed sleeping soundly. He moved quietly and kissed her on the top of her head, running his fingers over the smoothness. He eyed her a moment, his heart catching in his throat. No matter how many times he saw her, she looked so beautiful, even though the illness was slowly eating her alive. The chemo was helping, and they had seen a lot of progress and regression of the cancer, but that didn't mean her clothes fit well. She hadn't eaten a substantial meal in months, surviving on bits of soup and when she could stomach it, a slice of bread or two. Tom had lost weight too as a result. No point making a huge meal when there's only him to eat it. He changed her bed pan and got her morning medication ready with a drink of water next to her bed for when she wakes up.

Tom kicked off his boots and lay his head down on the couch

next to her, flicking through the tv channels with no real interest. He couldn't wait to see his wife open her eyes again so they could talk about what had happened on his shift, or lack of. The heat from the gas fire continued to swell and grow, melting the frost that gathered around his beard, his head nestling into the cushions, before his heavy eyes finally closed.

Pans and cutlery rattled around him. Tom opened his eyes lazily. It was still dark. Had he slept all day? Panic struck him. He needed to feed Jayne, give her medication. He sat up and saw her bed to be empty. His stomach felt like it had been plunged into an icy river. He got to his feet. He stumbled. He was woozy. Was he drunk? No, he hadn't touched the stuff since the oil rigs. Since Brad. The room was a blanket of darkness. The kitchen door was closed, only a band of golden light pushing through the darkness that encased him. Tom pushed the door open. "Jayne?" He whispered. "Is that you?"

The door opened and Tom felt the splash of sea water on his skin. Icy wind ripped through him and he closed his thick high vis jacket around him, zipping it up as fast as his thick cumbersome gloves would allow him. The tirading black sea smashed against the rig, huge waves of the abyss slamming and soaking him in a drenching downpour. The lights of the rig were flashing red, and Tom knew what that meant.

Man Overboard!

Tom raced, still falling over his own feet, the smell of whisky on his breath. The hard steel flooring digging into his knees and into his elbows as he crawled. He gripped the railings and eyed the scurrying men below him on the lower deck, pointing search lights into the never-ending sea. A flash of high vis in the water before it vanished again below the surface. Men and women throwing buoys and life rings out as far as they could, trying to command the flailing body in the water to grab hold.

Tom bolted awake, his arms flailing like he was sinking below the surface of dark water. Tom's face slapped with worry, sweating and panting. He was drenched. He hadn't taken his coat off from outside and he was lying in a pool of his own sweat.

"Bad dream?" Jayne said, nursing a cup of water, concern on her face. Tom nodded, running his hands through his hair and beard. "Want to talk about it?" She asked. Tom shook his head.

"I need a shower."

A few minutes later, Tom walked downstairs with his hair combed back, his beard washed and his teeth brushed. He looked less of a sasquatch and more of a groomed ape. He walked into the living room with his top off in a pair of loose gym shorts. His wife eyed him from her bed, nearly choking on the bowl of soup she was making her way through.

"Jesus," she said. "Should I be worried? You never walk around like that anymore! I was wondering if all that size under your clothing was just padding!" Tom let out a smile.

"I was hot. I needed to cool down."

"You can turn the fire down," Jayne smiled. "I don't mind." Tom looked out of the window and saw the frost gathering on the glass.

"No," he said. "I'll be fine. You need to keep warm." Tom moved and gave her a kiss on the head, and they shared a look of contentment between them. He gave Jayne the tv remote and checked the time. He had a couple of hours before he had to set out for work. Night shift number two. He was thinking he might actually make it the full week before he knew it. He made a cup of coffee and sat next to Jayne as she settled on a game show where people guess how much money is in boxes.

"I hate this show," she said, putting the remote down. Tom eyed her curiously.

"The hell you put it on for then?" He giggled. Jayne

shrugged.

"It's as good as any other crap on the tv these days. Plus, I like it every now and then when they win the big money." The two of them sat in silence for a few minutes watching the contestant cycle through every emotion known to mankind, before walking away with a little over a thousand pounds and them scoffing at the meagre amount.

"They walk in with ten in their pocket and leave with a thousand and they aren't happy," Tom said, sitting back, resting his coffee cup on his oversized gut. He wasn't fat, he was muscular coated in fat. Not like Jerry. Fuck that guy. Tom was prime steak with the fat left on. Jerry was a ball of lard. "Because there's a chance of winning more, people aren't content with what they actually win. Who gives a rat's ass if you could have won ten grand? You have walked out with one hundred times what you went in with." Jayne rolled her eyes. "What?" He said, taking a drink.

"This is why I hate game shows," she said. "So opinionated!" They laughed then. And Tom felt a wave of warmth in her smile.

"So tell me about your shift?" The two of them spoke about the dullness of the night. He thought about telling her about the footsteps, the book, the dog and even the near crash he had had on the way home. He thought against it however. He didn't want to worry her.

"Nothing much happened babe. Just sitting on my ass watching screens that didn't move, reading a couple of books I picked up from the store." They continued talking a little longer before Tom clocked the time on the television. He let out a sigh and stood up, stretching himself out. He adjusted Jayne's pillows and duvets and changed her bed pan once more. He did her medication, put the radio on the station she requested, and turned the fire low. He made sure the window was open just a crack but still on the latch to let a little air in, and tucked her sheets in just the way she liked it. He told her he loved her and touched her hands. They were so small inside his. He could feel every knuckle and bone inside that thin skin. He smiled at her and she smiled back. They locked lips, her mouth dry and lips thin, him devouring her in his face bush.

"I love you," he said.

"I love you too," she whispered, just about holding on to staying awake. "I'll see you in the morning." He stepped away, turning the light off, her silhouette illuminated a dark red by the fireplace. He put his key in the lock and pulled the door open, the hit of cold hitting him like the artic wind from that night.

"You better," he whispered, before slipping into the howling night.

10

The Second Night

Tom made another coffee. It was his third one in the last hour. Fuck he was bored. He couldn't even watch movies on his phone because the screen had fucked it in the near miss the morning before. He had only realised once he had gotten to work, and was running too late to try and go get a replacement for the shift. He had been meaning to write down all his emergency contacts on a piece of paper to keep in his wallet in case something like this happened, something which unfortunately, he had always put off. He was worried at the thought of not being able to contact Jayne if she needed him, but it was only one night, and she had been fine the night before, and she would be fine until the morning. His mind was his own worst enemy, something he had always struggled with. He didn't have anxiety, and was usually never an anxious person, but since the rig, since Brad, the thought of losing someone so close to him, knowing he could do something to prevent it, would be something he couldn't go through ever again.

He wandered around a little, stretched his legs, before returning to the only fun he could have had outside of masturbating at work, reading the book he found inside the cupboard. He had gotten a fair way through it tonight, seeing as it was the only thing he could do to stop himself either drifting off or start reading a newspaper. Fuck that, he had enough shit going on without reading about why the world was fucked or why global warming was going to kill everyone in the next thirty years.

"And as I found myself observing the blackness around me, I couldn't help but feel the touch of snow on my bare skin. I needed to find something soon, someone to pull me from this nightmare, for then I could truly dream of warmer days."

Tom put the book down and regretted what he had thought about the book being decent. It was not. There were tonnes of spelling mistakes, most of it was withered and he couldn't understand what was being said, and not to mention the absolute dribble it was filled with that didn't seem to go anywhere. No wonder it didn't have the authors name on it. Nobody would ever want to put their name to having spent hours writing such utter bullshit. He put the book down and checked through the cameras. Everything still. He checked the time. 1am. "Still a long way to go," he whispered, rubbing his eyes. He took hold of the torch and exited he SEC RITY room.

The beam from the torch licked the walls and shelves of the abandoned office, the busted clock in the corner stuck at *'03:15.'*

He had read a story about that once, about a man who loses his wife and is haunted by her memory. It didn't end well, so Tom stopped thinking about it. The office gave him the creeps. He imagined the monitors sparking on for a second and going dead again. He imagined seeing the draws fly open and papers spill out onto the ground. He imagined –

Shut up! He told that monkey in his brain to stop banging on the cymbals for ten fucking minutes. His mind was going into overdrive tonight, the worry in his heart bleeding into his thoughts.

He opened the office door into the main warehouse and made the rounds along the walkways and shelving's. He saw Gretta, the sorting machine. Its mechanical teeth not looking too friendly, and Tom dreaded to think what was left of that poor bastard's hand once Gretta had had his way with him.

The office areas were next. He put the keys in the lock and pushed the doors open, giving a cursory glance around the abandoned desks of HR, Payroll and Human Sacrifice. Then he went to the canteen, the backyard which was fenced off and had a few bicycles chained to the walls. Dusting the falling snow from his coat, he went to the back rooms where the elevator led down to the storage area of the unwanted mail. The ride wasn't nice. The elevator was a tiny box with a pull gate you had to manually secure yourself which rattled and shook violently when the ride got moving. All those years of dragging and hauling parcels down had taken its toll. Tom didn't want to think how long he would be trapped alone in the dark should the damn thing stop working. When the elevator made it to its destination, he threw the door open and jumped out like it was going to plummet to the deps of hell.

The storage room was more organised than Tom would have thought: boxes and mail stacked up in order of dates, locations and the amount of time they had been sitting there. Tom could see a few things poking out from behind the withered cardboard: watches, appliances, skates, shoes. All sorts of things. He made a mental note to jot this down when he got back to his desk. He's sure Jayne would love to see what she could find down here. He finished his rounds in the darkness, shitting himself on one occasion when a rat as big as a small dog ran from under the shelving, darting past him until the little furry bastard disappeared under a racking filled with stacks of toilet paper. He moved back to the elevator, then thinking better of it, decided to take the stairs. He didn't want to risk pushing the elevator too far. Plus he needed to pee, the cups of coffee coming back to say hello.

The stairs were freshly cleaned and the smell of bleach permeated the air. The cleaners must finish right before he starts. About halfway up those spiralling steps, he heard something which made his ball sack tighten to a tight set of plums. Footsteps coming up behind him.

Like his arse hole was rimmed with chilli flakes, he bolted up those damn stairs three at a time, the burning in his legs screaming for him to stop until he reached the top doors, pushing them open and stood away from the doors, waiting for whatever cocksucker was coming up behind him to show themselves where Tom would meet them with a face full of *fuck you!* Nothing came however, and as the minutes passed he began to doubt he had heard anything at all. The building was big, empty, and his footsteps would have made one hell of a racket. Easy enough to think that his own footsteps could be carried further, bouncing back into his ears and duplicated through some magic of physics he didn't understand. He turned his back on those doors, expecting some fiend from hell to burst through, dragging him down the stairs back to the basement, kicking and screaming. But he shook the thoughts away. He even laughed a little to himself, continuing his rounds, not wanting to look back to those doors in case it was stood there. He could feel it, his old friend again. It building up inside his stomach, soaking into his veins and nestling to the back of his head, and for a very real moment he felt something unmistakable.

Fear.

11

Later

Tom wasn't one for worrying about things that go bump in the night. When you've spent as much time alone in the dark as he had, the night became your friend. When the salt air mixes with the whisky in your blood, the world seems that little brighter. But tonight he was sober, as he had been for many months now. Eleven months, eleven days and six hours. Not like he was counting. So maybe that's why he was starting feel a little on edge? He felt his hands beginning to tremble as he held the torch and his brow start to sweat despite the cool air. He stopped and held his hand up in the dim light. He hadn't had the shakes since he had put the bottle down for good. Why was it happening to him now? He forced the thought of downing a few cold ones to the bottom of his mind, stomped on it a few times then threw it in the incinerator. He wasn't going to think about booze, no matter how much he felt the thirst all the fucking time. Tom got back to the SEC RITY room and grabbed the note pad.

Tuesday 00:12

I freaked myself out before babe. I was down in the basement doing the rounds and I didn't trust the elevator. I used the stairs. The smell of bleach was way too much for me to handle, I think it made my head go a little funny because I heard those footsteps again, like I heard outside on the first night. I think this place is driving me crazy, and I've only been here for two nights. Not to mention, and I don't want to admit this, but I have been thinking a lot about the rig and what happened, and I feel I might relapse.

He stared at those words under the dull light of the grey monitors. *I think I might relapse.* The thought of him going home to his wife who is having her body radiated so much he was surprised she didn't glow in the dark, and tell her he wanted to drink again because he had a bad time at sea made him feel sick. He tore out the page and threw it in the trash. He got the pen again –

I keep thinking of you while I'm here. Tonight has been tough knowing I can't call you. But I know *you're okay.*

I haven't seen anything on the monitors yet. Nothing but empty space. The snow is falling a lot though. Good job I brought a shovel with me for the morning.

Tom put the pen down and watched the monitors, giving them a quick flick through. All was quiet initially, but as he looked over the parking lot camera, he saw it. The dog was back, its head sniffing around the back of Tom's pickup that was slowly looking like an Igloo. Tom eyed the beast. It must be freezing, but he remembered what Jerry had said about the other guy feeding the animals that came wandering around the grounds. Tom touched the pages of his journal and he suddenly felt the creeping urge to write a little more. To revive that screwed up page, its words needing to be told. He fought internally, and after a minute, he pulled open a new page.

I can't help keep thinking about him. About Brad and what happened. I know it wasn't my fault. But that doesn't seem to comfort me much.

Tom put the pen back down. He didn't feel like writing anymore.

12

Later

He sat and watched the dog for a few minutes. It had been circling the back of Tom's truck, sniffing at the back door and then licking the bottom of his wheel. Maybe he had ran over a rabbit or something on the way in? Or maybe he had dropped a snack when he grabbed his bag earlier. The poor thing must have been freezing. The image wasn't crystal clear, and Tom could still see the dog's bones pushing through its fur. It was curled up under the bottom of the truck now, hardly visible to the camera.

Tom felt his heart begin to swell, like someone had dropped a hot coal in a frozen pond. The warmth spreading to his chest and out to his fingertips. He couldn't bring the dog inside, but he had more than enough snacks to see him through the next few hours. It was a little past midnight, and the cleaner would be coming in around six, before the day staff took over at seven. He didn't have long left before he could go home back to his wife. And he wouldn't feel right if he spent the next six or seven hours watching the poor animal freeze under his car without anything to eat.

Tom rummaged through his rucksack and found a pack of

mini sausages. The pack was the kind you normally buy if you were having a small buffet or hell, going away for the weekend in a camper. He let his mind drift back to the year him and Jayne had met. She was studying at university, some degree he couldn't possibly begin to understand, while he was working as a mechanic at the local car garage. He booked the weekend off work, or so Tom told her. Really he just phoned in sick and played hooky for a few shifts. They travelled to Galloway National Park in Scotland and lay under the sun in the evening warmth. They spoke of the star signs, the meaning of life, and the vastness of the black that loomed above them, a blanket of space scattered with millions of tiny diamonds, all so far away they could be long dead. Like an echo of what once was, an echo of something no longer around but you can still feel its presence if you listen close enough.

He did now as he did then, always packing way too much to eat. So as Tom eyed the pack of sausages mixed in with an assortment of other goodies: Oreos, cookies, crisps, dried meats and sandwiches. He felt much better about giving some to the dog. It wasn't having the Oreos though. They were his. The dog could have the apple too if it really wanted, but he didn't think even the animal was *that* desperate just yet.

He grabbed the sausages and went for the exit, but turned back, checked over the rest of the monitors to make sure the shadows hadn't grown teeth. He mentally checked himself, telling him that he was fine. It was all in his head. The dead weren't lurking in anywhere other than his mind. And still, as he thought this, he took the baseball bat out of his bag anyway.

It took around eight minutes to walk from the SEC RITY room to the front entrance of the building, and in that time Tom had managed to scare the shit out of himself at least twice. The first was immediately after he exited the office and saw his reflection in the surrounding office window. His face looked to be aged and ragged, and his beard, albeit already showing signs of grey, was completely whitewashed. He looked in his sixties, and his thick jacket looked ashen and weathered. His skin looked grey and his face withered, his eyes sunken. Tom squoze his eyes tight and looked again to find him still looking as ugly as ever.

The second time was he thought he had forgotten his pass for the front door, and then the thought crept into his mind of not being able to get back in should the doors close behind him. He found the pass around his neck, and swiftly told the intruding thoughts to *fuck off*.

The dog was still outside by the time Tom got to the main doors. The night was silent and the car park still. The snow had stopped falling and the sky above was clear. A good sign. It would still be as cold as dick when Tom left in a few hours, but at least he wasn't snowed in, which meant the dog should be okay too. He pressed the green button to exit the foyer and the hit of cold air made his boys shrivel up in his pants.

Tom whistled to the dog and it poked its head from under the truck. He dropped the pack of sausages down on the ground near the kerb of the car park and stepped back inside the building. The dog, seeing him now gone and food left there for the taking, emerged from under the truck and stalked cautiously to the meal. Tom crouched in the dark, staying still. The dog was actually pretty damn big despite it being withered. It was a Doberman: It's eyes a light brown, almost a dull green. Its fur was sleek and its ears pointed. Paws made firm indents in the snow and its snout pushed hot air into the surrounding cold. Tom felt that little better as the animal wolfed up the meal and retreated back into the car park and vanished into the tree line, the string of sausages hanging from its mouth. He stood, the cold seeping into his joints, and went back to the SEC RITY room, but not before taking a leak in the solitary toilet everyone was raving about.

13

Dawn

Tom once again found himself reading the book which he said he hated. He was a fair few pages in and frankly, was only reading it until the boss could come and tell him he could leave for the day. The main character, whose identity was still unknown, was lost in the trees and was looking for somewhere to sleep. The night was unrelenting, and from what Tom could fathom, there was something following him through the trees –

"I try to ignore the feeling that I am being followed, but it keeps returning to my mind over and over, like a mosquito you swat away but can't quite get rid of. It keeps coming back, and when I turn to check I am safe, I see no monsters behind me and the darkness does not grow teeth. No eyes of red glare at me, and the trees do not clutch at me with their finger like branches that bow overhead. But yet as I trudge through this never-ending night, the stars over me shining, and the moon low, swollen and red, I feel that there is something that wishes to do me harm. Be that from the outside world, or the monster within my own mind."

"Tom!" The loud voice bolstered Tom out of his seat. Jerry

was stood there his clothes layered with snowflakes. "Jesus I was shouting you for about a minute!" His face was red and his nostrils flared. "The second time now I find you staring at a book and not at the monitors? What the hell is wrong with you?"

"What time is it?" Tom said, confused about why Jerry was here so early in the morning. "You're early aren't you?" Jerry's temper seemed to surge greater.

"The fuck? You don't know what time it is? It's fucking seven thirty Tom! You fall asleep or something?"

"Seven thirty?" Tom repeated with horror, his mind trying to find where his time had gone. He had only just fed the dog, came in and sat down and was watching the monitors. Now he found himself missing three hours, face in a book he didn't care for, and the boss shouting at him asking to account for why the fuck he wasn't paying attention. "I'm sorry," Tom said, packing up his things. He took a drink of his coffee he had just made to find it stone cold. So cold in fact, the lip of the cup had gathered frost.

"It's freezing in here; did you not put the heater on?" Jerry said, rubbing his hands together.

"Yeah, I…" Tom whispered to himself. Did he? It was a few below freezing last night. He was so stiff. Where had the time gone?

"Whatever," Jerry said dismissively. "Get home and tonight,

I want you here that little earlier. I've got a few things to shoot out and do before you start your shift and we can't leave the place unmanned. I need you here for five, not seven. That okay?" He said, raising an eyebrow.

"Absolutely," Tom said, packing the last bits of his things up, putting the book back into the drawer. "I'll be here."

The ride back home was treacherous at best. The road had really begun to freeze up, but at least Tom didn't have a damn mobile phone to distract him this time. He still saw some cars in the snow, crawling morning traffic playing Candy Crush or some other shite on their devices behind the wheel, often needing to break at the last moment because they hadn't realised that the car in front had stopped moving a few seconds ago. Tom even leant out the window and blasted his horn at one driver in front of him who was reading something on an iPad whilst holding a cigarette in one hand and a cup of coffee in the other. He didn't give a fuck if he was driving a Tesla. It wasn't the point. It was the principle of the damn thing.

He arrived home a little before nine. The house was again all in darkness and as he went through the door, he noticed that the house was stone cold. Fear crept along Tom's flesh. He left the front door ajar, stepping in with snow covered boots.

"Jayne?" He said, trying to hide the trembling in his voice. He stepped into the living room, turning the corner of the door. His breath caught in his throat. He ran to her, picking her up from the floor, her half naked body covered in soiled blankets and sheets from the tipped bedpan. Her body cold to touch. He remembered screaming, running out into the street, begging a passer-by for a phone to use. He raced inside, touching her cold face, her lips turned a light shade of blue and screaming to the ambulance on the phone that she wasn't breathing.

14

Tie Those Boots

The paramedics came bursting through the door a few minutes after he had called them. He told them the address, and that his wife wasn't breathing. He wasn't completely sure, his mind a blur, not wanting to look into his wife's vacant eyes as they stared at the grey ceiling above. He shouted her name, stricken with worry, like all his muscles in his body were tightening at once, unable to release any tension.

They pulled him from her, taking over. Three of them converged onto Jayne, jamming IV drips into her arms whilst the other attached an oxygen mask and pumped a plastic balloon, forcing air into her lungs. They attached wires and mechanisms that beeped and buzzed, her vitals showing on a small machine that they carried with them. The paramedics exchanged a grave look, and then without a seconds hesitation, began CPR. Tom heard the cracking and splintering of his wife's ribs, a sound that shattered though any remaining resolve or hope that she would be okay, that she was just sleeping or in some kind of coma. They pressed over and over and then pulled her onto a gurney, one paramedic at all times keeping the sickening rhythm on her chest, her body moving out like a dead fish being slapped with a mallet before being served to hungry fishermen.

They raced outside, pushing the gurney between them, Tom pacing close behind. In the back of the ambulance, the harsh light pierced Tom's night time eyes, his body running on fumes and red lining with fear and adrenaline. The technician dove into the driver's seat and the paramedics put a seatbelt around the gurney so Jayne wouldn't go anywhere, oxygen being forced into her lungs that were being massaged by a very red faced first responder, him cursing at the unbreathing body in front of him.

They spoke so fast between themselves, all kinds of measurements being thrown out and being scribbled down on green paper: heart rate, blood pressure, carbon dioxide levels, toxicity of the blood, amongst other things. Tom stood helpless, like he was watching his wife be ravaged by wolves and he could do nothing but watch and hope they didn't take her too far over the edge.

The ambulance fired into life and the technician sped away, blaring the sirens as fast as she could without colliding with parked cars and standing traffic. The sirens filled the air as they hurtled in that tiny box which buzzed and blared, rocking and knocking them off their feet when the driver had to take evasive action.

"Do you know CPR?" The red-faced paramedic shouted breathlessly. Tom looked around; she was talking to him. This was his turn now, to drive his boulder hands into his Jayne's withered bag of bones wrapped in thin flesh. Her eyes still open, lips turning paler. He shook his head, feeling so small in a big world. The paramedic gave him a crash course, and on the count of three, Tom drove those sasquatch hands into his wife's sternum and began to press one third into her body at a rate of two compressions a second. He pushed and felt the crack of the ribs under his hands. He pulled back, the feeling cutting through him, knocking him sick. "Keep going!" The breathless paramedic said, wiping his face on his rubber gloves. "It's going to hurt her, but she'll just be sore. Better that than..." Tom didn't want to hear the next word. He dove on her once more, going hell for leather. His wife of thirty years, her life was in his hands, quite literally. He felt like he could cup her heart and massage it back to health. She had helped him through his addiction, got him away from crime, even when he was a wreck coming back from the rig. Now it was his turn to save *her*. He pressed down on that motherfucker like his own life depended on it. If she didn't pull through, then he wouldn't have a life left, and the bottle would soon be calling his name once more.

The ambulance flew through the grey streets, manoeuvring through streams of solid brake lights and pedestrians trying to wade through the thickening snow. After what seemed like a lifetime,

Tom was pulled away as more doctors and nurses from the ER burst through the back doors of the ambulance and pulled him away, taking over from him. He hadn't noticed they were at the ambulance bay at the hospital. A ride into hell that never seemed to end. Tom moved back, rushing after the squeaking trolley and the worried faces of the nurses that attached more probes, paramedics firing jargon faster than Tom could understand the sounds coming out their mouths to the doctors that hastily wrote it all down on their clip boards. They asked Tom some details about his wife: name, date of birth, address, blood type, medical history, next of Kin. Tom tried all he could but he was still walking, his thoughts running faster than a bunch of squirrels that had been set alight. They pushed through the ER reception doors and Tom saw the myriad of terrified and worried eyes that fell onto him, and he had never felt more out of depth in his life. Being stranded at sea was nothing compared to this, he was sweating, his clothes sticking to him, his adrenaline spiking and pupils dilating. He was breathless, catching himself on the reception desk, steadied by two security guards dressed in black body armour. They got him a chair, but he tried to fight them, screaming her name as she disappeared with doctors and nurses through a set of double doors, hearing them shout to do another shock, that she was flat lining.

15

The Third Night

Tom stared at the grey scale computer monitor with as much enthusiasm as a dog being told to give its favourite toy back. Nothing was moving, and the snow had fallen quickly since he had arrived at Welch Mill. The car park had been cleared by the shift before him, shovelling the white stuff in heaps and piling them on the side of the car park in huge mounds. Grit laid on the tarmac and the exiting cars scarring the remaining snow in thick black lines. They had since been frosted over, until they were now completely buried once more. Tom's truck sitting alone near the front of the building, shivering its mechanical arse off, coated in thick white. Tom thought of Jayne.

"You need to go back in tonight," she had said once she had woken up. She was a mess; her chest was bandaged and she had more wires and tubes poking out of her than a fuse box after a rat had gotten to it. "You need to go and take care of yourself. I am in the best place possible here. Sitting here will only make you worry." Tom sat by her bedside, listening to the various beeping and buzzing going off from the machines she was hooked up too. He stared at the floor, looking back at his reflection in the linoleum, the smell of citrus and bleach assaulting his nostrils.

"I should have been home," he whispered, trying not to crack. "I should have been at home with you last night. I could have done something; I could have helped you." He felt her fingers run through his long hair.

"Now you stop thinking like that Sash," she said. "You know that you couldn't have known what was going to happen, and that you did all you could. I am glad you got home when you did. The paramedics said that you saved my life."

"I should have been home," Tom said again bitterly. "I would have helped more. How do I know something like that isn't going to happen again?" He looked at her, his eyes bloodshot.

"The doctors have given me some extra medication to take for my heart. It's the cancer... it spread to my lungs and put pressure on the heart which stopped it beating for a short while." She sounded like she was talking about the latest upset in a reality TV show.

"How can you be so fucking calm Jayne?" He seethed, pressing his hands into the thin blanket. "You could have died. The damn doctors didn't spot the tumour was growing, didn't spot that your heart was under strain. This is their fault." He was caving into himself now, his stern exterior crumbling, the stone statue withered by the storm that just wouldn't stop beating it until it eroded and cracked. She touched his hands, leaning into him.

"You need to stop being so hard on yourself. You couldn't have known. No one could have! It happened, and I am fine."

"I'm going to quit the security job," he said, shaking his head. "I'm going to declare that I'm your full time carer. You need the help now more than ever." Jayne let out a sigh.

"We both know that that wouldn't be good," she said. "You need to keep busy. You need to be out of the house. You need something to keep you occupied." Tom let the words sink in. She was right. As much as he didn't want to admit it, she was right, as she always was. She was always the one that had the clearer, more rational head. *Sash smash*, as she would often say when Tom would think the best way to handle a situation was to throw might rather than reason at it. This was one of those occasions, and given by the bandages around his wife's ribs, Sash had smashed enough today.

An hour later, he managed to get a little sleep in the rigid uncomfortable waiting chair next to her bed whilst she got some rest herself. She would be in the hospital for a few days at most, then brought back home. Tom had agreed to stay working only if his wife had more care when he wasn't there, to which the home care company happily agreed, for an increased fee of course. Tom returned home after that, driving carefully on the roads that were growing more treacherous by the hour.

In his home he turned the light on, and the sight of the overturned bed and spilled bed pan made him weak at the knees. He cried then, allowed himself to breathe and let it out. He had nearly lost her. The realisation rampaging in his mind. He had nearly lost the woman he has woken up too every day for the last thirty years, other than his years at the rig. He got to work on cleaning the carpet and the sheets. Then, he eyed the large stack of half opened debt letters on his side table and realised Jayne was completely right. They had lived in the same house for last twenty years. They had always wanted children, but he had issues with his swimmers, and the IVF was too expensive, so they settled on a dog instead. Jasper, a little Yorkshire terrier. He had died a few years back after a long and happy life. Tom went to go work on the rigs shortly after that. When he got back, the doctor told him that the lump on his wife's breast wasn't just a cyst, and they had to remortgage the house to pay for the treatment. Eyeing those letters that hissed like a pile of rattle snakes, he knew that Jayne was right. Those wolves were howling at his door and he needed to keep them at bay.

Tom sat back in his chair, sleep wanting to find him. He checked the clock. It was only 9PM. He had a long shift ahead of him and needed to keep himself busy. Should the boss Jerry come back unannounced and find him sleeping on the job, it was bye bye salary, bye bye extra care for Jayne, and hello repossession letters.

He got to his feet, stretched himself out and gave the monitors one last flick through and seeing nothing but grey scale, left the SEC RITY room. He walked through the main office and into the warehouse. The sound of the wind rattled the large doors which let the wagons come through and the building creaked and ached with him. Tom shone his torch on the racking. He eyed frost appearing on the shelving, and knew that it was only going to get worse. Then, he spotted a small pool of icy water on the floor. He found a mop and wiped that sucker dry, putting out a wet floor sign, before the damn thing froze and became an ice rink.

Moving through the rest of the building, he found a small electric heater in the CEO's office and hauled it back to the SEC RITY room where he hooked it up, relaxing with a cup of hot coffee. Now, he had to fight off boredom. His phone was still busted, and he sat with the office phone next to him, hooked up to the wall. He had given the hospital his work's landline, another condition of him returning to work this evening, against all reservations. He hadn't even thought to bring any snacks or real food other than a small bag of spiced sausages he had bought at the deli counter of the gas station he had fuelled up in on the way to work. He tucked into one of the tiny delightful bastards. His stomach rumbled, yearning for fulfilment. He hadn't eaten in nearly 48 hours, and he was running on fumes. The spiced meat filled his mouth and he inhaled the morsel, hunger ravaging his body as he tucked into them famished, washing them down with a hot cup of coffee. He felt good, his mood getting better with the heat and the food. He felt a feeling of calm come over him. He put the rest of the pack back into his bag.

I could kill for a drink, he thought. *A nice little scotch with a little ice. 12 years aged. Beer or two to chase it down.* He shook his head, noticing that again, his hands were trembling. He held them steady. Why was he thinking again about the drink? Was it the stress? The job? The long hours alone or more likely, the fact his wife is dying? He remembered what his sponsor at the AA meetings had told him: *'You gotta keep busy. The bottle is the vulture on your shoulder. If you give it enough attention, it will get heavier until you can't ignore it.*

Easy for him to say, Tom thought. Try keeping away when you have your wife in hospital, in fuck tonnes of debt and you haven't slept properly in months. He didn't mean to, but without realising, he had opened up the authorless book from the drawer of his desk, and was falling into the pages before he realised.

'I move quickly, my assailant soon behind me. I come to a clearing, my friend nowhere to be found, by this creature that

follows me in this black, a friend they are not. He stands tall, withered and thin, a long grey beard and grey jellied eyes of blind man.'

'"Back beast!" I call, standing, facing my foe, hiding the fear in my voice. "I vanquish you to the hell you came! God has my side, and his light will force you back into the black which you spawned from!" I call and pray to my Lord, yet the creature does not retreat into the black. Its shoulders click and its thin ribs push through withered skin. Its face that of a man, an elderly man, its nose curved to its top lip, pointed and sharp. Its teeth bared, lines of yellow nubs pushing through blackened lips. Its fingers long, bony, nails sharp. It eyes me, then in my tongue, utters to me –'

'"Death is an echo. I may be vanquished by your false God, but I will remain until my debt is repaid." I turn to run, but the creature is there again in front of me. The blood moon above swelling once more, as the trees grow vines that strike me, wrapping around my legs and wrists.'

Tom turned the page. The last part of the story was missing. "What fucking dip shit tears out the back of a book?" He cursed, feeling the calmness that had befallen him melt like the falling snow. Tom opened the cupboard and tossed the book into the top drawer. He drove his hand into his duffel bag and pulled out his journal.

Wednesday. Night shift number three.

The last place on earth where I want to be is here. My wife is in the hospital and I am here sitting on my ass away from her through the night time hours, alone with my thoughts and a book that has no ending. Someone tore the pages out. Sadists.

The doctors said she would be fine, and I guess I have to give a little faith to them. They do wear lab coats and have thousands of pounds of student loan debt to justify their expert opinion after all. But I don't want to be here. I cleaned the house before I left, so that when I can go to the hospital and get her, I don't have as much to do. Fuck I'm tired. I haven't slept much at all since starting this job, never mind the last day. That was rough. Seeing her like that.

Anyway, I need the money, and what a shit state of affairs it is when a husband must be away from his wife to pay for the care she needs? She said that it does me good, keeping away, keeping my mind occupied, less I decide to drink again. And I guess she is right. But my god do I miss it.

Sorry, I thought I heard something. Why am I apologising to you? Sounded like something fell over in the other room. Just checked the monitors and nothing was there. Must be the wind or a rat or something. Ugh. I want to get this night over with, and it's still early yet. No food, no phone. It's going to be a long one... After I get my first pay cheque, I am out of this place. Jayne needs me.

He went to write more, but he caught something move on the monitors out the corner of his eye. The grey scale flickering, something emerging from the tree line. The dog. It was back.

16

Tread Lightly Kids

"Jesus," Tom spat with a shaky jaw. He hadn't noticed on the camera or through the thick glass of the automatic doors, but the sky had really clouded over. The thick spiralling blackness above him was giving way to a behemoth of snow, like a giant head of hair having a good scratch, getting the nails right in there and the flakes of skin peppering the world below. The snow was gathering around Tom's boots, and he knew that it would be there to stay. He wondered if he had brought some de icer and a shovel, but in a warehouse this large he was sure they would have something to help him out. A hammer and chisel, a flamethrower, sulphuric acid. He'd find something.

The dog was curled up underneath the bed of the pickup truck. Tom crunched the ground as he moved closer, hearing the electronic doors close behind him. At the back of the passenger side rear wheel, Tom eyed a clump of fur and a blood stain frozen to the rubber mangled into the trim. He must have caught a rabbit on the way in, the smell of a free meal finding the starving pooches' nostrils.

Tom pulled a couple of sausages he had saved from his pocket. They weren't much, but he couldn't sit by and watch the dog starve to death. Not in weather like this. The wind bit his fingers something nasty, icy teeth cutting into his skin and gnawing on the bone. He held out the meat to the shivering beast which perked it's head up and bared its teeth.

Tom placed another down by his feet and took a step back. The Doberman, its fur short, ears pointed and legs long, crept from under the truck and skulked forward, checking the coast was clear, before devouring the sausage once more.

Finally, Tom thought to be ballsy. If he was freezing his ass off outside and treating this runaway to some of the finest processed food money can buy from the reduced section at the local garage, God damn it he was gonna pet the damn thing even if it meant losing a finger. Figuratively speaking of course. Tom took another sausage, took a small bite and held it out in his hand. The Doberman was hesitant, those ears once more flattening, that tail tucking between thin quaking legs.

"It's okay," Tom said softly. "Come on." He wiggled the weaner in his fingers. The Doberman reared closer and with the swiftness of a spoilt child at a birthday party, snatched the meat quickly, its teeth gracing the end of Tom's fingers making him wince. It trotted back a couple of paces and ate the meat, not taking its eyes off the man with the big black coat and the baseball bat poking out the top of it. "Little shit," Tom joked to himself putting his bloodied fingers in his mouth. "Probably need a tetanus."

Tom turned and walked towards the front doors. The single street light illuminating him and the ever-gathering snow by his feet. Tom turned and saw the dog had gone, once again either hiding under his truck or had disappeared into the surrounding wood. He smiled to himself, saying farewell to his new night time buddy. He pulled out the pass from around his neck, touching the final sausage he had saved for himself in his jacket pocket.

He touched the black box which went from solid red to blinking green, making the glass doors open with a low whoosh. He went to step in when he heard the panting. He turned to see the dog once more, this time leaping for his hand, taking the meat from him. Tom recoiled, falling backwards onto the ground, snow hitting his face and the sting of concrete caressing his cheek. Dazed, he looked about the falling white on black, and saw the doors of the main entrance closing. He sat up, scrambling to wedge them open with his bat, but its head missed the last opening of the doors.

Tom eyed the Doberman through the glass, it sitting, panting. Its long tongue falling from those hungry snapping jaws. It shook the melting snow from itself, then disappeared into the black hallways, Tom's security pass attached to its paw, dragging him with it, his 2 x 5 picture smiling away at the world.   He touched the frosting glass of the doors.

"Fuck."

17

Watch Your Step

Tom sat up and brushed the gathering snow from his beard, holding the side of his head where he had made out with the concrete and gotten a bad hickey as a result. "The fuck am I going to do now?" He cursed to himself, frustrated with his stupidity more than anything else. He stood and moved to the black glass, thinking somehow they would open for him, but they didn't budge. Tom thought about smashing the glass open, but that was one way to get fired, and a sure way to lose what little money he would get from his first pay cheque. *Sash Smash* he thought to himself. He snarled again "Fuck!"

The building was huge, and he could feel the might of the clouds falling onto him. He was hungry, and the real fear of freezing to death crept into his mind. It was far below zero degrees, and he had had left his keys inside the office so he couldn't sit tight in his truck for the night.

Jayne entered his mind. Him lying in the corner trying to keep warm until the morning staff arrived. The cold hooking into his bones. The police telling Jayne he was found stiff, his face fixed in a permanent scream of her name. Tom pressed his hands to his temples and told the thoughts and images to disappear before he made them with his bat. *Think Tom,* he pressed himself. *There must be another way in.* Tom moved to the edge of the building and was met with a large wire fence where a security camera sat iced over, bleeping its red light on its big black eye. He studied the area but nothing jumped out at him. He couldn't climb something that large, not with how cold he was. Even if he managed to get to the top of the wire mesh fence with his fingers intact, there was still the problem of the huge loops of razor wire to contend with. He had seen what they can do to a man if they hook just the right part. Again he shook the memories from his mind.

"Fuck!" He hissed into the wind. He scrunched his face up tight, looking at the other security camera blinking at him. Tom saw a break in the razor wire, about half a foot long. At the base of the wall, there was a pile of empty storage boxes and a tonne of cigarette butts. Tom pressed the boxes with his bat and they were frozen solid, coated in a thick layer of snow. He picked up a couple, shaking the snow from them and bundled them under his arm, remembering his burglary days in his twenties.

The wind broke the still silence as its icy tongue licked his numbing face. He gripped hold of the wire mesh with his bare hands and the cold metal sliced through his flesh, sending a harsh burn through his fingertips. He felt the blood draining from his white knuckles as he took a handful of the wiring and hauled his frozen legs up from the ground. Another handful and the snow pelted his face a little more. The fence rattled under his weight like someone jingling a huge rung of old keys, the shaking fence dancing in the night, showering snow on the ground below. A little higher he went, and he could feel his fingers beginning to give way. He gritted his teeth, forcing the frozen digits to take another handful, before he was top side, the glint of the razor wire staring him in the face like a game of chicken with a great white shark, daring him to try his luck.

He took the cardboard and placed it in the gap of the wiring and placed it as flat as he could. Then, with one final yearning effort, he pulled himself onto the cardboard and flopped over the other side like a beached killer whale snagging a sleeping seal.

"Hey!" The voice slammed into Tom's ears like a dog singing a nursery rhyme. Tom missed the mesh on the other side and fell to the ground. He tumbled, grabbing out at anything but only finding air. He collided with the frozen ground, hard. He lay there for a moment, the wind knocked out of him, covered in snow and cardboard. A flashlight illuminated his face from the other side of the fence.

"What are you doing here? You're not allowed here! I'm

calling the police!" Tom hauled his ass up to his feet and eyed the man's darkened face. He was wearing similar clothing to him: dark jacket with blue jeans. His face obscured by the blinding light being shone in Tom's eyes.

"I fucking work here man!" Tom bellowed through the wind. "A damn dog took my pass so I had to find another way in!"

"Bullshit!" The torch wielding man said. "I saw you from across the way, scoping the place out! The fuck you got a baseball bat for if you work security? You're tryna rob the place?" With that, the torch man took out his phone and turned away from Tom. He put it to his ear and Tom heard him on the phone to the police.

"Yeah call the cops, I'm gonna get back to my warm desk. Let me know when they turn up." Tom turned on his heel and continued on, "now fuck off." The back court yard had tonnes of empty boxes stacked up against steel railings with more spikes you can shake a stick at, two open trailers left by HGV's, and giant dumpsters. Tom eyed windows lining the upper floor of the place, too high to reach, and he didn't feel like risking a climb again, his back throbbing like a snare drum on raw nerves. The torch man's voice yammering away in the background, carried away by the wind. He would have a story to tell the police when they got here. Those blue lights flickering on the horizon in the night. *Boom boom.*

A thought struck him. He knew his wife's number by heart, and the guy with the torch had a phone. Maybe he could let him use it? Doubtful, but this was all a misunderstanding. He was in the security uniform of the place after all and his car was in the damn parking lot. He would be able to talk his way through it. Where had the guy come from anyway? There wasn't another building around here for at least five miles.

Tom turned to shout the guy, but he saw no torch. He walked to the fence wiring again and got a good view of the parking lot. The guy was nowhere to be seen.

"Hey!" Tom called into the night. He moved to the wiring, pressing his face against the frozen metal, trying to find where the spectre had vanished too. Then he felt it. The pain in his leg. He looked up to the top of the fence. The cardboard had gone, and there was no hole in the wiring. Wet heat gathered around his quad. He looked down at the razor wire buried in his upper thigh, and the pool of crimson soaking onto the white blanket under his quivering feet.

18

Razor Wire Wet Kiss

The next few minutes of Tom Mackenzie's life were a runaway freight train of holy fuck. Tom began to spiral, his heart beat red lining. He gripped the razor wire with his bare hands and tore them to pieces trying to pull them out. He screamed more than a sailor with a bad hangover and then some. Stumbling, limping, him haemorrhaging into the abyssal white that surrounded him. His head spun, the ground meeting his back, snow pelting his face. Hot air spilling from his mouth and the darkening patch around his jeans.

Digging his bloodied numb fingers into the ground, he crawled and dragged his ass to the back door of the warehouse which was sealed tight. With all his strength, he took out his bat and flogged the glass of the window. A bullseye appeared, so he hit it again and again until the glass gave way. He pushed the head of the bat through the hole and pushed the glass out of the way which shattered loudly on the concrete floor on the other side.

The alarm was deafening, wailing and bright flashing red lights bounced around his vision, casting deep red glows in the inside floor and shelvings. He slammed his hand through the gap and fumbled numbly for the dead bolt. He found it and pulled as hard as he could. His teeth bared, leg drenching his junk in red hot, he forced the door free which came away reluctantly, covered in frost and ice.

He fell through the gap and splayed in the dark and glowing red. He clambered to his feet, leaving the mouth of the building wide open, allowing the ravenous winter blizzard to follow him through the racks of shelving. He got to the solitary bathroom at the back of the warehouse and pulled free the door. He hit the light and the porcelain white walls with stains from God knows what orifice greeted him like a dirty protest in a prison cell. Tom collapsed onto the freezing cold vinyl and tore open his jeans a little farther. He grabbed a small hand towel and wrapped it around his hands, then for good measure, put the handle of his bat in his mouth. He screamed and agonised behind the metal handle, digging his teeth deep into its leather grip as he took hold of the wire and forced it out, it gliding across his bone and tearing into his skin, hooking muscle and fat, flesh and fabric. The wire came loose finally, and Tom let out a breath of air, but he wasn't out the woods yet. He grabbed a bottle of disinfectant from the side of the ruined toilet bowl, unscrewed it, and poured it onto the fleshy wound.

If the razor wire hurt like a bitch, then the burn of the

disinfectant was the bitch's ugly fuck of an uncle. Red hot flames poured onto his skin and danced around his thigh, sending shocks of fire through his body as he rattled against the wall, screaming to whatever would listen to go fuck itself. Lastly, he grabbed a handful of paper towels and stuffed them into the wound, and then wrapped the hand towel over it as improvised bandage. He tried to hold on a moment before passing out.

19

The Phantom

The cold touch of a snout on his face woke him up. Tom opened his eyes quickly and recoiled at the sight of a hungry mutt licking his face and at the dried blood on his fingers.

"Fuck off!" Tom screamed at the Doberman, before it trotted away into the night. Tom put his hands to his face. His fingers were numb and blue, and then he felt the shivers start to take hold of him. He climbed to his feet, fighting for every inch of strength and to try and stop his legs giving way, using the bat to prop himself up, less he fumble and his head kiss the porcelain sink. Goodnight round two. Tom put the weight on his good leg. The bandage seemed to have stopped the bleeding, but he didn't want to chance it.

The back door was wide open, but the alarm had stopped. It must have been from a timer or something. He was surprised that it was the dog that woke him up and not the cops. Surely they would have been here by now? Or maybe an ambulance? How long had he been unconscious for? It was still dark out, and the snow seemed to have stopped. It had formed a nice rug of ice on the warehouse floor. Tom made a mental note to leave a wet floor sign at the back door before he went home.

Where was the hole in the fence? The thought hit him like an uninvited guest at a family party. He didn't have the strength to go check for himself, not right now anyway. Maybe he could check on the security cameras? There was one right next to the fence so it should capture the wall. But it *had* been there, otherwise he wouldn't have tried to climb back over. Had he mistaken the gap for something else? And who was the guy outside calling the cops? Nothing made sense at the moment. But regardless, he hadn't bled out, and he was out of the blizzard, so he thanked the heavens for small mercies, no matter how trivial they seemed in the moment.

Tom had never sworn more furiously, more loudly and damn it, more creatively than he did on that long painful walk back to the SEC RITY room. On a better day, he might have been impressed with the amount of different way you could curse all things under the sky, but this didn't seem like the right time for a pat on the back. Tom got into the room and closed the door behind him. By some miracle, his duffel bag was still there and he could still find the tiny amount of nibbles and snacks he had that hadn't been raided by the stray dog roaming the warehouse. He checked the time on the monitors. Only just gone three in the morning. He still had a few hours left before the morning shift came in. "Yeah fucking right," he cursed at the thought of staying another minute in this shit forsaken place. He needed to get out of here and fast. But first, he had a call to make.

He picked up the land line in the SEC RITY room and dialled the hospital ward Jayne was on. The phone began to ring, and in that moment he felt like the silence between the bleeps would eat him alive. Stretching tones of anxiety making his nerve endings like tort violin strings being caressed with a blunt razor blade. The call rang out until an automated message met his numb ears –

"Welcome to Nightingale Hospital. We're sorry, but –" Tom slammed the phone back to the receiver, rubbing his hands on his face. "Fuck," he strained, his mouth arid. Tom sat his ass in the spinning desk chair. He noticed it then. His notebook had been left out, a fresh page staring at him. There, written in scratchy writing read the word –

'*Home.*'

Tom stared at the offending word in the dull light of the monitor. Had he written that? No, he hadn't. He would remember. But then again, he hadn't slept properly in nearly three days. The stress, the anxiety, the loneliness. The *fear.* He turned the pages of the journal and horror ripped through him. Every page. Every fucking page. Written over and over again, over his own writings, his own thoughts.

'HomeHomeHomeHomeHomeHomeHomeHomeH

omeHomeHomeHomeHomeHomeHomeHomeHomeHo

meHomeHomeHomeHomeHomeHome'

Tom threw the notebook across the room like a snake about to bite him. He put his head in his hands. He tried to think, but he couldn't find anything to make sense of what had just happened. The wiring, the dog, and now this? Tom tried to speak, tried to say something that would make sense of it all. The room seemed that little darker, that little tighter, like the night had grown teeth. Hungry ghosts lurking in the darkness of the walls, waiting for someone to stray that little bit too far.

"I'm losing my fucking mind." He saw something move on the monitor. He turned his head, his neck creaking and popping. Standing in the main warehouse in the darkness, a few metres from his office. A figure draped in shadow looking up at the camera.

20

Shadows With Teeth

Tom eyed the spectre on the camera. His body went tight, gripping his baseball bat. He watched the figure cross the threshold into the office. Tom could hear the footsteps from behind the door. The figure on the monitor standing still at the foot of the SEC RITY room. He tried to call out, but the vice of fear clenched around his neck like a stranglehold of an MMA fighter. He sat there, waiting. The air still, his heart pounding in his ears, his breath deep. The handle of the door began to rattle. Tom struggled to his feet, standing with the bat primed like a baseball player ready to score the big win. His leg ached and yearned for release, it shaking, trying not to buckle as his muscles burned. Tom forced the pain to the back of his mind. The handle turned once more, and the SEC RITY room door pushed open.

The torch was blinding and Tom put his hand over his eyes. "Come any closer and I'll bash your fucking skull in!"

"Hey, hey no need for that now," a voice said. "I'm here to check the alarm." Tom felt the fear drain from him.

"You are?"

"Yeah," the torch holder said. "You the nightman?" Tom nodded.

"Hey, you mind lowering that damn light? Fuckin blinding me over here."

"Oh, sorry," the figure said, lowering the torch. Tom lowered his hand and let his eyes adjust once more to the night. He sat back down on his chair, putting the bat across his lap. "I didn't mean to startle ya," the figure said, his accent a mix of American and Northern English. "I tried to call the office line but no one answered so I had to make my way here. Everything good?" Tom thought of that question.

"Everything is fine," he said. "I got locked out before and had to break my way in. That's what set the alarm off. Everything's fine though," Tom said with a resounding sigh. The figure nodded his head. He was tall, real fucking tall, maybe around six eight, six nine, no hair on top and as thin as a coat hanger. Tom thought he had a slight resemblance to Jack Skellington. "Hey," Tom began.

"Yeah?"

"You didn't happen too..." *Write in my notebook did you? Tell me I'm not going crazy.* "Come by earlier on? We speak before?" The tall man's face contorted, his greyed features dull in the light of the monitors.

"No," he said flatly. "No this is the first time I have been here in a few months."

"Oh," Tom resounded, more confused than before. "I spoke to someone outside when I was locked out. I thought that might have been you." The tall man shook his head.

"No," he repeated. "Not been here in a few months." Tom felt something off about the guy, a little unnerved.

"Well, thanks for checking in," Tom said, turning away from the guy and going back to the monitors. He checked the time and confusion slapped him once more. It was still three AM. But that was impossible? He had been back in the SEC RITY room for at least twenty minutes. Was there a problem with the computers? *Great,* he thought. "Listen man I'm not being rude, but I just wanna get my night done with. So if you don't mind?" Tom began flicking through the monitors, waiting for a response, for the sound of the door closing. But it never came. Tom noticed something on the monitors. The car park. Only his car was there. He sat back, that icy chill slowly filling his stomach once more. "Say," he said, trying to hide the shaking in his voice. "How did you get here?" No response. Tom clenched his eyes shut, then with every part of him screaming not to look, he opened his eyes once more and turned the chair round. The tall man was still standing there, his face etched in a long grin.

"I walked," he said, his fingers clicking together.

"You walked?" Tom said, gripping the handle of the bat once more. The tall man's eyes fixated on the bat. His smile widened.

"Yes," he said, "From the woods." Tom felt the horror firmly cup his balls and squeeze. "Did you like my book? I left it for you. Have you seen my dog?"

"What the fuck did you say?" Tom stammered.

"Are you going to give me a gift like the last one?"

"The last one? A fucking gift?" The tall man nodded.

"Yes. My home. You're in my home. The last one gave his blood. What will you give?" Tom stared at the spectre in stunned terror. *The last one? Walter? Wallace? He heard Jerry's voice in his head -*

'He was a weird guy. Was still alive too when the cleaner found him. Taken away in the ambulance. Kept on talking about 'The Night.''

Tom stood once more, finding the bravery that had been trodden on by the dark, pulling it back into his heart. He held the bat by his shoulder, ready to knock this weird fuck's head off if he took a step his way.

"Get the fuck out of here right now," Tom spat. "Go on! Beat it!" The tall man smiled once more.

"The Grey Man will come for you," he said. "The Grey Man knows your fears. Your past. He will take you soon." The figure rushed to Tom, howling, screaming, long arms outstretched. Tom swung the bat, the head of destruction cutting through the air. He lost his balance, cascading to the floor near the tables of the coffee machine. The carpet licking his cheeks. His breath was ragged, sweat pouring out of his flesh, his leg screaming in hot agony. Tom turned, expecting to see the creature over him, but he was alone once more. He turned again and faced the darkness under the table. He heard breathing coming from under there. *Ghosts with teeth waiting for someone to stray too far.* Tom remembered the torch in his pocket. He licked his lips, the breathing, panting, coming from under the desk growing louder. *The dog?* He wondered. *Have you seen my dog?* He pulled out the torch and clicked it to life. The beam pierced his dead eyes first. His mouth was stretched in a scream. His beard frosted over. The yellow and grey Kevlar overalls covered in sea weed.

Tom dropped the torch, as Brad's swollen face stretched into a toothless grin.

21

Some Things Should Stay Buried.

Tom bolted back to the other side of the room, his leg erupting in agony, the bandages coming away, re opening the wound. He stared in horror at the blackness. The torch still in his hand shaking furiously. He wanted to scream, but his voice couldn't find the air. He shook his head in fury. *It's not real. It's not real.* He knew he shouldn't. He knew he wouldn't. He knew he couldn't. But he knew he would. He bit down on his fear and lowered the bright beam of light to the lip of the table above, and then in one quick flash, the torch found under the base once more.

Brad's smile was stretched from ear to ear. A long toothless grin that fixated on Tom. His eyes met the dead holes in Brad's head.

You left me. He heard the corpse whisper, lips not moving. That grin waxy. Holding itself. *You left me alone on that rig. The black tides pulled me under, as you went to get another bottle from your cabin.* Tom's mind fractured. He didn't want to blink, fearing what he would see when his eyes re opened, but the clicking and popping of those dead bones forced him to focus on that pale bloated skin. The impossible in front of him.

"I...," he started. "I didn't..." He felt his eyes begin to well. "I didn't leave you. It was an accident."

Liar. The word stretch like nails on a black board. *You left me on there to man the rig. Tides were high. Never leave someone alone on the rig at night.*

"I wasn't gone long," Tom pleaded. "I was gone only a minute."

Liiiiieeees. The mound spoke. *You left me. You were drunk, and wanted more. I called for help when the tide got too rough. Then the black swallowed me up.* Tom remembered hearing the sounds of screaming, the siren blaring. The flashing of red in his blurred vision as the rig rocked, or his drunken legs shook him as he clambered onto the deck. The rest of the crew throwing life rings over board. Spotlights shining over the pelting rain into the deathly black abyss. The sight of a man taking lung fulls of salt water, his head vanishing under the waves.

I'm still down there, Brad hissed. *In the black. Fat and swollen, my eyes eaten by hungry fish.*

"You're not real," Tom cried, the torch heavy in his hands. The light begin to flicker, splutter and die. Tom saw Brad's face vanish into the darkness once more. He felt the wind in his ears.

The taste of salt on his lips. The monitor went dead. Tom sat silently in the darkness. The beating of his heart in his head. The sound of shuffling. Wet heavy footsteps on the floor. The sound of dripping. Sliding. Getting closer. Tom held his breath. The torch came back to life. He was above him now. And he found his voice in a scream as the icy finger tips wrapped around his throat.

22

Dead Men

Tom fumbled and screamed as the grip of Brad's fingers squoze around his throat. He could feel the air of the Atlantic hitting his face. The deafening sound of the sirens in his ears. The taste of sea salt on his tongue. *You left me, you left me, you left me* the corpse's voice bounced around Tom's mind over and over. *It should have been you, you drunk! You criminal! You waste! It should have been you!* Tom felt shells and rotten fish fall onto his face, Brad's withered face cast in shadow from the shaking torch. His nose missing, the torch light pushing through the holes in his face. Tom squoze his eyes shut, the sound of the tide ravaging him, the feeling of water consuming him, he thrashed, his arms and fingers gliding through black heavy sea. He tried to breathe but a mouthful of salt water forced its way into his lungs. He saw the torch lights blurred and hazy above him as he sank deeper into the Atlantic, before all light vanished, and he was left sinking in the consuming depths.

Tom heaved gulps of air, turning on his front, the taste of salt water lacing his tongue, his nose and eyes stinging. He forced himself onto all fours, coughing until his lungs felt that they were going to give out, spewing bile and retching until nothing more came. As quickly as it had come, it was no more. Tom reluctantly opened his eyes, his face sweating. His breath fast and shallow, whimpering quietly to himself. He was alone. The security monitors still blinking as they always were, switching camera lenses from the white out of the car park, the dead space in the offices, and the empty warehouse. The torch was by his feet, solid light beam engaged.

Tom took hold of the torch and shakily checked the shadows for monsters, but he found none there. Brad was gone. The depths of the abyss vanished. The feeling of weightlessness and water a memory that lingered in his mind, if it had ever been there in the first place. He tried not to think, but he was exhausted, his mind red lining so fierce it had broken, the cogs and pistons from the engine had come loose. He got to his feet, grabbed his bag, and stumbled for the exit. He stopped. He needed his pass to get out of the car park otherwise it was a long fucking walk home. He reluctantly moved back to the monitors and flicked through. The Doberman was in the cafeteria sleeping on one of the couches, his pass still wrapped around its leg. *Have you seen my dog?* The voice in his head crept in once more. Tom told it to *fuck off,* no longer giving himself to the fucking delusions of his own mind. *I'm going insane,* he thought once more, and that, somehow, was more comforting than the alternative.

Tom put his bag down and pulled out some small chicken bites. He couldn't remember what food tasted like. The touch of water on a dry throat a distant memory. He noticed his hands were shaking. He wanted a drink of Vodka so badly.

The warehouse was deathly silent as he stepped out from the SEC RITY room. He could see his breath in front of him, a gust of ghostly mist leaving his mouth. He began to shiver and wrapped his jacket tight around him. The metal walls of the warehouse creaked and groaned as the winter wind ran through them like an uninvited guest. Tom moved through the corridor, shining the torch into the corners, waiting to see those dead eyes once more. In front of him, the light from the cafeteria spilled through onto the floor. He could hear the soft snoring of the dog, and Tom took his bat out of his bag. His leg was hurting badly, and he could feel the warmth leaking out of him, his trousers sticking into him with each step. Tom flicked off the torch and placed it in his bag and gripped the bat with both hands. He turned into the cafeteria, and the bat fell from his grip, rattling on the floor.

He stumbled as his legs went weak and caught himself on the counter. The room had transformed. It wasn't the cafeteria anymore. The blue couches had disappeared. The busted TV and coffee machine no longer there. The room wasn't brightly lit with harsh strip lighting. It was dim, the smell of bleach pushing up his nose. The sight of her, lying there, tubes coming out of her arms, face and stomach. The machine she was strapped too keeping her breathing as the dull bed side lamp flickered on her hospital bed.

"Jayne?"

23

Closer

His throat swelled and finally, the tears pushed through. His hands and knees met the vinyl flooring as he crawled to her bed. The itchy blue blanket crumpling in his fists as he clambered to her. The steel bed frame meeting his palms. His face met hers. His eyes searching for something, anything that would make sense. He could smell her. He could touch her. He could feel her warmth on his fingertips as he held her face.

He tried to speak but he couldn't. He wouldn't. Nothing he could say would bring her back. Nothing he could do would make her wake up. Just like that day when he got home from the rig. When she had been lying there in the hospital. He climbed on the bed and it creaked and yearned under his weight. He lay next to her. His eyes burning, his cheeks red. The touch of her hair through his fingers. She was here but so far away. A skeleton wrapped in withered skin. He fell into that space he didn't want to visit. That place of despair, when all has crumbled around you, and you can't find the strength to pick up the pieces.

Tom went to speak, to say something. That he loved her.

That he missed her. That he was sorry he wasn't there for her. That he leaned on her too much when he got back, about his drinking, his past. All the bad shit he had done and she had given him nothing but unconditional love in return. That he was sorry she couldn't come home. He told her about the day they first met. A friend's birthday party. The blue dress she had worn and he pointed out she had spilt cream from the buffet on the cuff. They laughed and she put the stray dab on his lips before taking it with her own.

How he had touched her and held her that night as they made love. When two became one, and he had been a part of her ever since, and she him.

"I'm sorry," he whispered finally. His despair bleeding into his words like paint mixing together on a soiled carpet. "Wake up baby," he cried, stroking her face. "Wake up baby." Tom closed his eyes and held her hand in his, falling into her embrace.

24

Little By Little

Tom opened his eyes and saw his wife gone. He was on the ground, his arms stretched out onto the floor, his face on the cold flooring of the cafeteria room. He felt fur brushing his face, and then the cold of a snout. The room was how it had been, his wife no longer here. A projection of his own fear. The Doberman sitting next to him, the pass around his paw, its tongue long and pink panting away, drooling on the floor. Rage gripped him then. He lunged at the animal, it recoiling from him, baring its teeth. The dog snapped those hellish jaws to him, its teeth burying into his leather jacket. He felt the power of its jaws as it latched on. Tom howled at the beast to let him go, to fuck off back into the cold. The dog thrashed and its teeth tore through his jacket sleave and found the cold skin underneath. He smelt the potent sharp odour of blood permeate the air. Tom reeled his hand back and punched the mutt in the snout. It didn't release, he punched it again, the pain of the night, of what he had seen, his misery coming to the forefront. The other shit of the night might have been his own head playing tricks, but this dog was real. He punched it one last time and the animal moved backwards, nestling behind the blue sofa. Tom snatched at the Dobermans back paw, unlooping the tangled lanyard of his ID and stuffed it into his pocket. He stepped back quickly, less the dog want another go of him. His arm erupted in agony, the blood flowing freely, dripping on his pants and the ground like a painter with too much liquid on the brush and too far from the canvas.

Tom turned and moved for the corridor, lanyard in hand, and the smell of freedom permeating the air. He hobbled through the dark corridor, his leg shaking, his arm bleeding, his car keys firmly in his hand, his bat and duffel bag over his back.

Outside the double glass doors, he saw his truck sitting there, encased in thick ice. He pushed the release button on the wall. A flickering red light met his eye. His heart plummeted. He pushed it again. Still nothing. The doors didn't budge. He hammered the button over and over, trying to hold back the panic which sat on his shoulder like a hungry vulture. He dropped his back to the ground and took out the bat. He swung that motherfucker as hard as he could against the glass, the head of bat bouncing back, sending a violent tremor through Tom's wrist and shoulder. He dropped the bat to the floor where it rattled on the ground. Tom eyed the bullseye in the glass, and then, before his eyes, it reformed into a flawless, smooth surface. Tom moved to the glass and put his hand to it. From the bottom of his lungs came the scream he had been holding back all night. He thrashed and bashed at the glass.

"Let me out! Let me the fuck out!" He picked up the bat once more and went hell for leather, each time the bat bouncing off the glass, the bullseyes reforming, and the tremors racing up Tom's shoulder.

"Sash?" The sound struck him like a truck blindsiding a soccer mom with too much gin in her system for a Sunday morning. Jayne was standing there, looking as beautiful as she did the first day they had met. The thought of her in the hospital bed.

"You're not here," he said through gritted teeth, tears gathering on his lip. She moved to him, and he felt her warm touch on his face. She dressed to his front, those green eyes piercing his through the night. She touched his lips with hers, running her hand through the back of his hair.

"I'm here baby," Jayne said. "I'm here. I won't leave you to face this alone. We need to stay here; you won't make it back to the hospital in the state you're in. You won't make it baby."

"I have to get back to you," Tom said. "I need to get back to you, make sure you're okay." She smiled, that same smile that always melted the worry from his heart, that smile that pierced through his most stubborn moments, her face soft, melting away the ice in his heart.

"I'm here," she whispered. She kissed him once more and he held her tightly. "I want you to stay with me Sash, stay here with me. Don't leave me alone in the dark." Tom tried to think of what to say, what reasoning for what was happening. The lights in the foyer came to life and the hallway lit up in bright, warm light. "Come on baby," Jayne whispered again, holding his face in both hands. "Stay here with me forever."

25

Jerry

Jerry scratched his stomach as he hauled himself up and sat on the corner of his bed. His phone had lit up and a notification stared at him. He picked it up and read that the alarm had been activated at Welch Mill. Jerry felt the dread creep along his skin. He took out a cigarette from the pack by his bed side and lit it, letting the thick smoke fill his lungs as he dialled the number for work. The call didn't connect. He tried once more and still nothing. He rubbed his eyes and checked the time. Nearly 4am. Memories plagued him of Wallace, and he felt worry enter his heart as he got out of bed and threw on some clothes.

He was downstairs and had his shoes and coat on within five minutes. This wasn't supposed to happen. Not Tom. He wasn't like the others; the dark couldn't take him. Not like the others. Not like the murderers and other convicts he had given to the night. Tom wasn't like that, but death knows no morality of men. We are all worm food in the end. Jerry moved through the house and caught a glimpse of a photo. There, in six by nine, a picture of his daughter before they had gone to the beach. The last photo he would ever take of her. He would have her back again soon, but the long nights of insomnia, drinking himself to sleep, his body and mind destroying at the price he had to pay. He couldn't do it anymore. He had to make it stop.

Jerry walked out and the cool winter air bit his skin. In his car he put the heating on and brushed the gathered snow from his windscreen. It was still falling, and he hoped the roads were clear and he could get there before it was too late.

He reversed out the drive way and took off down the long empty streets, streetlights gliding over him as he drew closer. He saw the sign for Downtown and took the exit of the freeway, his thoughts running around his head.

Jerry checked his pockets to make sure he had everything he needed. He needed to be more prepared this time. After the last guy had called him in the middle of the night, there wasn't much left of him by the time he got there. He touched his coat pockets. He had his cigarettes. His phone. His wallet, and more importantly, his gun.

His heart was in pieces since the first day Tom had walked through the front doors of the building. He had a record, yes, but he wasn't a bad man. Not like the others he had offered. Not like the others at all. *It wasn't time* Jerry thought. *It's not supposed to happen yet.* He wasn't like the others. He wasn't like the other pieces of shit that worked the night shift: ex-convicts, drug users, killers. The kind of people they would normally hire to do the night shift. The one which the entity wanted. Those that could have *accidents* on sight. Those who society wouldn't miss. Those who had more darkness in their hearts than good. Tom wasn't like them. He should have never given him the job. He passed the interview; Carl was sure about that. He was a candidate, no one would ask questions if he got a little squirrely with what he had been through. But he couldn't do it. Three nights was far too much for him. Normally the Mill would be more gentle, erode them slower. But it appeared that was happening much faster this time. More aggressive. The shadows with teeth.

"When death asks why?" He whispered to himself as he drove down the snowy highway. "When death asks why."

Jerry arrived at the Mill around fifteen minutes later. He checked his watch. He still had some time left. He needed to get Tom out. He needed to stop this thing once and for all. He pulled up to the pick-up truck Tom had left to be devoured by ice. He killed the engine and stepped out of his Sedan. His boots crunching under his feet as he moved to the entrance of the building. He shone his torch through the dark glass. A baseball bat and spats of dried blood on the carpet. His mouth turned dry. He hoped he wasn't too late to save him. He lifted his ID to the door to open it, but the doors came open freely, the darkness welcoming him inside. He took a deep breath, took the pistol out from his coat, and stepped into the foyer, the doors closing behind him.

26

The Dark

Jerry eyed the bat on the floor and the lanyard discarded next to it. *He nearly got away,* Jerry thought, remembering the last time this had happened. The sound of Gretta's teeth crunching around the poor bastards' fingers. Jerry finding him lying on the ground in a pool of his own blood. Then glimpsing the hounds' eyes as it slunk away into the warehouse racking's, drips of blood dotting from its long pink tongue.

Jerry crossed the threshold into the hell mouth, smelling the sodden carpet and the fresh potpourri left out on the counter. He heard the sound of growling coming from behind him. He ignored the rod of ice creeping up his spine. He knew better than to look the death hound in the eyes.

The pistol in his hand, Jerry stalked slowly through the hallway. It was dark, but luckily he brought a torch. All the lights were off in the warehouse. Not even the cafeteria light was on anymore, and that damn thing was *never* off. Jerry liked to keep it that way, like some kind of safe haven. Monsters don't like the light. That's why it's always safe to stay away from the shadows. That's why he hated staying here too late.

It was silent at first, only the sound of Jerry's heavy breathing pushing through the black. *Tom could be anywhere* he wondered. He touched the door handle of the HR office. He pulled down slowly and the door released with a reluctant *click.* It was dead inside. Only two empty desks with black monitors. Nothing of concern. The door closed too and Jerry continued to walk towards the main hall.

Again, the sound of growling behind him. Closer this time. So close, he could feel the dog's hot panting on the back of his jeans. Jerry didn't turn around. He knew what would happen if he looked that thing in the eyes. Those big brown spheres of the death hound. The evil this place holds. Like staring into the heart of a murderer. Nothing good will come of it. Two more heavy steps and Jerry swallowed dryly. The sound of a whimper behind him. He passed the door of Management, his own office. Maybe Tom had taken some sort of solace inside there? He had tried to call him, however, now he thought about it he wasn't sure it had been Tom calling him or it was the being that fed from him inside this place. Jerry didn't believe in ghosts, but he did believe in evil. This place wasn't haunted. He hadn't ever seen a ghost or a spirit, no poltergeist throwing toilet paper or hiding people's car keys. But something did live in these woods and the surrounding area, and he had seen that with his own eyes, the day his daughter died. Like it fed off his grief, and offered him a way back from it.

The hound was in front of him. Those eyes dark pits of death. The tongue pale and flat. Its lips crumpled, teeth coming out to play. Tom averted his gaze, putting his hand to his face. His heart jack hammered and he felt icy rain wash over him. The hound moved closer. It pawed at his leg and its snout nestled his pockets and licked at his coat. Jerry tried not too look, like a child watching someone butchering a rabbit at a magic show. They know they shouldn't watch, but they just can't help it. We are drawn to the things that wish to damage us the most.

The hound stood up on its hind legs. It was nearly as tall as him. Jerry pushed back into the wall, tried to catch himself but fell backwards. The hound was over him low, licking at those tightly closed eyes. Jerry could feel its bare rib cage against his fingertips, the flesh dangling from its insides. The gun in his pocket being squoze harder than a desperate virgin's dick who just discovered online porn. Its nose was cold, touching Jerry's reddening cheeks. He tried not to breathe, the stench of rot making him gag. That, and it was the only way he could hold back the scream that wanted to burst from his lungs.

The hound sat back, panting heavily on his face. It growled again, and Jerry wanted so badly to shoot the thing in between the eyes. But if he did that, the creature would have him. He would be inviting it in. Inviting it to hurt him, to ravage him. Jerry could only wait. Wait until the torment was over. Resist the urge to look into that hollow skull that still moved. Those empty eye sockets. The thing that should have died but still wandered the halls of this place.

The creature leaned in and barked. Spittle flying into Jerry's face. He squoze his eyes tighter, the grip on the gun turning his knuckles white. He heard the sound of shouting coming from the warehouse. The sound of a man screaming, wailing and begging. His eye lids snapped open and sweat bled into his eyes making them rampage like dipped in lemon juice. He eyed the doorway. It was open, light spilling through the dark corridor. The glow of the emergency lighting in the warehouse casting the shelving and desks in a dull red, reminding Jerry of the old dark rooms of photo production.

He could feel the hound's snout on his cheek. The brush of its teeth on his face. He closed his eyes again just as the jaws of death opened wide to sink its teeth into his flesh.

27

Bargaining

Jerry pushed the beast off him. He crawled to his feet. He stumbled and caught himself on the wall. He turned and saw the hell hound gone. The keeper of the gate. The bringer of souls. Jerry pushed harder, reaching the door to the warehouse where Tom was. He grabbed the handle but it was burning hot. He pulled his hand back, the handle steaming into the night air. He looked around him, hoping to see an answer, maybe to see God staring back at him? Or even the Devil himself...

"Haven't you had enough!" He screamed to the encroaching blackness. "Haven't I given you enough!"

I gave you your daughter back the voice bled from the black. *You have a debt to be paid. You have a debt to fill.*

"I have given you many!" He screamed, tears of pain flowing freely, his teeth bared.

I desire one more. I desire this one. The voice called again, swirling around Jerry's ears. *I require one more to take. One more to feed. Why do you care about this one?*

"Because I can't live like this!" He screamed. "I can't go on living like this! He isn't like the others, he has a wife, she needs him. He isn't like the others! He has done wrong but he is not a bad man, he has demons like all of us!" The darkness paused, then, the sinister voice filled his mind once more.

One more soul, or I will take her back. A light in the foyer flickered then died. A figure, small and thin, approached him. A silhouette with short cut hair. A tube through her nose. A small stuffed bear in her hand, as she moved towards him. The light blinked, and she was closer. Step by step, closer and closer, limbs popping, arms and knees dislocated, crunching and warped as she moved. The light flickered out, and black surrounded him. One last snatch of a glimpse through the etched window and he could see Tom on his knees, the entity before him. The dog by its side, and the tall man with it. He turned one last time. His daughter, what *looked* like his daughter, was standing behind him, her eyes sunken to the back of her head, her cheeks eroded, maggots falling from the fleshy black wound.

Daddy...

Jerry took out the gun from his pocket and kicked at the door until it blasted open and bolted through the entrance.

28

Headrush

Jerry raced through the door which exploded in a barrage of twisted steel and flying wood. He raised the gun, screaming at Tom, screaming at him to move away. He saw the entity touching him. The *Grey Man. Its* skin withered, teeth black, hair thin and a soiled cloth that wrapped around its emaciated body. It was leaning over Tom, drinking him, his soul being devoured in front of his eyes and *The Grey Man* took it hungrily. His mouth wide open, eyes rolled to the back of his head. "No!" Jerry howled. "Not this one! You can't have another one! Enough is enough!"

One more soul or I will take her from you spoke the darkness. Next to the beings, his daughter appeared once more, a white bead of light coming from her chest to the Grey Man's chest. The Tall Man snarled. He touched the thread of light and tightened it between his long, bony fingers. Jerry recoiled.

"No!"

Jerry raised the weapon and took aim at the Tall Man. It reeled its head back, then lunged its long face to him, his eyes pits of black, mouth hanging low as darkness spewed out the wails of hell. The room closed black and shadow fell around him. He was blinded in blackness. Jerry searched the empty void around him, his voice sounding far away, echoing around an empty abyss. He took out his torch, trying to find someone, something, but the beam continued stretching, the cold pricking Jerry's skin. The light stretched and stretched, finding nothing but empty space around him. He called out, and he heard only his voice disappearing in the emptiness faster than he uttered it. He was in *that place* again. The place beyond this world. The place he had seen in the eyes of those he gave to the Grey Man.

I require one more the darkness said. *I require one more. One of darkness. One of pain. I require one more for my collection. I require one more. Only one more, or I will take her from you and bring her back to me.* Jerry searched the darkness more but found nothing.

"You can't have him. I can't do this anymore. I can't feed you more!"

Then I will take her from you the dark said. Jerry screamed in protest, howling for his daughter, howling for mercy. He dropped to his knees, his heart rampaging. The torch fell to the floor. Tom saw the pair of feet in front of him. His daughter standing there. The thread from her chest like a streak of light in the blackness. Her face unmoving. Her skin healed, no longer ridden in maggots or decay.

"Please don't take her from me," Jerry cried. "Please, let him go. Take me instead." With that, the Grey Man appeared in front of Jerry. It reeled in closely, touching his face. Its teeth were tombstones of black and yellow, tongue and gums eroded and blackened. Its nose curved, face wrinkled, skin grey and yellow, like thin leather draped over bones. It touched a long finger nail to its chest, and from it, a thread of light followed. The Grey Man hovered its finger over Jerry's chest.

"When death asks you why?" It said, it's breath like decayed meat.

"I can't live with myself anymore. What kind of monster am I? I have taken so many. Given you so many."

"Deservedly of the fate they suffered," it spoke. Jerry shook his head.

"I was desperate. I did anything I could to bring her back, but I can't do this any longer. I can't give you another. Not this one." Jerry saw Tom lying on the ground beside the Grey Man, a thread of light from his chest leading into the creatures. He thought of his daughter once more, tears falling onto the ground. "If you're not breathing... why am I?"

"We had a deal," the creature spoke. "Your daughter's life for one day a year, for the lives of the damaged." It lingered its fingertip over Jerry's chest once more. "When death asks you why?" Jerry felt the answer burning in his throat. The same question the Grey Man always asked. The same question it always asked before it took someone. Before it gave him his daughter back in return for a soul. He put the torch once more to his daughter's face. She was perfect, the tubing from her nose now gone. Her bones no longer broken from the car accident. "When death asks you why..." The Grey Man said, pointing to the black. Jerry followed the darkness and shone his torch.

Seven. Seven in total standing there. Each driven mad by the darkness as an offering to it, until it consumed them. One with a chewed-up hand. *Wallace.* The rapist. A woman with a ligature mark on her neck. She had done it in the bathroom. The thief. Another, a faceless man holding a torch, blood leaking from his skull and barbed wire tearing into his legs as he tried to climb the fencing to escape. The drug dealer. A woman screaming, banging on the walls of the elevator who had suffocated. The fraudster. A man in his thirties frozen to death. The violent. The Tall Man, the first of them, who was lost in the forest in a blizzard, finding the Welch Mill with his hound, begging Jerry for shelter but was met with a box cutter to the stomach instead. Standing there, their heads facing the floor. Their eyes closed. "When death asks you why..." The Grey man said once more. His daughter moved to him, the bear in her hand. Her small digits wrapping around his neck, holding him tightly.

"Because I love her," Jerry said, squeezing her tightly in his big arms. The Grey Man lifted his head. Jerry stood and moved to him. He held out his hand and he understood. He cast his eyes on the blackness, on the hound, on the victims of his cruel creation. He stared into the eyes of his daughter who held out the pistol. The Grey Man touched his chest, the string of light complete. Jerry put the gun to his temple, and the darkness consumed him.

28

Cycle

Tom awoke on the floor of the foyer to the feeling of someone slapping his face. He opened his eyes and saw the morning cleaner, a tanned lady with fake lips as plump as bee stings, scalded him.

"Get up!" She howled. "Get up now! What's the matter with you? I've been knocking for thirty minutes! I'm late to work now! Get up before the boss gets here!" Tom sat up, his body ached. He turned to see the morning sun breaking through the thick clouds above. He got to his feet and checked himself over. The wound to his leg had gone, and so had the bite on his arm. He stared at himself, checking his clothing and his body intently, like he had woken up from a surgery with a pair of breasts when he went under for a root canal.

"I'm okay?" He said, astonished. The cleaner held him with contemp.

"You night workers are all fucking weirdos. I think it's the dark. Drives you all crazy." Tom didn't care, he stretched out his body and let the pops and clicks come. He hadn't felt this great in a long time, his first real night sleep. He tried to remember what had happened, how he had gotten to the foyer? But as much as he tried, he couldn't quite snatch the memory from his mind, like trying to grab fleeting smoke. "So go on," the cleaner said, her arms folded. "What did you go to jail for? That's all they hire here for your job. Convicts, weirdos. You're on camera so don't try anything. I do Krav Maga." Tom scrunched his face and let out the biggest laugh he has in a long time.

"I'm going home back to my wife," he said as he exited the foyer. "Fuck this place." Tom walked along the icy tarmac to his truck. He de iced the windscreen and cracked the door open. He turned the ignition on and let the car warm up and de mist. Getting into the driver's seat, he cranked it in reverse and pulled out the car park. He couldn't wait to see his wife, to tell her he had quit, that he was leaving that place for good.

As he drove steadily down the long country high way, he tapped the steering wheel to his favourite song that played on the radio, him singing at the top of his lungs. He didn't see them watching him as he moved away through the trees, or the Doberman that crossed the road behind him, looking for its next meal. Eight of them. Eight in total. Waiting for the next person to take over the Night Shift.

About the stories –

Lorna -

This story was inspired by true events. The nature of a dysfunctional and abusive relationship is that prevailing feeling of confusion. The plot is disjointed for a reason, the facts constantly changing and told from the narrative of a character who we see change as the story continues. I hope I got the tone right, and left you, dear reader, wondering about aspects of the plot. Rather than it be a straight narrative and plot, I liked to play around with it. Not just the timeline, but the intentions and lives of the characters too.

If you are left both satisfied with the tale, and still wondering about certain points, then good. I have done my job. The nature of toxic love is exactly that, its poisonous, and lingers long after the ride is over, leaving you wondering what happened.

The Eyes –

Children are afraid of the dark, and as a child I was terrified of it. If I didn't have every light on in my house then I couldn't sleep. I often thoug3ht I could hear something tapping on the windows during the night, and the large tree that stood outside my window would grow a sinister toothy grin. Now, add a little poetry, and you have something really nightmarish...

There's Someone at the Door –

This one was really fun to write. I have an interest in folk law, as you may have seen in some of my writing, and have always been interested in Changelings and Doppelgangers, creatures that take the form of another creature. Now, add an elderly couple, a tragedy, and something knocking on the door, and you have a cold winter night sprinkled with a little more terror.

The Ghost in the Mist –

Ahh, the classical tragic love story. Heathcliff and Catherine, Romeo and Juliet. The inspiration for this story was the song 'House Carpenter,' originally an English folk law song, adapted by the American rock band 'Hurt,' in which a soldier goes off to war. I took the initial premise and built a story from the idea. I tried to capture the desperation, the despair, and also, the love, never dying and never ending, from the two characters. I hope I brought a tear to your eye...

The Strain –

I always wondered what would happen if a zombie outbreak happened? We have seen the movies, read the books and played the games, but I had never approached the idea myself. Then, The Strain popped into my head, of just that idea. Locked in a custody suite filled with murderers, with no chance of help coming, and throw some zombies in the mix and see what happens! Its like getting every bad scenario you can think of and throwing them in a blender...

The Nightshift –

This story basically wrote itself and I loved writing it. I used to be a delivery driver, and part of my job was going into old offices and warehouses in the dead of the night to drop off parcels, mail etc. You see some creepy stuff in those buildings, and I remembered wondering what it would be like to work a night shift in one of those places? So, a little imagination and some unfortunate events or two, and there we have it. I wouldn't take a night time security job if you paid me. I'm not brave enough for that.

If you enjoyed this title, please leave a review. Reviews are how indie authors make a name for themselves and are able to keep releasing content for you hungry readers to eat up.

Thank you for taking the time and spending it reading my work. I thoroughly hoped you enjoyed it. If you would like to see more of my work, look below —

For my books, head to Amazon Kindle Store and search 'Jay Darkmoore.'

For my website, blog and mailing list of exclusive content, head to www.Jaydarkmooreauthor.com

For my socials, head to Instagram Jay_Darkmoore_Author, Twitter - @DarkmooreJay

For my YouTube channel of original horror stories found nowhere else, search 'Jay Darkmoore.'

See you soon.

-   J

Printed in Great Britain
by Amazon